Meet the team

Cover Designer: Francessca's PR & Design
Editor: Rebecca Vazquez
Proofreader: Jackie Ziegler
Formatting: Nicola Miller

Disclaimer:
Playing Vinn is a stand-alone story, however, Vinn has appeared in the Kings Reapers MC books, also written by Nicola Jane.

This book is a work of fiction. The names, characters, places, and incidents are all products of the author's imagination and are not to be construed as real. Any similarities are entirely coincidental.

Spelling Note:
Please note, this author resides in the United Kingdom and is using British English. Therefore, some words may be viewed as incorrect or spelled incorrectly, however, they are not.

NICOLA JANE

Acknowledgements

I'm so excited to bring you Playing Vinn. This is my first self-published book, and I thank each and every one of you who has helped me get to this point. Especially Rebecca for being super supportive and amazing, for also helping me put a team together and advising me on the best in the business ;) And Jackie for picking out the bits we miss.

As always, thanks to everyone who has downloaded, bought, shared, reviewed, and helped spread the word. You're all amazing! xx

Trigger Warning

This story is a mafia romance. It's contains bad words, violence, aggressive behaviour, far fetched situations and drama. It'll twist your heart and make you want to launch your kindle/book into the garden. But please remember, I write whatever is in my head, my imagination is not going to be the same as yours and therefore you might feel like some situations should be different. This story is not based on real life, it would be boring if it was! So try not to get too vexed with the characters. . . or me, Vinn made me do it!

Contents

Playlist	IX
Get Ready	X
Chapter One	1
Chapter Two	11
Chapter Three	22
Chapter Four	35
Chapter Five	44
Chapter Six	55
Chapter Seven	69
Chapter Eight	86
Chapter Nine	98
Chapter Ten	106
Chapter Eleven	118
Chapter Twelve	129
Chapter Thirteen	141
Chapter Fourteen	151
Chapter Fifteen	155
Chapter Sixteen	163

Chapter Seventeen	173
Chapter Eighteen	181
Chapter Nineteen	191
Chapter Twenty	201
Chapter Twenty-One	212
Chapter Twenty-Two	221
Chapter Twenty-Three	227
Chapter Twenty-Four	233
Epilogue	243
VINN	245
A note from me to you	246

Playlist

Maybe Don't - Maisie Peters ft. JP Saxe
   Favourite Ex - Maisie Peters
   Tell Me You Love Me - Demi Lovato
   Love Don't Cost a Thing - Jennifer Lopez
   Picking Up the Pieces - Paloma Faith
   Arcade - Duncan Laurence
   Gangsta - Kehlani
   Foolish - Ashanti
   Flames - MOD SUN ft. Avril Lavigne
   Please Don't Say You Love Me - Gabrielle Aplin
   Little Did I Know - Julia Michaels
   Hate That I Love You - Jonathan Roy
   Playing With Fire - N-Dubz ft. Mr Hudson
   Do I Wanna Know? - Arctic Monkeys
   Lost In Your Light - Dua Lipa ft. Miguel
   Dancing With The Devil - Demi Lovato
   Hate The Way - G-Eazy ft. blackbear
   Good Guy - Eminem ft. Jessie Reyez

Chapter One

SOFIA

I wake, stretching out on the king-sized bed and running my hands over the cool silk sheets. I hate silk. I glance around the white room, I groan aloud. White walls, white furniture, and white silk sheets.

I make my way to the en-suite bathroom, which is twice the size of my family bathroom back in Italy. *Italy*. Damn, I miss it so much. I step into the walk-in shower with white tiles adorning the walls and stare with hatred at the white towels hanging innocently on the white wall radiator. I hate white.

Next, I open my wardrobe and run my hand along the many items of clothing hanging there. Some things are mine that I brought with me from my home, but the rest, well, who knows where the rest came from. Obscenely-priced shops, mostly. I glance at a price tag on a cream trouser suit and arch my brow. Who the hell would wear this unless they're over sixty? I close my eyes and pull out the first thing my hand lands on, it's a game I've played every day since I came here. I laugh at the low-cut, bright orange summer dress. It's short and way too revealing. He'll hate it. I smile as I pull it on.

Downstairs, I pass the usual security men, I call them Bill and Ben after an old television show my mama loved, but I have no idea what their names are because no one bothered to introduce us. They nod in greeting, and I smile politely. I hear pots and pans banging as I head for the kitchen, and Josey looks up as I enter. She's sweating and looks flustered. "Sofia," she says, smiling and wiping her head on her forearm, "did you sleep well?"

I pull myself up onto a chair at the breakfast bar, where no one ever seems to sit. "Yes, thank you. Did you?"

"Yes. Breakfast?" I shake my head and reach for the coffee pot instead, pouring myself a cup. "You really should eat something."

"I'm not really a breakfast person," I admit.

"Vincent came looking for you this morning. He wasn't happy that you didn't eat with the family again." I lower my eyes. What does he expect? I never know when he's here or away on business. We communicate through his staff or occasionally through his mother.

It's hard to believe we've only been married a week.

It was an arrangement made by our fathers years ago. His father died, so you'd think that would release me, right? Wrong. My papa still reached out to Vincent Romano and asked him to marry me. It's his name that makes him hugely desirable—not to me, of course, but to many men who have daughters. Connecting your family with the Romano name can open all kinds of opportunities, and when you're part of the mafioso, opportunities are everything. "Anyway, he said to tell you he's in his home office today and he'd like to see you." When I remain quiet, she moves to where I'm sitting and places her hand over mine. "It gets better, Sofia, I promise."

PLAYING VINN

As I approach the ground floor office, Gerry is just leaving. He looks surprised to see me, so I guess I've been hiding away in my room a lot. "Good morning, Mrs. Romano."

I shudder, hating that name. "It's Sofia," I mutter. He leaves the office door open, and I step inside. Azure, or Blu, as everyone calls him, is pacing back and forth, and Vincent, my husband, looks angry. Both men turn to glare at me.

"You should knock before entering," barks Vinn. I roll my eyes and step back over the threshold, raising my fist and banging on the door. Blu almost cracks a smile but recovers fast when Vinn stands angrily. "I don't find you amusing, Sofia."

"Josey said you wanted to see me. I can go, it's fine."

He takes a deep breath and turns to his brother-in-law. "Blu, leave us." Once he's gone, I step closer to the large oak desk. "My mother is offended," he begins. "You don't join us for breakfast . . . or any meal, come to think of it."

"How would you know, you're never here yourself."

He stares at me, unblinking, "I have to attend to business, it can't be helped."

"Okay," I say, shrugging. I turn on my heel and head for the door.

"What does that mean?" he snaps. "Will you be joining us for lunch?"

I check my watch. "No. I have a date."

His laugh is cold. "Really? I'll see you in the dining room at one o'clock. And change your dress, unless you want my men dreaming about you."

I head out, not bothering to answer.

NICOLA JANE

Zarina spots me entering the restaurant at one o'clock exactly. I hate to be late. She stands to greet me and hugs me excitedly. "You look amazing."

"So do you," I say, holding her at arm's length and taking in her beauty. It's all natural, from her long black lashes to her pedicured toes. She's stunning. Zarina is my cousin and closest friend. She was also a bridesmaid at my wedding, the one condition I had when the event was arranged. She knows everything about me, and when she discovered I was moving to the UK, it was the perfect opportunity for her to check out what London had to offer. Her father is my papa's underboss, and it took some convincing to allow it, but he eventually agreed she could stay here for three months. Secretly, I think he's hoping Vincent will find her a nice Italian man.

"So, tell me everything," she demands.

"Like?" I ask casually.

"Like how is married life? What's Vinn really like? Is he as scary as his reputation?"

"For this conversation, I need a drink," I mutter, catching the attention of the waitress.

"Drink," repeats Zarina. "You never drink."

I order a white wine and lemonade. I've heard some of Vinn's sister's friends order it and always wondered what it tastes like. Zarina sticks with water. "It's awful, Zee," I whisper, glancing around like I'm going to be heard. "I'm always on my own. It's like I'm a prisoner. I had to sneak out today just to see you."

"You did what?" she hisses, her eyes wide.

"I told him I had a date for lunch, but he didn't believe me. And why should I tell him my business? I know nothing about him. He leaves before breakfast, and God only knows when he returns. Is this it? Is this my life forever?"

PLAYING VINN

Zarina offers a sympathetic smile. "Sofia, we talked about this a hundred times. You have got to make this work. For you, for your family, and most of all, for Mario."

My heart twists at the mention of my brother's name, and I nod. She's right—this marriage will make everything right again and Mario will be able to come home where he belongs.

VINN

I tap impatiently on the dining table. "Vinn, please," whispers Mother.

I check my watch and sigh heavily when I see it's almost ten minutes past one. "Get her," I order Conner, one of my men. He heads up to Sofia's room, where she's always hiding out since moving here. It doesn't bother me—the less I see of her, the better, so I can forget the marriage and all that comes with it. But it's upsetting my mother, and I can't allow that to happen.

Conner returns without Sofia. "Boss, she isn't there."

I frown. "What do you mean, she isn't there?"

"I checked her room, her bathroom, and the library, all places she usually goes. She isn't there." "Then check the other rooms. She'll be here somewhere."

"Actually," comes Josey's voice from somewhere behind Conner, "she said she was having lunch today with her cousin."

Conner visibly swallows. "Did you know this?" I ask, and he shakes his head. "Who was watching her today?"

"The new guy."

"Bring him to me now."

Mother pats my hand. "She'll be fine, Vinn. It's just lunch."

I nod stiffly, not wanting to snap at her. "But I told her to be here."

NICOLA JANE

"It's nice she's going out and enjoying herself. If she's staying in London, she'll need a life."I snort. "She has a life here, in this house. It's my job to keep her safe."

Conner returns with the new man I hired two weeks ago. "Well, you're not with her," I state, "which means my wife is out there alone."

"I'm sorry, Boss, she never said she was going out. I checked her diary and everything," he explains.

"It's not an excuse," I reply, trying to stay calm.

"But I'm not a mind reader," he snaps, and Conner nudges him, telling him to shut up.

Blu enters, and when he feels the tension in the air, he stops and looks back and forth between us. "Everything okay?"

"This clown just spoke back to me, Azure. Get him out of my sight before I kill him."

Blu doesn't need asking twice before he takes him by the upper arm and guides him out.

"I'll go find her now, boss," says Conner.

"Don't bother," I snap, grabbing a set of car keys. "I'll go myself."

Sofia's cousin responds to my text message immediately. I like her, she's obedient, why the fuck didn't I marry her? Arriving at the restaurant, I spot the pair inside, eating lunch and chatting animatedly. When I step inside, the waitress rushes to greet me, but I pass her, ignoring her extra nice greeting, and head straight for Sofia's table. Zarina keeps her eyes downcast, her expression filled with guilt as Sofia glares at her accusingly. I sit down, shoving her farther along the booth. "You never said you were meeting your cousin."

"Yes, I did. I specifically told you I had a lunch date."

I push my face into hers, and she backs up against the seat. "No, *mia cara*, you told me you had a date, and I thought you

PLAYING VINN

were making a joke. I should have known that wasn't the case, since I don't think I've ever seen you crack a smile."

Sofia squares her shoulders, defiance in her eyes. "Firstly, I am not your darling. Secondly, pay attention when I talk next time."

My tongue runs along my lower lip while I try to gain control of my boiling rage. Twice in one day I have been spoken back to. It's a new record, and I wonder why the fuck everyone suddenly thinks it's okay. "Zarina, my driver will take you home. Please join us for dinner tomorrow evening. I'll have you collected at eight."

Zarina nods, sliding from the seat. "But we haven't finished eating," hisses Sofia.

I swipe my hand across the table, sending everything clattering across the floor. "Now, you have." She gasps, glaring at me like I've lost my mind. She's lucky I didn't throw it across the room to release some of this anger rushing through me. "Get your things."

She's angry too, breathing in through her nose sharply. Good. Maybe it's time we cleared the air. I stand, and when she doesn't, I grab her upper arm and force her to her feet. I take a bunch of notes out of my wallet and drop them on the table, apologising to the waitress about the mess as we leave.

It's beginning to rain and she's wearing the damn summer dress I told her to change out of. I offer her my coat, but she turns away, so I shrug and grab her by the arm again, marching away from the restaurant. As we pass men in the street, they stare at her with appraising expressions, and I glare at every goddamn one of them until they avert their eyes.

The orange dress is now a darker shade as rainwater soaks into it. Her hair looks matted, sticking to her face and chest. She's practically popping out the top, showing way too much skin for a married Italian woman. I look away, tempted to forcibly wrap my damn jacket around her body. We reach Enzo's, the nightclub I own, and she stops abruptly. "I'm not going in there."

"I have work to do."

"Then I'll go home. I'm not sitting in your office while you make eyes at your assistant."

I smirk. She found me kissing Raven a few months back and hasn't stopped reminding me of it since. She even delayed our wedding because of it. "Sofia, as much as I'd love to stand here in the pouring rain, discussing my assistant, I don't have time."

"I'm not going in there."

I growl, bending and tossing her over my shoulder, and she screams angrily. "Like I said, I don't have time." Raven looks up as we enter the office, mainly because Sofia is hitting my back and shouting curse words in Italian. I dump her back on her feet. "Watch her. If she tries to leave, tie her up."

Raven laughs. "Vinn, I'm not tying up your wife. That's your job."

Ignoring her, I head into my office and slam the door. I close the blinds, so I don't have to see either of them, and then I sit at the desk and stare at the picture of my father. "This is your fault," I mutter. "You and your stupid promise to your stupid friend. You said I should always honour a promise, and I did, Pops, but shit, you owe me big for this."

SOFIA

I fiddle with the hem of my dress. "So," says Raven, "things going well?"

"Perfectly," I mutter.

"Look—" she begins.

"You told me he was a nice man," I butt in accusingly.

"In all fairness, you were locked in the bathroom, refusing to come out and marry him. The alternative was to let carnage happen amongst the two families, and I'm sure you didn't want that." It was my husband's mistress who talked me into marrying him on the morning of my wedding. Ironic, right? I never wanted this in the first place, and when it came down to it, I was terrified to walk down that aisle towards a man I didn't know. But it was Raven who convinced me to do it . . . that and the fact I had no choice. My father needed this marriage. I sigh, looking around the office. "Why does he like white so much?"

Raven looks around too. "I dunno. Maybe cos it's clean-looking?"

"Or maybe he's just boring."

"Boring?" Raven chuckles. "Vinn Romano is the least boring person I know."

"In or out of the bedroom?" I quip, and she blushes. I shouldn't be unkind, because she was just as hurt by Vinn. Besides, she's been nothing but nice to me, and she and Vinn are well and truly over. She's happy with her new man. "Sorry," I mutter, taking a breath. "I hate it here," I admit, and her eyes soften. "His house is so . . . cold and lonely. He's never there. How am I supposed to get to know a man who's practically invisible?"

"Have you talked to him?" asks Raven.

I shake my head. "I don't think I want to. He looks at me like I'm an annoying bee buzzing in his ear. Neither of us are happy."

"Sofia, you have to talk to him. You're both in this whether you like it or not, and if you feel the same, air it and find a solution."

I glance at the office, seeing the blinds are still closed. "I'm going to the bathroom," I say, and she eyes me suspiciously.

"You're not gonna run, are you? He'll kill me."

NICOLA JANE

I shake my head, not wanting to lie out loud. I take the stairs but pass the bathroom and continue to the ground floor, where I head for the exit. There's no way I'm hanging around here all day. I have shit to do.

The house is quiet when I get home, apart from the usual house staff. I head for my room and send a text off to Vinn, letting him know I'm home safely. I don't want to get Raven into trouble, and there's no point in antagonising him by letting him think I've wandered off and am roaming the streets of London alone.

Opening my laptop, I go to my secret files, load the document I've been working on, and smile. The trouble with Vinn Romano is, he thought I was quiet and maybe a little stupid. He might think he's the boss in every sense of the word, and he might even think I've forgiven him for ripping me away from my family while fucking his personal assistant, but he's about to discover I'm not who he thought I was.

Chapter Two

VINN

I glance at the text on my phone. Why can't she do as she's fucking told? Raven knocks on the door, and I see her silhouette through the frosted glass. "If you're coming here to tell me she's gone, I already know," I say dryly.

She steps inside. "Actually, no. I just got a call from my inside woman at the London Daily Spy and your number one fan has made contact." I sit a little straighter. "Contact?"

She nods. "Bad news, Vinn, they're running the story."

"Are you fucking joking me? What's the story?"

"I don't know, she's trying to find out. All she knows is it's going on the gossip page."

"That whole newspaper is a gossip fest. Nobody buys it, anyway, so I'm not worried."

Raven leaves, and I turn my chair to stare out at the busy streets below. Some dickhead had taken it upon themselves to write to the press about my life. They've accused me of being a chauvinistic pig, exposed my affair with Raven, even though Sofia was already aware, and now this. I need to find them and put a stop to it before it gets serious. I don't need bad press when I'm trying to expand businesses, and who knows what they'll uncover if they keep snooping into my life. Maybe this is the reason people suddenly think it's okay to disrespect me.

NICOLA JANE

"Word on the street is you're going into the gossip pages tomorrow," comes Blu's amused voice from behind me.

I slowly turn to face him, annoyed by his smug expression. It's a permanent fixture on his face ever since he married my sister. "Word travels fast."

"Raven told me," he says sheepishly. "What gossip could they have on you?"

"It's probably a lie. Newspapers don't give a shit as long as it fills a column."

"Maybe this person is a disgruntled ex?"

I shake my head. "I don't have any, not that were serious. There's only . . ." I frown. "Well, just Raven, but she wouldn't."

Blu glances over his shoulder to see Raven on the telephone, then he pushes the door closed. "Are you sure about that, Boss? You hurt her pretty badly."

I shake my head. "She wouldn't dare. Besides, she came running when the first story hit the Gazette and sorted all the positive PR bullshit. It's what got her to come back to work for me." "I'm just saying, don't rule her out too quickly. Women are clever, and revenge is a dish best served cold." He sits and places his feet on my desk. I eye his boots with a scowl. "Anyway, how's married life?"

"You ask me every time I see you, and every time, I tell you the same thing. It's fine."

"Things good between you two?"

"Why do you ask?"

He sighs. "I'll be honest, Boss, your sister is worried about you both."

"Gia needs to stop worrying and concentrate on her own marriage. Maybe she could teach you some manners," I say dryly, pushing his feet from my desk. "Now, if you don't mind, I'm busy."

He checks his watch. "We have a meeting in ten minutes."

PLAYING VINN

I glance at my diary. Fuck. My head is not in the game right now. "Mr. Hicks. Right."

"Gia thinks Sofia is miserable and that she's missing home."

"Impossible. She's at home right now."

"You know what I mean. Italy. Plus, you're never together."

"We were together this morning."

"Look, Boss, I don't wanna have this conversation either. I told Gia to keep me out of it, but you know what she's like when she gets going. She wouldn't leave it. She's gonna speak to Sofia today and see if she's okay."

"I can assure you, she's fine."

"Gia mentioned—" I groan, and he sits up straighter, grinning. "Hear me out. She said you have separate bedrooms." I stare at him. There's no way we're discussing this. Blu's eyes widen, and he laughs. "You're shitting me, right? You mean to tell me you haven't . . ."

"That's none of your business. You're overstepping."

"So, shoot me," he says, relaxing in the chair.

"You're not safe just because you married into my family."

"You're the boss, the top man, and you haven't—"

"Azure!" I suddenly yell, but he doesn't jump in fright. It's in his blood not to react. It's the way he was trained, just like me.

"Look, you have a reputation to uphold, and as your second in command, I'm telling you, you need to sort this out. She's your wife, and that comes with responsibility. Isn't it time you taught her that?"

"I'm not gonna force myself on her."

"You already did when you married her. You have to go through with it, Vinn. Back in the day, the families would have checked the sheets to make sure you'd consummated." He laughs. "Things have changed, but still, you need to complete the marriage. How the fuck are you gonna have a son?"

"It's temporary. I'm letting her settle in."

NICOLA JANE

"You're letting her think she's the boss. If this gets out, people will think you're an *omosessuale*, that you're hiding behind a fake marriage. It's not the first time a mafioso boss did that. People will think you're weak." I hear Raven greet our guest, and I sigh with relief. "Hicks is here. Concentrate on making us money and securing this deal, and forget about my marriage."

SOFIA

I smile as I press the telephone to my ear. "Oh my god, Sofia. You can't send that story," yells Zarina.

I emailed her my undercover story just minutes ago. "There's no way you've read that fully, I only just sent it."

"I don't need to. The headline says it all." I hear her suck in a shaky breath. "Sofia, have you lost your mind? What if he discovers the truth? What if he finds out the mysterious 'Revenge' is you? This is out of hand now."

"He won't."

"He'll kill you. You can't fuck over men like him."

"Zee, relax. He won't find out. Besides, what else am I supposed to do, sitting in his fucking white tower every day, bored out of my mind?""You do what housewives do, Sofia. You make friends. Have lunch out. Go to the damn library. But you don't write shit about a mafia boss."

"He underestimated me. He shouldn't have." I'm angry she's defending him when she knows how unhappy I am.

"So, you want to write shit about him? Embarrass him just because he underestimated you? Christ, Sofia, listen to yourself. He married you to help your family. Think of Mario. If Vinn finds out about this, Mario might never come home."

"I don't understand why you're defending him, Zee. Anyway, you're killing my vibe. He won't find out."

A few stories in a gossip rag are hardly gonna bring down the great Vincent Romano. Maybe when the Gazette were printing my work, I'd have stood a chance of getting under his skin, but since he shut that down with his violent threats, I've had to go to less known news outlets. Now, it's just a bit of fun.

I head down for dinner at six, the same time as almost every evening. Josey and Lorenzo share dinner duties. Lorenzo once had his own restaurant and he's an amazing chef. Josey mainly sticks to breakfast and lunch as well as housekeeping. Both are fantastic at what they do.

I'm surprised when I step into the dining room to find Vinn seated at the head of the table. He glances up from his laptop, and when he sees it's me, he closes it and moves it to the side. "You're home," I say.

"I thought you might want to spend time with me," he says, smirking. I take a seat away from him, and he sighs impatiently, then pulls out the seat to his left. "Here," he demands, so I move. "You seem to want my attention, *mia cara*. No?"

"Why would you think that?"

"You keep defying me. I can only assume it's because you want more attention."

I roll my eyes. "That's the opposite of what I want. I like eating dinner in the kitchen and chatting with Josey."

"And Lorenzo," he chips in.

I laugh. "You're not going to ban me from speaking to your oldest employee, are you?" It bothers me that he knows what I do when he isn't around. How does he know my every move? I glance around the room, looking for cameras, but see nothing obvious.

NICOLA JANE

"Why did you leave the club today?"

"Because I was bored."

"So, you'd like something to keep you busy when I'm not around?"

"No, I can amuse myself," I say, arching a brow.

"I can get Gia to show you the local salons or the best places to shop," he suggests, and I inwardly groan. This arrogant arse is a chauvinistic dick.

"I'd rather you didn't."

"What else would you like to do, if not shop?"

"You know, Vinn, not every woman is a shopaholic with an addiction to lip fillers and facials."

He smirks, nodding. "I feel like I've been tricked," he murmurs, and my heart rate picks up a little. "Your father portrayed you as a quiet virgin, but now, I see you have your own opinions and an unruly mouth."

"Shocker," I mutter sarcastically.

"Let's hope some of what your father told me is true."

His eyes are burning into me. I feel the colour drain from my face, then sigh with relief as the food is brought out. Once the food is set before us, the waitress leaves. "Where were we?" asks Vinn.

"My mother taught us not to talk at the table."

"Did she teach you how to be a good wife?"

"What's that supposed to mean?"

"Well, we've been married for a couple of weeks, maybe it's time you moved into my bedroom?"

I almost choke on my own saliva. It's not what I was expecting him to say. "That's not happening," I manage to splutter.

"We are married," he repeats.

"And that means shit," I snap, and he narrows his eyes. "I don't even know you. You haven't spent any time getting to

PLAYING VINN

know me at all. We went on a three-day honeymoon where you spent the entire time glued to your phone and laptop."

"So, you want to spend more time together?" he asks.

"No . . . yes . . . no! I don't know," I cry, frustrated and flustered all at the same time.

"You know, eventually, we'll have to . . ." He leaves the sentence open, but we both know what he's referring to. I drop the white napkin on the table and stand. "Where are you going? You haven't touched your food."

"I've lost my appetite." I head for the door.

"Am I that repulsive?" he yells. "There are other women out there who would love to share my bed!"

"And I'm sure you'll let them. I haven't forgotten about Raven," I snap. "How can you expect me to act like a real wife when it's been a sham from start to finish?" I spin back to face him, suddenly feeling the need to get everything off my chest. "I never agreed to this marriage. I was happy in Italy. I had a life that I've been ripped away from and brought here to live in this . . . this big, empty place that is too white and has far too much silk." I take a deep breath. "I don't love you, Vinn, and I can't ever be the wife you want me to be."

He stands slowly and his eyes darken. I'm suddenly reminded of why men are scared of Vinn Romano. He moves towards me menacingly, but I refuse to take a step away. I will not bow down to a man who forced this life on me. "You have a responsibility, Sofia."

"If you want me to bear you a son, it'll be through force, no other way."

He sniggers, his face so close, I can feel his warm breath on my cheek. "You *will* have my child. It's not up for discussion. But I won't force you, Sofia. You'll come to me willingly and you'll beg before I lay a finger on you," he whispers.

NICOLA JANE

My head feels light, and the second he leaves the room, I grip the back of a chair for support. I hate him, so why the hell do I find his words hot? I let out a slow breath, glancing around the large room to check there were no witnesses to that moment of madness I'd just experienced. I scoff. "Beg him, please, not if he was the last man on Earth," I say aloud.

VINN

I like the sound my shoes make as they crunch over the dusty floor. It's deathly silent, apart from that sound, and I feel like it sets the mood for what's about to happen. Blu removes the black sack from my guest's head, and I smile. "Good evening."

The man's eyes widen and terror fills them. Before this moment, he probably wondered what the hell was going on. Before this moment, he probably thought he'd be able to talk his way out of whatever trouble was awaiting him. But now, as he makes annoying noises behind his tight gag and struggles against the thick rope binding him to the chair, he knows this will be his last night on Earth. Because nobody crosses me and gets away with it.

"I hate that it's come to this," I say, and I mean it. I'm sincere when I say those words, because if I wasn't, what kind of a monster would that make me? "But I tried to be kind. I sent my men to talk with you and explain everything. Didn't you understand the terms of our agreement?" He nods wildly, desperate for me to hear him out. "Then I don't understand where it all went wrong." I like a dramatic pause, so I wait a moment before continuing. "Wait, I know." I pull out a piece of paper and hold it up. "It was around the same time you emailed Raymond Clay and offered up information about my organisation." My captive makes more stupid noises, and I roll my eyes and wave my hand for Blu to remove the gag.

"I swear, Boss, I didn't. He wouldn't leave it, put money into my account. It's a set-up."

"So, these emails are not between you and him?"

"It wasn't how it looks—"

"Really, Carlo? Because it looks pretty bad from where I'm sitting. I moved you up in the ranks. You're a made man, even though everyone around me thought you weren't good enough. I thought you were worth the risk because I liked you, Carlo. You had fire in those eyes, and I knew you'd run the soldiers with no problem. But then, you screwed me over, you screwed the mafioso over. You know I can't let that slide."

"Please . . . please, Vinn, I didn't mean to. It was a mistake, and I fucked up, but I'll make it right. I'll do anything."

"There's no way back."

"I gave my life to you," he suddenly yells, and I smirk. The begging is over because he knows it won't work, so now, the hate is pouring from him. "I killed for you," he hisses.

"You killed for the family. You wanted in, and I gave it to you," I growl out, pushing my face close to his. I feel the darkness lingering as I crack my neck from side to side. "I gave you everything, and you fucked it up. Now, you have to pay."

I hold out my hand for Blu to pass me my knife. Gripping Carlo by the throat, I dig my fingers into his clammy skin. He stills, accepting his fate, and I slowly push the blade into his eye. He begins to scream and thrash around. I close my eyes, absorbing his cries of pain, and inhale the stench of his dirty blood pouring from the wound.

I took this kid in when he was seventeen and taught him everything he needed to know. Making him part of my clan was a big deal. He wasn't from a family I knew well, and I took a big risk, one that didn't pay off because his loyalties were too easily bought by my enemy.

NICOLA JANE

The crimson fluid turns black as it mixes with brain matter and trickles down his lifeless face, and Blu is already on the phone arranging a clean-up. I remove my gloves and throw them in a nearby metal drum, followed by my jacket, the material now soaked by blood splatters. Blu runs an ultraviolet torch over me to check for any lingering evidence. There's nothing, so I head back to the car where Gerry is waiting.

"You might want to look at this," he says, passing me an iPad. It's open on an article. The picture of Sofia and me standing apart screams unhappy, and as my eyes take in the headline, I grip the tablet so hard, the screen cracks.

Gerry drives me home, and as I take the stairs two at a time, my head is full of rage. I push Sofia's bedroom door open, slamming it hard against the wall. She sits up, dazed and confused, blinking through tired eyes. Grabbing her wrist, I haul her from her bed, causing her to scream out. She stumbles as I drag her across the landing, open my own door, and shove her inside.

"From now on, you sleep in here," I yell, slamming the door closed and locking it. Sofia stares at me, her whole stance ready to fight. Her breathing is rapid, and her fists are clenched. "Do it," I hiss, pushing her to carry out her attack. "I dare you."

"I'm not scared of you," she says through gritted teeth.

I smirk, moving close enough to feel the heat from her body. "Oh, you should be, *esuberante*."

"I'm not feisty," she hisses. "I'm an enraged woman, and I'll never be scared of you."

I take in her shorts and low-cut vest, the swell of her breasts taunting me for the second time. I might be a bastard, but I won't ever force myself on her. "Go back to sleep."

She turns, looking at the super-sized, four-poster bed. "It's not white," she mutters.

PLAYING VINN

I head to my bathroom, ignoring her.

Chapter Three

SOFIA

The deep red cotton blankets are a nice change from the cold white silk. I slip in and close my eyes. The bed is soft and comfortable, but the thought of sharing it with Vinn has me wide awake and alert. I hear the shower stop and turn onto my side so my back is to him. When he steps into the room, he pauses for a minute before passing me to go to his walk-in wardrobe. I open one eye in time to see his naked arse disappear. When he returns, he's wearing bottoms. I watch as he rubs his wet hair with a towel, taking in his large, muscled physique. I can see why women drop at his feet—he isn't exactly ugly.

Vinn throws the towel into his laundry basket and climbs into bed. I lay frozen, awake and hardly daring to breathe, for the rest of the night. When the sun finally rises, I feel Vinn stir. Without a word, he disappears back into the bathroom, showers and dresses, then leaves the room.

I sit up, staring at the closed door. He always seems to be mad about something, and now, I realise he even wakes up like that. Biting my lower lip, something tells me it's about to get a lot worse when he sees that article today.

NICOLA JANE

Downstairs, I hear Gia and Blu. I join them at the table, taking my seat beside Vinn, who is staring at his mobile as usual. "Good morning," says Gia brightly.

"Good morning." "What are your plans today?"

I shrug. "She's spending the day with me," says Vinn coldly.

We all turn to him, but he continues to stare at his phone. "Doing what?" I ask.

"Smiling for the fucking cameras," he snaps.

My heart drops. He knows about the story. "Cameras?" I repeat.

"Ignore him. He's got his panties in a twist over some gossip in the paper. It's nothing."

"Nothing?" yells Vinn, looking up. He snatches the nearest newspaper and opens it. "High-flying businessman Vincent Romano is living a lie," he reads.

"Come on, Vinn, nobody reads that paper," says Gia.

"The business mogul who recently married Italian Sofia Greco is living a lie. It's not the first time a man of his status has married to keep their love life secret. Our source revealed he has yet to consummate his marriage to the Italian beauty, leaving everyone wondering if it's female company he really desires." Vin throws the paper across the room, and it spreads over the wooden floor as it lands. "Whoever the fuck this 'Revenge' person is, I want him found."

"Vinn, you have a million enemies. It could be anyone," says Gia.

"Then I'll kill every single one of them."

"What if it's not an enemy?" asks Blu. "What if it's someone closer to home?"

"I told you, Raven wouldn't do it," snaps Vinn. "She's not like that." It annoys me how he jumps to her defence, but I feel some relief they're not looking in my direction.

"You did hurt her," I mumble.

PLAYING VINN

"We sorted that out and moved past it."

I arch a brow. "And how exactly did you sort it out?"

We stare at each other angrily, and I feel Gia shift uncomfortably. "Anyway," she continues, "I thought we could spend the day together."

"I told you, she's coming with me," snaps Vinn.

"Maybe I don't want to."

He takes a calming breath. "You're my wife, and you will act like it."

I scoff, folding my arms over my chest. "Fine." He wants a wife, I'll fucking be the doting wife.

Vinn's mother enters the room, and we all fall silent. She takes in the newspaper scattered across the floor. "Keep your head, Vinn. Do not respond to negative lies and show a united front with your new wife. It will die down." Then, she calmly takes a seat.

When we arrive at Vinn's office, Raven is already yielding calls. She smiles sympathetically. "It'll blow over."

"It's not that." He glances at me. "Let's go to my office," he says to Raven, releasing my hand. I ignore the sting of hurt in my chest. Why should it bother me that he can talk to her? After all, she knows him much better than I do. Instead, I head for the stairs. "Where are you going?" asks Vinn, but I ignore him.

I'm halfway down before I hear him chasing after me. "Sofia," he hisses angrily.

"I'm acting like a wife," I say, forcing a bright smile. "Isn't that what you wanted?"

"You're not leaving!"

"You just asked the assistant you were fucking to step into your office so you can open up to her about how hurt you are," I say, mimicking a baby voice and sticking out my bottom lip. "Do you think a wife would react well to that?"

"She's my P.A., and I have business to discuss."

"Great, then I'll be on my way."

"Sofia," he shouts as I take another step away.

"You told me to act like your wife, so I am. I will not be made out to be a fool. Unless the story is true," I accuse, narrowing my eyes.

"Don't be ridiculous," he barks.

I close the gap between us, a smug smile on my face. "Is that what you need to talk to her about? Does she know the real you?"

He moves so fast, I don't see it coming until his hand is around my throat and his lips are an inch from my own. "You'd like that, wouldn't you," he whispers, "a reason to get out of this marriage." I swallow. His thumb idly rubs along my jaw as he stares at my mouth. "Just say the word and I'll prove it isn't true." His other hand takes mine and he holds it against his pants. His erection pushes against my palm, and my eyes widen. "Say it," he whispers.

I pull free. "Never."

He grins, his eyes still fixed on my lips. "Never is a long time." Our heavy breathing fills the silence and then he steps back. "Now, get back upstairs, Sofia."

VINN

"I can't let anyone think I'm gay, Raven. I can't lead the organisation like that. I'll have men trying to say I'm not up to running it. They'll think I'm weak." "That's bullshit. Gay men aren't weak."

"I know that, but things are different in this life. There are beliefs. I must have a son. It's expected."

She shrugs. "If you ask me, it's all outdated crap. You're the boss, change the ways."

I laugh. "If only it was that simple."

"Then get her pregnant, shut them all up."

"That's proving a little more difficult than I imagined," I mutter.

"She can't have kids?" gasps Raven.

"I wouldn't know. We'd have to try to know that." She stares at me for a few seconds, absorbing what I've said, and then she laughs.

"You're kidding. You haven't had sex?"

"I don't know why this news shocks everyone. Blu laughed too."

"Well, it's just you're so . . . well, let's just say you're insatiable. It's been weeks . . . months since you and I . . . so where are you going?"

"I'm not going anywhere else. I'm married," I say, defensively. "I'm waiting for my wife."

"Oh. I bet that's hard." She laughs at her pun, and I roll my eyes.

"How're you and Mac?" I ask, changing the subject.

"Actually, there's something I should tell you. It's early days, but as my employer, you should know. I'm pregnant."

My mouth falls open. "Pregnant? Since when?"

"Since before Mac left for Nottingham. I did the test at your wedding."

"Shit," I stand, and so does she. "Erm, congratulations."

She smiles, and I wrap her in an awkward hug, inhaling her strawberry scent. "And it's definitely his?"

She hits my chest playfully. "One hundred percent."

NICOLA JANE

I nod again, not wanting to push too much. Would she even tell me if I was this baby's father? As if reading my mind, she smiles softly. "This baby is Mac's, not yours. I'm only eight or nine weeks, and it was months ago for us."

I ignore calls all day. The other Capos want to speak with me, but the fact they'd even question these lies makes me want to kill them all. "There's nothing else for it," states Blu when I turn up at the Kings Reapers clubhouse later in the day. "You'll have to get her pregnant."

"It doesn't mean anything," says Riggs, the club's president. "People deny they're gay all the time. They lead full lives with the opposite sex and come out later in life."

"How about I shoot every man who asks me if it's true?" I ask, staring hard at Chains. He grins wide. "Go on, try me," I tease. We're always looking at ways to piss each other off.

"Chains, don't," warns Riggs. "If Vinn kills you, my sister will kill me."

"It might be worth it," Chains replies, smirking.

"Better still," I murmur, standing just in case my next words touch a nerve, "let's ask your wife." I turn to where the women are chatting with Sofia. "Leia?"

"Jesus, Vinn, she's my little sister," snaps Riggs.

"Don't push me for a fight because some nutcase ex is selling shit about you," drawls Chains. "I got the girl, get over it." He's right, I need a fight and I'm pushing him. Leia would never forgive me if I hurt her husband, and when she joins us and snuggles into Chains' side, he winks at me, reminding me that he did in fact win the girl.

"What's wrong?" she asks.

PLAYING VINN

"Vinn's in a mood cos of the story in the paper today," says Chains. "And he isn't getting any."

"Any what?" she asks innocently.

"Any of what we did an hour ago," he responds, smirking.

Riggs shoves him hard. "Some shit is private," he hisses. He hates any talk like that about his sister, as would most men, but Chains laughs and kisses Leia on her head. They have a kid together, so Riggs can't exactly do anything about their relationship.

"It's nice you've brought Sofia over," says Leia, and I nod. "She's really lovely."

"Just say what you really need to say, Leia," I mutter.

She kisses Chains before taking my arm and leading me away from everyone else. She's the only person I'd let drag me around like a damn puppy dog. We sit down at a table, and she clasps her hands like she's about to get serious. "She looks so sad, Vinn."

I glance over to where Sofia is sitting with Anna, Riggs' wife. I've never really taken the time to watch her, but I guess I can see sadness there. Her smile doesn't quite reach her eyes. "There's nothing I can do about it."

Leia arches her brow. "Nothing?"

"Yah know, I did her family a favour. They're hardly up there in the family ranks. By giving her my name, her father went to the top. She acts like I forced this on her, but she should be grateful."

"Sheesh, if you say shit like that to her, no wonder she's miserable. You know she had a boyfriend back in Italy, a life with friends and a career?" she asks, and I narrow my eyes. It's new information, and Leia wouldn't understand the gravity of what she's saying. Our lives are not the same, and we have expectations. Sofia was promised as pure, saved for me. It was her father's job to keep her safe until the day she married. There should never have been a boyfriend.

"So, she's pining over some boyfriend?" I snap.

She gasps. "God, no, that's not what I meant. I just wanted you to understand she had a life, and now, suddenly, she's here with you. It's a huge change."

I stand and straighten my tie. "I married Sofia because my father was a good friend to her father and he set it all up. It's not a marriage for love but for convenience. We both have to get on with it."

"Vinn," says Leia, trying to grab my hand, "it doesn't have to be like that. You could be happy together."

I scoff, shaking my head. "This isn't a fairy tale, Leia. It's life. I'm not the kind of man to love or to be loved. As long as my bloodline continues, my job is done.""Bullshit," she snaps. "I know you, and I know you could treat her so good. You could fall in love and be happy."

"Nobody truly knows me, Leia. You know what I allow you to."Hurt passes over her face and her hand falls in her lap. I feel a pang of guilt as I step away. Diesel, the dog I bought Leia, rushes past me to get to her, and she makes a fuss of him. "I know you, Vinn. I don't care what you say," she mutters from behind me, and I smile to myself.

We're in the car heading home when Blu calls me. "You're not going to be happy," he greets, and I brace myself. "Planning permission for the apartment complex was turned down."

I grit my teeth. "How? That was supposed to go straight through without any hitches." I've sponsored an entire campaign for the local councillor, costing me thousands, all so this planning permission would go through smoothly. "Today is the gift that keeps on fucking giving," I utter, leaning towards Gerry, who's up front driving. "Take me to see Councillor Jones."

"I'll meet you there," says Blu. I disconnect and note the annoyance on Sofia's face.

"It won't take long," I explain. As the car slows to a stop outside Jones's small office, I take a deep breath. "We have dinner with your cousin. Afterwards, we'll talk." She doesn't respond. Gerry opens my door, and I direct her, "Stay in the car. I won't be long."

Blu's already waiting, and he bangs on the door. Jones isn't popular amongst the locals, hence why he keeps his office door locked. He appears at the other side of the glass, looking mildly irritated when he spots us. "How hard would it be to hide his death from the public eye?" I mutter as he unlocks the door.

Blu smirks. "I'd make it work."

"Gentlemen, I'm about to head home," Jones says, faking a smile.

"Too bad." I shove my way in, and Blu follows. "Azure just delivered some very upsetting news," I drawl, picking up a photograph of his wife from his desk.

"Yes, well, as I explained to Azure, it can't be helped. If I was allowed to vote alone, I would pass it. You know that, Vinn. But there are twelve people on the board, and all of them had reservations."

I place the photograph down and turn to face him. "I don't think you understood the assignment. Your mission was to quash the reservations."

"Vinn," he gives a condescending chuckle, "throwing your toys out the pram won't get the planning permission granted." I glance at Blu, hardly believing my ears. I've spent years

NICOLA JANE

listening to my father tell me I should always show respect, ask nicely, and reach agreements with as little violence as possible. But this is one dick too far today, so when my hand wraps around Jones's throat and I force him to take a seat, it's almost a natural reaction, and I wonder which Vinn is the true me. "I have been very patient," I seethe. "I've helped support your ridiculous campaign."

"Vinn," he whispers, choking when I squeeze harder.

"You told me it wouldn't be an issue. You said you had a strong say on the panel."

"I'll talk to them," he croaks. I release his throat and hold my hand out as Blu passes me a small knife. "Our next meeting is in a month," he splutters.

I grip his leg, and he frowns, confused. I take the small, sharp knife and push it into his thigh, twisting it. It's painful, and it'll take a hospital visit to close the wound. When he realises what I've done, he opens his mouth to scream, but Blu shoves a handkerchief in there and it muffles the noise. "I have had enough of people thinking they can take the fucking piss. You have twenty-four hours starting now. I want that planning permission."

I withdraw the knife, and he cries harder, gripping the wound. Blood pours through his fingers as he looks at me with panic in his eyes. "If I was you, I'd call an ambulance. That's pretty deep. It'll need packing and stitches." I pat him on the shoulder and hand the knife to Blu, then I wipe my bloodied hand down Jones's jacket. "You should be more careful using knives when opening your mail. I'll have my P.A. send you one of my company letter openers."

Outside, Gerry and Sofia are leaning against the car, chatting. I narrow in on the way she's smiling as she watches him smoke a cigarette. As if my day's not bad enough, I have to contend with her breaking all the fucking rules. "Get in the car," I growl. My voice makes her jump. Gerry flicks his cigarette and gets into the driver's side without a word. Sofia utters something under her breath as she gets in the back seat, slamming the door.

Blu's behind me. "Remind me again, what exactly did her father tell you about her?" he asks.

"That she was a good girl."

"She's a fiery one, that's clear."

"She's pushing me too far, Blu. I'm gonna snap." He pats me on the shoulder. "Sometimes it's easier to work with them. Gia is much calmer when I agree to whatever she wants."

"Sofia wants to be in Italy with her old life."

"Oh. Well, show her it's better here, with you."

I shake my head, getting into the car. I don't have time to settle her in, she's just got to suck it up and stop being such a spoiled brat.

I arranged for dinner to be on the terrace this evening. It's a warm evening and with this being Zarina's first visit to our home, I thought we should make the effort. If I can win over Sofia's cousin, maybe she can talk her into making my life easier and complying.

Sofia smiles wide when Zarina arrives, and I watch as they embrace. They're close, it's obvious. I stand and kiss each of Zarina's cheeks. "Your home is so beautiful," she gushes, and I smile.

"Thank you." It's something Sofia has never commented on apart from the other night when she made a confusing statement about it being too white and full of silk. I got the impression it wasn't a good thing.

NICOLA JANE

The waiter pours us wine as we settle into our seats. "How long are you here?" I ask.

"Three months. My father agreed to a short-term arrangement, although I have fallen in love with London and would love to make it a permanent thing."

"Yes, it's magical on the first visit. What do you do for a living?"

"In Italy, I'm a beautician."

I smile wider. "Yes, it shows." She blushes under my compliment. "Maybe you can give my wife some tips. We have a charity dinner tomorrow evening."

She glances towards Sofia and offers a guilty smile. "Actually, Sofia is amazing at make-up. She taught me."

I smirk. "I have yet to see that side of her."

"I am actually sitting here," Sofia says brusquely.

"Oh, I'm aware," I drawl, sipping my wine. "Tell me, did she show that side of herself to her boyfriend?" They exchange a look, and I drain my glass. "Your father never mentioned it."

The waiters bring out the food. "This smells wonderful," says Zarina, relief in her voice. I stare at the homemade salmon pasta, Lorenzo's speciality, then we eat in silence.

Afterwards, the women make polite conversation with each other while I check emails on my phone. I'm angry at the thought of Sofia with someone else. Not because I'm jealous, although I am, but because her father lied to me, and now, I have to deal with that.

I finish the bottle of wine seeing as both women stick to one glass. "What did you do back in Italy?" I ask Sofia, interrupting the conversation they were having about a fashion designer.

Sofia stares for a second before replying, "Why?"

"Why can't you ever just answer a fucking question?" I yell, taking her by surprise.

"I was a hooker," she spits, smirking when my eyes blaze with anger.

Zarina stands. "It's been lovely, but I should go," she mutters.

"I'll see you out," says Sofia, leading the way to the exit.

I remain seated, tapping my thumb on the table and counting silently to try and calm myself. When she returns, she stays on the other side of the table and rests her hands on the back of her chair. "You can't even be nice for one dinner. Isn't it exhausting being so angry all the time?"

I stand abruptly, knocking my chair back. "Who was the boyfriend?"

"Nobody important."

"Did your father know?" She stares at me blankly, which angers me more. "Think about your answer, Sofia, because it could get someone killed."

"It was a stupid fling, nothing important. Why does it matter? You don't even like me!"

I stalk around the table to her, and she stands tall, keeping her eyes locked on mine. "It matters if your father lied to me, *moglie*."

"Why do you do that?" she yells, throwing her hands in the air. "You have pet names for every fucking woman in your life, but you refer to me as 'wife' or something equally as distant and unaffectionate."

"Answer my question!" I shout, slamming my hand on the table.

She swallows. "Yes," she whispers. "Yes, he knew."

Chapter Four

SOFIA

Vinn closes his eyes briefly, and when he opens them again, they are darker than I've ever seen them. "Did you have sex with him?"

"I don't have to answer that," I sputter, feeling my face heat. This wasn't the plan. Papa never said what to do in this situation. "I need to speak to my papa."

He shakes his head, sneering. "No."

"Then I'm going to my own room," I hiss, turning on my heel.

His arm cuts across me, stopping me. "Did you have sex with him?" he repeats. When I don't reply, he growls and spins me until I'm facing the table. His hand wraps in my hair and he shoves me over the table. "Should I find out for myself?" he yells. I close my eyes, trying to hold back the tears. *Don't show fear*. I repeat it like a mantra in my head, zoning out from Vinn as he holds me pressed against the table and kicks my legs apart. "Tell me!" he shouts.

"Yes," I mutter, digging my fingernails into the cotton tablecloth. "Yes."

He shoves away from me, but I remain where I am, scared if I move, he'll carry out his threat. I hear each heavy breath as he falls into his seat. "Get out," he mutters. It takes me a second to realise what he said. I glance up, and his eyes are

NICOLA JANE

now cold and vacant. "Get out," he repeats. I slowly push up from the table and straighten my hair, tears leaking from the corner of my eyes. "Go to your own room," he adds, and a pang of hurt hits my chest.

I lie awake. Maybe I should tell him the truth just so he doesn't look at me like I'm dirty, but he might see it as a green light to do what the hell he likes to me. Maybe my papa is right, and he'll use it as an excuse to disrespect me further. Mama said men like Vinn don't forgive and forget. She said he'd look at me like dirt forever, like my papa looks at her. I wipe another tear. I don't want to be like her, yet here I am, stuck in this marriage with a man who hates me. Eventually, he'll do exactly what papa did to her—he'll spend his nights with other women and return when it's convenient for him. He already spends as much time away from me as possible, and now he knows about Dante, it'll always be that way.

Maybe it's good I've kept him at arm's length, at least his rejection can't hurt me.

As predicted, I eat breakfast alone. Gia breezes through but tells me she has a busy day, so she doesn't have time for breakfast. Josey tells me Vinn's mother requested to eat in her room, so I tuck into pancakes and coffee and chat with her about her life outside of here.

When Vinn saunters in, I almost choke on my mouthful of pancake. "Phone," he says coldly, holding out his empty hand.

I stare at him, waiting for an explanation. "Give. Me. Your. Phone."

"Why?" I notice Josey rushing out to give us privacy.

"Make me ask again," he warns.

"I wanted to call my mama today."

"Then you'll call from my office, in front of me."

I narrow my eyes. "Why?"

"That word is banned from this point forward," he snaps as I place my phone in his hand. "You question me again and you'll regret it."

He clicks his fingers, and a male and female enter wearing grey suits and shades. I smirk because it's almost like a comedy sketch with the way they obey his clicky fingers and stand together with stony expressions. "Frazer and Ash are now your personal guards. Everywhere you are, one of them will be there too." He flicks his hand, and they leave as quickly as they appeared.

"What's going on?"

He grabs a handful of my hair and tugs my head back. "Did you question me, *puttana?*" His use of 'whore' sends another dagger to my heart. I wince as he tugs harder. "You'll be pleased to know we're flying home to Italy at the weekend." I keep my mouth closed, not daring to question him. "I have business to attend to there. In the meantime, you need to do this test," he says, pushing a small box into my hand. He releases me, and I glance at the ovulation test. My blood runs cold. "Now, *puttana.*"

"I . . . what do I . . . I don't know what to do."

"Pee," he hisses, grabbing my arm and hauling me to my feet. He gives a small shove out of the kitchen, and I move forward.

"I don't need a pee," I mumble feebly. He follows me to the downstairs bathroom, holding the door open for me as I enter.

NICOLA JANE

He also steps inside. "You're staying?" He folds his arms across his chest and watches me coldly.

I sigh, opening the box and emptying out the contents onto the sink unit. Glancing over the instructions, I find it hard to concentrate with his moody arse glaring at me. With a shaky hand, I open one of the pee sticks. "Could you at least turn around?" I ask, and he rolls his eyes, turning to face the door. I will myself to pee but only manage a dribble. Fuck knows if it's enough, but honestly, I'm past caring. How dare he make me feel so fucking cheap and worthless? I put the cap on the stick and slide it across the marble floor until it hits his shoe. He glances down at it, then at me with an arched brow. "Apparently, you're looking for a smiley face," I snap.

He lowers gracefully and swipes the stick from the floor. He stares at the small window. "Looks like you're off the hook, for the next two nights anyway. We'll test again before we fly to Italy."

"What happens?" I ask, and he pauses to look at me. "When we get a smiley face?"

A grin spreads across his handsome face. I don't think I've ever fancied and hated someone all at once. "You'll spend the night in my bed."

"Why would you want a child with me when you hate me so much?"

"Because something good has to come out of this fucking nightmare that you and your father trapped me in." "Trapped you?" I repeat, hardly believing my ears. "I didn't trap you. This was you and my father. I'm the one trapped!"

"Two days, *puttana*."

"Stop calling me that!" I scream, clenching my fists.

He laughs. "I thought you wanted a pet name." I glare after him as he leaves. My mama was right—he looks at me differently now. Imagine how he'd be knowing the truth. I rush to my bedroom, needing to get my words down on paper. It's the only way to release the hatred I'm feeling.

VINN

"What's with the mood, Boss?" asks Blu warily.

I glare at him. "Maybe I'm just sick of everybody questioning me." "Hey," he says, holding up his hands in defence, "I ain't questioning you, I just haven't seen you so angry and agitated."

"Get used to it. It makes me feel better."

"Is this something to do with Sofia?"

"She isn't a virgin," I blurt out, and he raises his eyebrows in surprise. "Her father told me she was." "Maybe he didn't know?"

"Or maybe he took me for a mug."

"Is it really important to you?" he asks carefully.

"You're missing the point," I snap, speeding up the running machine.

"I much prefer running in the park than in this sweaty gym," he complains, starting up the machine beside me. "So, what's the point I'm missing?"

"Her father lied. She told me he knew about it. He lied and let me marry her. Why would he do that?"

Blu shrugs, "Maybe to get her off his hands? She's a mouthy one."

I shake my head. "No, there's a reason he wanted her to marry me. He fed me lies to agree. He said she was quiet, shy, a virgin who never left the house. It was bullshit. He sold me a dream wife, and I got her."

Blu laughs. "Is she that bad?"

"Worse."

"Why do you think he wanted her to marry you? It could just have been the deal he made with your father back in the day."

NICOLA JANE

"He's practically an outcast in Italy. The families don't trust him. I agreed because it's what my father would have wanted. Diego was his closest friend at one point."

"Are you gonna tell him you know?"

"Damn straight."

"And what will you do if he laughs in your face, Vinn? You're married now, there's nothing you can do." "We haven't consummated, so we can get the marriage resolved." Blu slows his machine until it stops, and I feel his eyes on me. I glance over to him. "What?"

"You'd seriously resolve the marriage? Why?"

"We're not right for each other. I want someone I trust to raise my son, and I don't trust her. She's keeping secrets from me, and her father lied." "Did you ever ask her if she was a virgin, or did you take her father's word for it?"

I shake my head. "It doesn't matter."

"I just think you're overreacting, Boss. You weren't exactly pure when you met her. What if she wanted a pure man?"

I laugh. "Are you coming to Italy or not?"

"Of course. Where else would I be when my boss is starting a war with an Italian mobster?"

SOFIA

I'm not used to travelling in style, so when the car drives directly onto the tarmac at the airport and Ash opens my door, I stare out at the private plane. "Are you sure this is right?" I ask her. It's only been a couple of days since Vinn hired the duo to follow me around, but I quite like Ash and she's growing on me.

"Yes, ma'am."

PLAYING VINN

"It's Sofia," I remind her again, and she smiles.

I head up the steps of the aircraft. Vinn avoided me for two days straight, and I was instructed to meet him here at six p.m. for our flight to Italy. It's now five-forty-five.

Gerry is seated at the front of the plane, tapping away on a laptop. He nods in greeting. I'm not sure if I'm imagining it, but he seems off with me these last few days, just like Vinn. Gia and Blu are in the next seats. She's resting her head against his shoulder with her eyes closed, and he's staring out the window. He doesn't acknowledge me, so I slip into a seat in the next row.

Five minutes later, the curtains at the back of the aircraft open and Vinn steps out, grinning. He's followed closely by the air hostess. His eyes land on me and his smile fades. "You're early," he mutters. I roll my eyes and turn to stare out the window. And he has the nerve to call me a *puttana*? He slips into the seat beside me, and I shift further towards the window to get away from him. "Have you eaten?"

"I'm not hungry." I haven't joined him for any mealtimes these last two days, not wanting to be in his cold company for a second longer than I have to. But Josey has made sure I've eaten by bringing food to my room.

"You need to look after yourself if you're going to carry my child."

"What does that mean?" I snap.

"You're welcome to use the gym I own."

I spin to face him. "You think I'm fat?"

He scoffs. "I think it wouldn't hurt to hit the gym."

My eyes widen. "I think it wouldn't hurt for you to keep your opinions to yourself." I straighten my shirt, glancing at my stomach. I'm not overweight, not even a little. I've always been lucky enough to eat what I want and never gain a pound, but hearing someone say I need a workout offends me.

NICOLA JANE

"Sofia, I just meant—"

"Stop talking to me," I hiss, turning back to the window. I hate him so much.

I spend the next hour watching the air hostess as she flutters her lashes and constantly touches Vinn's arm or shoulder as she serves him whiskey and laughs at his stupid remarks. I hate him. I hate him. I hate him.

I can't help but compare her tiny waist to my normal one. I buy size ten to twelve, and she must be a six, if that. Christ, maybe I am overweight. I rub my stomach subconsciously. Why do I suddenly feel so unattractive? Gia's the same size as me and she's gorgeous. I sigh heavily, and Vinn glances at me. "Are you hungry?"

"No," I snap. "Christ, I don't eat that much."

"I didn't say you did," he mutters.

"But you think I'm fat?"

Blu glances back at us, a warning look in his eyes aimed at Vinn. "No, I didn't say that," Vinn says.

I stand. "Why am I letting you make me feel like this?" I ask aloud even though I'm talking to myself. I pass him, wondering if my arse looks as fat to him as I do. Oh god, what's wrong with me?

I go into the small bathroom and stare at myself in the mirror. "Jesus, woman. Sort your head out. Why do you care what that Italian prick thinks of you? You're gorgeous. Stunning. He's lucky to be sitting next to you," I say aloud to myself. "Now, stop doubting yourself. Own your curves." The door opens, and I yelp in surprise. Vinn steps in, pushing me back against the wall. "Who were you talking to?" he asks, placing a hand either side of my head and staring down at me like a predator about to eat his prey.

"Myself."

PLAYING VINN

We stare at each other for a moment. Every so often, he glances at my lips, and I subconsciously lick them. His eyes darken when I do. "I wasn't trying to insult you back there. Apologies," he whispers. "You're beautiful. I read that mothers-to-be should work out to keep fit, that it helps their bodies go back to normal after birth. I should have explained myself better." He moves in closer, sniffing my neck, and I shiver, closing my eyes and willing myself to be strong. "You smell amazing," he mutters, his nose brushing my hair.

"We should go back out," I squeak.

"Actually, I have this," he says, holding up an ovulation test. I stare at it, then reality washes over me and I snatch it. For a second there, I thought we were making progress.

I sit on the toilet, not bothered that he's watching me this time. I pee on the stupid stick and push it into his hand, not caring it's wet with my urine. He glares at it with disgust. There it is—the look I'm used to. I wipe myself and as I stand, he smiles, turning it to face me. "Oh look, it's smiling." I feel the colour drain from my face as the smiley face mocks me. "And just so we're clear, nothing happened with me and the air hostess."

I scoff. "And I should believe you?"

"Yes. I don't lie." His words cut deeper than they should as I head back to my seat.

Chapter Five

VINN

I forgot how ridiculous the heat gets in Italy this time of year. Add in the mountains and winding roads, and by the time we reach Sofia's parents' house, I'm too hot and very irritable. I'd booked a hotel in the same village, but I'd also agreed to a welcome dinner with her parents, and we're already late, so there was no time to change.

Her father greets us at the door, which is unusual, but I let it slide. Maybe he gave his staff the night off. He kisses Sofia on each cheek, smiling proudly. She flinches slightly as he booms his greeting like he wants the whole damn village to hear. "Go through, your mother is so excited," he adds, pulling her inside. He holds out his hand, and I shake it, eyeing him cautiously. He's nervous and jumpy, glancing behind me as I step inside.

"Is everything okay?" I ask suspiciously.

"Fine, just tired. Flying back and forth to London is hard work." He set up his property development business in the UK, hoping to get more work. He's built his business here in Italy, but like me, he follows the money. He's already working on a few of my projects, including the apartment development that was finally agreed on earlier this week by the council.

NICOLA JANE

"We should go over the property plans for the apartments while I'm here," I suggest.

Sofia is talking in a low whisper to her mother, Angela, and she stops abruptly when I enter the room. "Vincent, how lovely," her mother greets, standing. She grips the chair and winces like she's in pain.

Sofia shakes her head, glancing away like it hurts her to see her mother struggle. "Are you okay?" I ask, catching her hand.

"Yes, my hips are acting out."

I kiss her cheeks, and she lowers carefully back into her seat. "I'll make us some drinks," says Sofia, disappearing into the kitchen.

"How are you both?" asks Angela as Diego joins us.

"Good," I lie. "Will Mario be joining us for dinner?"

They exchange a look at the mention of their son. "Not this evening," says Diego, the lie rolling off his tongue. "He's very busy."

I nod. "Are we eating here or out?"

"We're joining some of the other families up on the rooftop," says Diego. "Everyone is looking forward to seeing you."

Sofia re-joins us with a tray of iced tea. "Dinner on the rooftop?" she repeats. "I thought we agreed we'd have a family dinner this evening?"

Diego glares at her, and she lowers her eyes. "The families are our family."

"Of course," she mutters.

"Is there somewhere I can freshen up?" I ask, and I'm pointed to the downstairs bathroom. Pulling out my mobile, I call Blu, who headed straight for the hotel with Gia and Gerry. "Look into Mario Greco, he's missing."

"He didn't attend the wedding either, right?"

"Correct. They said it was a passport problem. I didn't care to question it, but for him not to see his sister at all since . . . I want him found. Also, Diego was acting shifty when I arrived. He's arranged for dinner on the rooftop this evening with the families."

"Interesting. You'd think he'd want to spend time with his daughter." "My thoughts exactly. He's showing us off, wanting everyone to know we're here. I'm delaying my conversation with him about his lies."

"Probably for the best. I'll check out Mario and let you know what I find."

Rooftop dinners have not changed. I remember them from when I was small. Everyone from the village gathers for tapas and drinks. It's a regular occurrence, one I sometimes miss, and it's a good way for the families to keep an eye on each other. The main man of this part of the organisation, the capo, isn't here, and it surprises me. If he was to come to London, I'd make sure I was available as a show of respect. It leaves me questioning how happy they are to have me here in Italy despite having two connections, one through Gia and Azure and now through Sofia.

I make polite conversation, occasionally looking over to where Sofia sits with her mother and some other older ladies. She takes a limoncello from the centre of the table and knocks it back, taking a second and doing the same. I've never seen her drink apart from the occasional glass of wine.

SOFIA
I wince as the sweet, sticky liquid slithers down my throat. It doesn't even taste that nice. Why do people insist on drinking

this stuff? "Are you okay?" whispers Mama. I nod, taking my fifth drink, and she watches me warily. "Are you sure?"

"Yes. Are you?" She knows what I'm really asking. "Hips." I scoff.

"What did you expect me to say? That I fell down the stairs? That old cliché?"

I sigh. "Have you heard from Mario?"

"He's doing well, Sofia. Please don't worry."

"I haven't seen or heard from him in months. I miss him. When can I talk to him?"

Papa joins us, shifting his chair closer to mine. "Why are you here?" he whisper-hisses.

"I have no idea," I snap. "He announced the trip two days ago and took my phone so I couldn't warn you."

"Have you argued? Have you told him anything you shouldn't have?" I shake my head, my mind wandering back to my conversation with Vinn about Dante. Papa eyes me warily. "What, Sofia?"

"You told me to say I had a boyfriend, right?"

He nods. "Yes, if he questions your virginity."

"Well, he did. Sort of."

Papa leans even closer, his eyes full of rage. "What happened?"

"He asked if you knew, and I wasn't sure what to say. He took it like you did and got mad."Mama squeezes my hand. "Why didn't you use your brain and tell him I didn't?" Papa hisses.

"Because I'm not good at lying. I told you that."

He shakes his head angrily. "You had one job," he hisses.

Vinn's shadow falls over us. "Sofia," he says sharply, and I look up guiltily. He holds out his hand, and I take it. "I just need to speak with my wife for a second," he tells Mama and leads me away. I snatch a glass off a nearby table as I pass, drinking it fast before Vinn notices.

The alcohol is making me lightheaded, so when we stop at the terrace edge, I grip the wall to steady myself. "What's going on?" asks Vinn.

"Going on?" I repeat.

"I'm not stupid, Sofia. I can see something isn't right. Tell me now, because if I have to find out for myself, it won't end well."

I shrug, and he narrows his eyes. "I don't know what you're talking about. Why are we here, Vinn?"

"Here on the rooftop or here in Italy?" he asks, his face serious. "I have things to discuss with your father."

"Because he lied?"

"Is your boyfriend here, Sofia?" he asks, looking around the crowds, but I shake my head. "Tell me who he is."

"It's in the past, leave it there."

"Did you love him?"

"Do you care?" I counter.

"I could kill your father for lying to me like he has."

"He didn't know," I blurt out, and Vinn laughs.

"Get your story straight, did you, when you were just chatting?"

"He didn't lie."

"Gerry is on his way to collect you. He'll take you back to the hotel."

I panic. "But I thought tonight was . . ." I swallow, not wanting to say the words. "You know, the night."

Vinn smirks, running a finger down my bare arm. I shiver. "I'll join you later. I have business to attend to."

I grab his arm, desperate to make him listen. "Vinn, please, Papa doesn't know about Dante, I swear it."

His face darkens. "Dante?" he repeats.

NICOLA JANE

"Shit! Fuck," I hiss. "Danny . . . I meant Danny."

Vinn removes my hand from his arm and glances at his mobile. "Gerry is here. Go."

"Please," I try one last time, "don't hurt my family."

"Then tell me what you're hiding."

I take a shaky breath. "Papa is the reason Mama is hurt. He's violent. But she loves him, and without him, she'll die. I love her so much. Please don't hurt him, or he might take it out on her."

"That's not the secret, Sofia," he says, smirking. "Try again."

I glance to where Papa is watching us. "There're no secrets."

He looks past me. "Take her back to the hotel, Gerry."

I glance back as Gerry makes a move towards me. I grab Vinn's arm, and he stares at my hand with disgust. "Vinn, please," I beg desperately.

"Good night, *puttana*."

At the use of that name again, I spit at his feet. It's a huge insult to spit at the feet of a capo, but I want to distract him from my papa. His hand dashes out fast, gripping my hair and pulling me close to him. People nearby are staring wide-eyed. Disrespecting my husband is one thing but disrespecting a capo in front of everyone cannot be ignored. Vinn's eyes are blazing with fury. "For that, *piccola vagabonda*, I'll be extra hard on your papa," he warns, shoving me towards Gerry, who catches me.

"Little tramp," I repeat, laughing in his face. "At least I've had sex. I'm beginning to wonder if the news story was true." I'm antagonising him in the hope he takes me back, leaving my papa here, alive.

Vinn takes a deep breath, forcing a smirk in place of the seething anger. "No more alcohol, Sofia. You can't handle it. Take her now."

PLAYING VINN

Gerry wraps an arm around my waist and lifts me from the floor, carrying me to the car. "That was stupid," he hisses in my ear. "What were you trying to achieve?" I begin to sob. "He's going to hurt my papa. You have to stop him."

"You know as well as I do, I can't stop Vinn Romano. Nobody can. Disrespecting him like that in front of the families was a huge mistake. He's going to make you pay."

I break free, almost stumbling. "I'm already paying with my life," I yell. "I'm tied to that monster forever."

Gerry shakes his head, his expression full of disappointment. "I thought you'd be the one to change him, but I was wrong."

"What's that supposed to mean?"

"He wasn't always this harsh. Since his father passed, he's . . ." Gerry trails off as he unlocks the car. "Well, let's just say he's not as calm as he once was. I put it down to a broken heart."

I scoff. "He'd have to have a heart for it to be broken."

"And I thought you'd heal it. Heal him. But you're causing more drama than is needed."

"I can't just take it lying down. I didn't want to be in this marriage, and then I caught him cheating with Raven and God knows who else."

"I have no time for your dramatics. Something is going on here," he says, pushing me to get in the car. "And when he finds out, which he will, we'll all suffer."

VINN

I invite Diego to sit away from the families. Most of the women have gone, leaving the men to drink. "Why did you lie to me, Diego?"

He looks almost bored, but it's forced, and it only confirms what I already know—he's hiding something. "Lie?" he repeats. "I haven't lied." "You're lying to me right now. You know what the punishment is for lying to me?"

"Can you be more specific?"

"Who's Dante?"

He sits straighter. "Who?"

I slam my hand on the table angrily. "I am trying to be patient for Sofia's sake, but if you don't start talking, I'm going to kill you right here," I hiss through gritted teeth. Diego glances around before sighing. "I didn't know until after the wedding," he lies. "I still don't know the whole truth."

I take out my gun and lay it on the table, resting my hand on it. He eyes it warily. "Sofia lied to me too. I only found out because Angela slipped it out," he says. "Is that why you beat her?"

Diego pauses, his nostrils flaring. "What happens between a man and woman in their marriage is private business."

"I feel like I've been taken for a fool, Diego. I promised my father I'd help you, should you ever need it, and I upheld that promise. The least you owe me is the truth."

"He's Colombian," he mutters reluctantly.

My eyes widen at his confession. "But not mafia? Surely not the Colombian mafia?"

His eyes flick to mine before landing on the gun again. "I don't know how she met him or what happened. She's yours now, he's not around."

"You handed me used goods, and not just any used goods, Colombian used goods!" I snarl and click off the safety on the gun. "Give me a reason not to kill you."

"Sofia will hate you."

"She already hates me," I yell, pointing the gun to his head.

He stares me in the eye, and I respect that he's showing no fear. "Teething problems. All marriages have them. Take her to dinner once in a while, buy her flowers."

PLAYING VINN

"I don't need relationship advice from a man who lies and beats his wife," I snap. "Why me?" I demand, pushing the barrel of the gun hard against his skull. "Why didn't she marry him?"

"Italian and Colombian? I'd have been cast out."

"That's all that matters to you, isn't it? And now, you have my name to help you climb that ladder a little bit higher." I slam the gun against his head, and he hisses as blood trickles down his cheek.

"Vincent, Benedetto would like to see you," says a voice from behind me. I turn to find three men in suits waiting patiently. They lower their heads in greeting. Benedetto, the Capo of this Italian clan, is my age, having taken over from his father recently. If I was still here, he'd be my capo too, but since my father made it alone, we have our own clan back in London. It's respectful to agree, so I follow the men to a waiting vehicle, where Benedetto is seated in the back. We shake hands.

"Apologies I wasn't there this evening," he says, handing me a whiskey. "I had things to discuss."

"Not a problem. I was going to come and see you tomorrow."

"I hear things have been heated this evening."

"Nothing I can't handle."

"Diego Greco and his daughter, Sofia?"

"Like I said, nothing I can't handle."

"There were rumours about Sofia," he says, sipping his drink. "And then she was shipped off to London."

"What rumours?" I ask.

"That she was fucking the Colombian mafia."

I swallow the liquid in one. "I hadn't heard."

He chuckles, leaving me feeling uneasy. "Strange. I thought you'd do your homework before committing. Rookie error."

NICOLA JANE

"My research didn't bring anything back," I say through gritted teeth. "Diego goes way back with my father, as he did with yours. I was honouring an old agreement."

"Yes, to tie the Romano and Greco families together. With your ties to the Rossi family too, it makes you very powerful."

"Are you worried I'll take over?" I ask, smirking.

Benedetto laughs, but it doesn't reach his eyes. "You wouldn't want Italy. You have your hands full with London. Besides, if the rumours are true and your wife is fucking the Colombian mafia, you'll have bigger problems."

I place my empty glass down. "It was great to see you, Benedetto. We'll talk soon."

"I look forward to it." He smirks, and I exit the car.

Gerry is parked up behind. I pull the door open with more force than is needed and get in. "Jesus, what a night."

"I don't think it's going to get any better, Boss. Sofia found a bottle of Jack back at the hotel, expensive stuff left for you from someone in the village. She wasn't in a good way when I left, so I hate to think how she'll be when we return."

I sigh. "Fucking great."

Music is playing loudly from our hotel room, and I find Ash standing by the door inside. "Where is she?" I ask.

"Bathroom," she says.

"Thanks. Get some sleep."

She nods once and leaves. I lock the door and go to the speakers to turn them off. Sofia comes scrambling into the room wearing only underwear. "What happened to the music?" she wails. She freezes when she sees me. "Vinn."

"Hi, honey, I'm home."

PLAYING VINN

"My dad?"

"Is alive."

She sags with relief. "Thank you."

"I didn't do it for you."

I shrug out of my jacket and loosen my tie. "I'm not a bad person," she almost whispers, but I ignore her. "Why do you hate me?"

"Colombian?" I ask, and she pales. "You were fucking Colombian mafia?"

Her mouth opens and closes before she finally mutters, "It wasn't what it seemed."

"I can't even look at you," I spit.

"It wasn't how everyone is saying," she snaps.

"Where is your brother, Sofia?"

She shrugs. "Working. He's on the oil rigs."

"More lies," I yell, unhooking my cufflinks. "You keep lying. You disrespected me in front of everyone," I throw them on the table, and they skid off, hitting the floor. "You're making me out to be a fool."

She rushes to me, gripping my arm. "I'm not. I don't mean to."

"Get some clothes on," I snarl in disgust. Hurt passes over her face. "You look like a whore."

She covers her mouth, and I wait for her tears to flow, but instead, she bends slightly and vomits down my front. I stare at the bright yellow fluid as its warmth soaks the thin cotton and clings to my skin. "Oh shit," she croaks. She scrapes her hands down my shirt, trying to scoop the vomit off. It splats on the floor, and I suck in an irritated breath. "Sorry," she whispers.

Chapter Six

SOFIA

I wait patiently while Vinn showers, my head pounding. Why the hell do people drink regularly if this is how it makes them feel? I've spent ten minutes on my knees scrubbing my own puke from the floor and trying my hardest not to repeat the incident.

When he returns, Vinn snatches a pillow from the bed and heads for the couch. I watch as he lies down. "I'm sorry, Vinn." He doesn't reply. "I'd understand if you wanted to divorce or leave."

He scoffs. "Maybe I should let the Colombian have you."

"If it makes you feel any better, I hate myself."

"Don't!" he hisses, glaring at me. "I'm not gonna feel sorry for you. How the fuck did you meet a man we consider to be an enemy?"

"Vinn, do you trust me?"

He laughs, shaking his head. "I don't trust anyone. Trust gets people killed." I nod sadly. "You're probably right. I trust the wrong people. That's why I'm here, in this mess." I lie on top of the blankets, turning my back to him.

"And don't think I don't know why you got drunk this evening," he snaps.

NICOLA JANE

Part of me wanted to test what kind of a man Vinn is. Would he still force himself on me if I was drunk? It would have been easier on us both. He thinks I've drank in the hope he'd leave me alone, but in reality, it was to numb the pain I'm going to feel the second he lays down with me. It's not that I don't find him attractive, I do. And it's not because of Dante, fuck no. It's because making love, having a family, should be about choice, and I am so sick of having my choices taken away.

When the sun rises at exactly five-thirty, Vinn is banging around and making as much noise as possible. I groan, throwing an arm over my eyes. "Up," he orders, ripping the sheets from me. His eyes linger a second on my body, then he turns away and begins rummaging through a suitcase. "Now," he adds, throwing some clothes at me.

I sit up and hold my spinning head. God, I feel awful. "Where are we going?" Taking in Vinn's running gear and trainers, I groan and flop back on the bed. "No, I don't run."

"I'm still extremely pissed about your father lying and I'm undecided how to make you both pay for tricking me into marrying you. I suggest you do exactly what I ask before I go on a rampage and take half the families out." He says it so casually that it takes a second for his words to hit my brain. "Running is a good cure for a hangover," he adds more softly.

Ten minutes later, we're standing outside the hotel while Vinn stretches. "Even in this heat?" I complain.

"There're other ways I like to burn off my anger," he says, raising a suggestive brow, "but I don't think you'll handle that, so running it is." He begins to jog away, and I groan. Why didn't I marry an overweight, ugly, out of shape Italian? Then at least when he says things like that, I'd be repulsed instead of . . . well, instead of not.

After thirty minutes of me constantly stopping and complaining, we reach a clifftop. I bend, placing my hands on my knees, and try to suck in more oxygen before I pass out. When I look up, there's a car approaching. It stops beside Vinn, Blu steps out, and they shake hands. "What's going on?" I ask warily, glancing around. It's pretty secluded here, and we haven't passed a house in ten minutes.

Gerry steps out from the driver's side and opens the back passenger door. He reaches inside and struggles for a second before dragging a man from the back. The man's hands are bound and there's a black bag over his head. Gerry shoves him hard towards Blu, who pulls him to the cliff edge. Vinn smirks at me as he removes the sack from the man's head, and I gasp as my papa's pale face stares over the cliff edge. He doesn't move, doesn't make a sound. My screaming pierces the silence, causing birds to fly from the trees in panic. Gerry wraps his arm around my waist, holding me back. "Now, *cagna*, start talking," whispers Vinn with a satisfied look in his eyes.

"Bitch? Oh, the names get better," I yell. "But nothing sweet yet, I'm disappointed." He laughs. "Your precious papa is about to go over the edge. You have five seconds before I give the go-ahead."

"You can't kill him without Benedetto's permission," I shout.

"Five . . ."

"You'll be killed yourself . . ."

"Sofia, keep your mouth shut! This piece of shit cannot threaten me!" my papa shouts.

"Four . . ." says Vinn in a sing-song voice.

Blu moves closer to the edge. "Vinn, be reasonable. I'll give you whatever you want. A son, a family, whatever."

"Three . . ."

I shake my head, tears wetting my face, and I plead with my eyes for him not to do this. "You don't have permission. You'll never make it out of Italy," I whisper.

NICOLA JANE

"What makes you think I don't have permission?" he asks, grinning. "Two . . ."

A silence falls over us all, the sound of my heavy breathing echoing, then Vinn nods to Blu. "One—"

"Okay!" I scream, and Blu pauses, glancing at Vinn for confirmation.

"Sofia, no," my papa yells.

"I was attacked," I continue. "The Colombian raped me." Vinn's mistrusting eyes narrow. "It's true," I add. "I saw a private doctor. There were notes, you can check."

Vinn tips his head in the direction of the car, and Blu drags Papa away from the edge. "You stupid girl," he snaps as he's shoved back in the vehicle.

Vinn steps closer, and Gerry releases me. "Tell me everything." I hesitate, and he arches his brow in warning. "I can get him back out here."

Gerry and Blu leave us, waiting in the car for their next order. "Mama said it was best to keep it to myself because it would start a war." I tangle my fingers together in a nervous knot. "Benedetto doesn't even know." "How did this happen? How did they get to you?"

"I was taken from my uncle's private boat. We'd spent the day at sea, me and Zarina with some of our other cousins. They took me during the night."

"You were on a boat with no security?"

"Papa is struggling financially. He had to let the staff go. Nobody knows," I mutter.

"He's setting up in London," says Vinn, confused. I shrug, unable to explain where Papa got all the money from for a new business and flights back and forth. He doesn't share that sort of information with me. "And your brother?"

"Papa said he's working on the oil rigs, but I don't believe him. I haven't spoken to Mario in months, not even on my wedding day. Papa said he didn't want to have him return in case he found out about the attack and started a war."

"Who knows about the attack?"

"Just my cousin. A video of the attack was sent to Papa. He says they are blackmailing him and that's why he has no money. The marriage to you was supposed to put an end to everything. They wouldn't want to war with you, or so Papa thought."

"Blackmailing him how?"

"I don't know. Papa said if word got out, I'd be accused of working for the Colombians, and Benedetto would have me killed."

Vinn sighs, nodding to Gerry for them to leave. Once the car has gone, he pulls me against him and wraps his arms around me. I stiffen, surprised by his show of kindness, and then I relax, letting him hold me. Suddenly, I'm tired . . . so very tired. Vinn scoops me into his arms and heads back down the path as I rest my head against his chest and close my eyes.

VINN

I carried Sofia back to the hotel, putting her straight to bed. Now, I'm watching her sleep as her eyelids flutter occasionally, her dreams clearly not good because she whimpers and flinches. Blu stands behind me. "You believe her?"

I shrug. "Find the doctor."

"Already done it," he whispers proudly. "He's meeting us here in thirty minutes."

"It doesn't add up. Why would they blackmail him over Sofia? Unless he's hiding something?"

"You think she was taken as a warning?"

I nod. "I want to know who this Dante guy is. We need to dig deeper into Diego Greco. We're also taking her mother back to England, so make sure she has a passport."

NICOLA JANE

"And if Sofia's lied again?" asks Blu.

I stand, grabbing my jacket. "No more chances. I will kill her."

The doctor shakes our hands and takes a seat. The barman brings over a tray of espressos. "These are the notes," he says, handing me a file.

"Tell me," I say coldly, and he nods.

"Ms. Greco—"

"Mrs. Romano," I correct him, and he nods again.

"She was assaulted sexually and physically." He opens the file and lays out a few close-up photographs of Sofia, bruises on her face, her thighs, and her neck. Her lips are swollen, and her eyes are bloodshot. The doctor uses his pen to point to her red eyes. "Consistent with choking. These marks on her neck are rope burns. She was held for six hours and raped repeatedly. Internal bruising was extensive, but she healed well and there should be no lasting scars."

"And this was definitely an attack?" asks Blu. "Yah know, it couldn't be consensual, rough sex?"

The doctor shakes his head. "Very rarely do I see anyone with these kinds of bruises. Mrs. Romano was extremely lucky. The culprit didn't care for Sofia, and he made sure to leave traces of who he was." He pulls out another sheet of paper. "He left DNA behind, which is very unusual in cases like this. It's almost like he wanted her to know who he was."

I stare down at the name. "Dante Arias," I say aloud. I pass over the envelope of cash, and the doctor tucks it inside the file. "Thank you."

PLAYING VINN

When I get back to our room, Sofia is sitting on the bed with her knees pulled to her chest, staring out the window. "We fly home this evening," I say.

She starts at my voice. "Can I see my parents before we go?"

"No."

"But my mama—"

"We're having dinner with Benedetto and his family. Dress."

"I don't feel like—"

"Dress, Sofia!" I snap impatiently.

She slowly rises from the bed and heads for the bathroom, slamming the door closed. That's better. I can handle things when she hates me.

Benedetto's home is much like my father's used to be. There're men hanging around playing cards and drinking whiskey, and the atmosphere is light and jovial. When I replaced my father, I changed things. I decided to keep my family close, and although I still have my closest men hanging around, it's not how it was before, not like this.

Benedetto greets us like long-lost family, ushering us inside a quieter room with a table laid out with tapas and wine. I'd forewarned Sofia to act like my wife today, so her hand is firmly gripped in mine, and as we're introduced to Benedetto's wife, Caterina, I release her so she can make small talk.

"Did you ask your wife about the Colombian?" he asks, pouring me a glass of dark liquid.

"I want to tell you, Benedetto, I really do, but I don't trust you," I tell him bluntly.

NICOLA JANE

"If you were in Italy, you'd be under me and you'd have no choice but to confess all. Vincent, this is my family, and I'll do anything to protect it."

"I hope you're not talking business," says Caterina, smiling and seating herself on Benedetto's lap.

I smirk. Sofia stands awkwardly beside me, and I hook a finger around hers, guiding her towards my lap. I pull her down and wrap an arm around her waist. "You're right, apologies," I say.

"I was just telling Sofia about my pregnancy," she adds, holding up a grainy image. "We had the first scan yesterday."

"Congratulations," I drawl, rubbing my hand along Sofia's thigh.

"We've been married for a month and weren't expecting to catch so quickly, but we're excited," Caterina says.

"Any news for you two?" asks Benedetto. "Everyone is wondering after that ridiculous story in the news." I laugh. "It's hardly news, Benedetto. It's a gossip page for bored idiots. I'm sure we'll make our own announcement in time." I grip the back of Sofia's neck and pull her down for a kiss. Her eyes widen as I press my lips lightly against her own. "Right, *bellissima*?"

SOFIA

I shudder when Vinn addresses me with the same name he uses for Leia. I don't know why it annoys me, but it does, and as he pulls away, I place my hands on his cheeks and kiss him back, only I take it deeper, sweeping my tongue against his and taking my time to taste him. It's our first proper kiss, and as I pull back, I feel my cheeks flush. For the first time, I see heat in Vinn's eyes instead of anger. There's desire and maybe even a little shock. Turning back to the couple, I smile, gasping when I feel Vinn's erection pressing against my arse.

PLAYING VINN

"That's right," I manage to squeak out.

"Wine?" asks Benedetto.

"Not for Sofia," Vinn cuts in before I reply. "We're flying home this evening."

"It'll help me sleep on the flight," I say, taking the glass offered to me.

Vinn removes it and places it on the table. "We have plans for the flight," he warns, and my cheeks burn again.

We eat while Vinn tells Benedetto about London and some of his businesses. It's boring really, but I do find out more about his property plans that my papa's drawing up. Vinn needs him, so there's no way he'd have pushed him over the cliff today.

※

I'm nervous for the flight home, so when I climb aboard the private plane and see my mama sitting beside Gerry, I'm in shock. "What's going on?"

"A visit," says Vinn, moving past me and heading for whatever is beyond the dark blue curtain at the back of the craft.

"Are you okay, Mama?" I ask, crouching before her and taking her hands in mine. She nods, glancing at Gerry nervously. "Have you hurt her?" I snap, glaring accusingly at him.

He smirks. "I've been a gentleman."

"We'll talk," I whisper to her, then I storm after Vinn. "What are you doing?" I hiss.

He looks amused, and I take in the small kitchen area as he pours himself a drink. "I'm having a drink."

"I mean about Mama."

"I told you, she's coming to visit."

"She's never away from Papa," I snap. "What did he say?"

NICOLA JANE

Vinn slams his now empty glass on the counter and pushes his face close to mine. "Your papa didn't have a choice," he growls out. "I call the shots." "What could you possibly want with her?" I wail.

"Maybe I did it for you."

I scoff angrily. "You don't do anything for me, Vinn."

His hand wraps in my hair at the base of my neck and his lips almost touch mine as he smiles. "I'm gonna set the world on fire for you, *ragazza dolce*."

"Sweet girl?" I repeat in a low voice. It's the first nice thing he's said to me and meant it.

"Men will burn, Colombia will fall, and it'll all be for you, *cara ragazza*."

I suck in a sharp breath. Nobody has called me 'dear girl' since my nona. "That's not for me, Vinn. It's for you. It's to save your reputation."

His nose brushes mine and his eyes stare at my lips. "Think that, if it makes you hate me more, but I know the truth." His lips press against my own in a slow, careful movement, almost like he's waiting for me to pull away. I don't. I wait, and as he tilts his head and his thumbs angle my face perfectly to connect with his, I close my eyes and let him kiss me. It's the kind of kiss that curls your toes and makes you press your legs together to ease the building ache.

Vinn's lips move across my mouth and then my cheek. He brushes the hair from my shoulder and runs his lips down my neck and across my collar bone, occasionally nipping the skin. His hands skim my stomach, which is on show thanks to the cute, cropped shirt I chose to wear, and then they travel underneath, his thumbs drawing circles as they make their way up to my bra-less breasts. He guides the shirt up and leans down to trail kisses over my chest, towards my pebbled nipple. I grip the counter behind me, throwing my head back when he takes my nipple into his warm mouth and circles his tongue over the sensitive nub.

His hand tugs at the button to my denim shorts, and when he slips it inside, I gasp, feeling slightly exposed as he runs his fingers through my wetness and smiles. He moves his finger in circles, and I jerk as sparks zap through my body. His other hand gently wraps around my throat, and he tears himself away from my breast to thrust his tongue into my mouth, kissing me with hunger.

Vinn rubs his erection against my leg, groaning into my mouth as he pushes a finger into me. My hands grip his wrist, trying desperately not to cry out in pleasure when he presses his thumb against my swollen clit. Knowing there are people just on the other side of the curtain is as much a turn-on as the thought of getting caught.

He pulls his hand away, and I resist the urge to grab it and put it back in my knickers. He holds his glistening fingers between us and grins before sucking them into his mouth. "Are you ready to beg yet?"

I stare open-mouthed. "Huh?"

"I told you before, *moglie*, you need to beg me, because I'll never force myself on you."

His words hit me like ice water. I straighten my clothes and take a deep breath. "I don't beg, *marito*. Ladies don't beg."

He laughs. "Very well. I'll sort this myself." I watch as he loosens his trousers, and my eyes widen. "Are you going to watch?" he asks, amused. I shake my head, backing out of the kitchen area and almost crashing into the air hostess. Vinn smirks, opening a door behind him and disappearing inside. I leave the curtain open just so I can keep an eye on the hostess, who sets about making drinks as I take my seat.

NICOLA JANE

"Mama, what happened?" I whisper, leaning across to her.

"Vinn told me I was coming to visit London," she says with a shrug. "Your papa wasn't impressed." "I'm so sorry," I murmur. Vinn returns looking relaxed as he slips into the seat beside me.

"Are you looking forward to your visit?" he asks.

"Very much," smiles Mama politely. I can tell by her fake expression she's nervous and wondering what the hell is going on. I turn to Vinn, making sure my mama can't hear.

"Please don't hurt her, Vinn. She knows nothing about my papa and his dealings, she won't be able to tell you anything ." "Relax, it's just a visit."

"Why?"

"Did I not warn you about questioning me?"

"Swear on Gia's life," I whisper.

"I won't hurt your mother, Sofia," he says firmly, but I note how he didn't swear it on his sister's life. "Don't you want some company at home?" I nod. "Then be happy."

Mama loves London. She always has. She'd visited before the wedding and then again for the big day. Her eyes light up at all the hustle and bustle, and even being followed by Ash and Frazer doesn't dampen her mood.

We've been here for three days, and we've spent every single daylight hour sightseeing. Ash knew all the best places to go despite Frazer's reservations of safety issues. We finish our day with a coffee in our new favourite cafe.

PLAYING VINN

"You don't spend much time with Vincent," Mama remarks, stirring her latte.

I half smile, "I've been spending time with you." "I spoke with Josey, and she said you seem unhappy."

"Mama, don't let Vinn hear you're checking up on me with the staff," I hiss, groaning. "He'll send you home." Despite her reservations about coming here, she's really enjoying herself, and honestly, I think the break from Papa is doing her a world of good. It's the first time in a long time she's walked straight without cowering or wincing in pain.

"I have to go home one day, or your papa will come looking for me. Why aren't you happy?"

I shrug, picking up my napkin and tearing pieces from it. "It's a big change."

"We talked about this already. Vinn will keep you safe."

"Mama, he can't stand me. He isn't going to keep me safe."

"He will. You'll have his child, and then he'll have to."

I avert my eyes, and she places a hand on my cheek. "Sofia, what's wrong? You are trying for a child?"

"Not exactly," I mutter, and she gasps, looking around like it's a shameful secret someone might overhear.

"Dear girl, Vincent is your safety net. He was your way out of Italy. Don't let him slip through your fingers. You're his wife!"

"Like I said, he hates me."

"It doesn't matter, Sofia, he'll learn to love you. Just be yourself and the rest will come naturally, but you have to give him a child."

"Did you learn to love Papa?" I ask, and she stares down at the table.

"It was a difficult relationship from the start. My family was poor, and I didn't have the novelty of choosing a man like Vinn. Your papa was just a soldier back then. He worked hard to become a made man. Benedetto's father gave us a chance

NICOLA JANE

to be who we are, and I'm grateful. I don't have to eat from the garbage these days." She laughs. "I love your papa, but he's a complicated man with a lot going on."

"You could stay here, with me."

She shakes her head. "I have a duty to him, until death do us part. Italy is where I belong."

"I'll need help with your grandchild one day."

She smiles, taking my hand. "Good girl, you'll make me proud."

"Mama, why did Papa choose Vincent?"

"He knew his father, you know all this."

"Just . . . he seemed so insistent on it. Vinn said he hadn't seen Papa for years before they met to discuss the wedding. I wondered if there was another reason."

"It doesn't matter either way. You have a decent man, so look after him like a wife should."

Chapter Seven

VINN

It's late when I finally climb the stairs to bed. I'm so exhausted, I can hardly see straight, and the bottle of whiskey I shared with Blu didn't help. As I open the bedroom door, I pause. Sofia is asleep on top of the blankets in a sexy nightdress. It's short, riding up her thigh, and it's shaped around her breasts. I frown. She's been sleeping in her own room since I yelled at her and told her we'd only share a bed when she was ovulating. She'd not even attempted to step one foot in here let alone dressed like that.

I carefully strip down to my shorts and sit on the edge of the bed. She looks peaceful, and even though my cock is screaming at me to fuck her until she wakes, I know I can't. So, I lie down beside her stiffly, trying not to disturb her.

I wake sometime later, feeling too hot. Glancing down, I find Sofia nuzzled against me with her leg over mine and her arm resting across my stomach. Her head is laying on my chest, angled up so I can see her beautiful sleeping face.

I brush my finger over her cheek, and she mumbles to herself. I smile—she's cute when she isn't talking back and asking questions. I gently kiss her lips, and she mumbles again, this time clearer. "*Frazer.*" I stiffen and it disturbs her, causing her to wake with a start. She glances around, takes in the

NICOLA JANE

way her body is wrapped around mine, and scoots away like I've burned her. Maybe she was expecting someone else, I think to myself angrily. Jealousy burns through me at the way her cheeks flush and her lips are slightly apart. "Vinn," she whispers, sounding confused.

I climb from the bed. "Sorry to disappoint," I snap.

"I waited for you, but you were late," she mutters, tugging her nightdress strap back to her shoulder.

"Why are you dressed like that?" I ask, and she blushes deeper and shrugs. I grab her ankle, tugging her until she's flat on her back, and she lets out a yelp. I climb over her. "Who were you waiting for?" I take her tiny hands in my own and hold them above her head.

"You," she whispers.

"Then why the fuck were you dreaming about Frazer?"

She frowns. "I wasn't."

I grip her chin in my free hand and push my face to hers. "You said his fucking name."

"I-I don't know . . . I don't think I was dreaming about him. I can't control my dreams."

I run kisses along her jaw, and she closes her eyes. "Maybe I've left you alone too much and now you're fantasising about other men."

"I have spent a lot of time with Frazer," Sofia reminds me.

I grip her throat, not enough to hurt but enough to let her know I'm pissed. "You don't wanna bring out that side of me, Sofia. I can't control him."

I tug the strap of the nightdress down her arm until her breast is exposed. She's breathing fast and watching me through hooded eyes as I go back to kissing along her neck and collar bone. I avoid the one place she's desperate to feel my mouth, and she whimpers every time I move around her breast. "What do you want?" I ask, smirking. She presses her lips together, refusing to answer me. I grin and go back to teasing her.

I move down her body, releasing her hands, but she keeps them above her head and occasionally strains her neck to watch me kiss across her stomach, over the soft material of her nightdress, and down her thigh. I gently part her legs, taking one foot in my hand to rub it. She groans aloud, and my cock twitches. I run my hand up her calf and over her knee, almost to the top of her thigh, before running it back again. She fidgets impatiently. "Tell me what you want, Sofia."

"The same as you," she whispers.

"Which is?"

When she doesn't answer, I laugh at her stubbornness. Without warning, I rip her panties, exposing her to me. She tries to close her legs, looking shocked and just as turned on as me, but I pin her knees to the bed and lean closer. She smells amazing. I press my tongue against her opening, and she cries out in surprise. I run it over the bundle of nerves and concentrate on teasing the sensitive bud. She grips her fingers into my hair.

"Say it," I whisper, but she still doesn't answer. I place my hands underneath her arse and lift her pelvis slightly. "You just have to say the words, Sofia." I suck her pussy into my mouth, lapping her juices. I rub circles over her clit with my thumb, and when I feel her clench, I pull away.

Sitting back on my heels, I wipe my mouth on the back of my hand. Sofia stares at me with a lost expression. "Just say the words." I crawl over her, placing a hand either side of her head, and I flick her nipple with my tongue. "Say them." She bites on her lower lip. "Do you trust me?" she asks.

I frown. She asked me this already, and again, I shake my head. "I told you, I don't trust anyone." I roll from her, hating that I feel the loss immediately. "Do you trust me?" I ask.

NICOLA JANE

"No."

"Probably for the best," I admit, turning onto my side and pulling the sheets over. I hear her sigh as she lies back down.

SOFIA

I'm not sure if I'm sad or angry. I dressed sexy, and he didn't show until God knows when because I fell asleep waiting. Then, I give into his sultry smile and his skilful tongue without so much as a fight, and he leaves me wanting more, so much more. I know what I have to say if I want him to finish what he's started, but there's a fear deep inside me that worries I'm asking for more than sex. I was adamant, from the second I knew I had to go through with this marriage, that I wouldn't give him that part of me. At least not willingly, and yet here I am, hooking my leg over his half-naked body and sleeping on his hard, muscled chest like some wanton whore. I roll my eyes. I'm an idiot . . . a desperate one.

When Vinn's alarm rings an hour later, I'm still awake, feeling frustrated and annoyed. Vinn showers and dresses for work like he didn't come home stinking of whiskey in the early hours. How does he do that?

"We're attending an important dinner this evening. Get a cocktail dress," he orders, throwing his credit card on the bed. "And maybe get your hair done?" I narrow my eyes behind his back. *Dick.*

Once he's gone, I dress and head to the library. It's on the top floor of the three-story home and it's the only place, as far as I can tell, where there are no cameras and his men won't bother me. I've yet to explore the rest.

I curl up into a cosy armchair and open my laptop. Vinn still has my mobile phone, and I won't give him the satisfaction of asking for it back. I open my emails. My heart beats faster when I spot the editor from the Daily Spy has sent me something. I scan my eyes over the email, picking out the important bits, and then clap my hands in delight. Just wait until I tell Zarina.

I arranged lunch for me, Mama, and Zarina, and it's the perfect time to tell Zarina my exciting news. I wait for Mama to go to the bathroom before leaning across the table and grinning. "Guess what, the editor loved my story. She said it was Tweeted about loads. She wants me to write another." "Oh, Christ, please tell me you said no."

"Are you joking? Of course, I didn't. Can you imagine if this becomes my career? I could be a journalist like I always wanted." It was a dream Papa squashed, saying no one from our community would trust us. "Or the decomposing ex-wife of a mob boss," says Zarina, shrugging.

I laugh. "It's gossip. No one cares about gossip."

"Vinn will care that his wife is the one writing it," she hisses. "You're crazy if you think he'll laugh this off."

"I can't pass up this opportunity. Do you know how long I've waited for this? He shut down the Gazette, and that was huge. The editor at the Spy doesn't seem to give a crap what Vinn says. She's a female editor and all for women's rights."

"Will she campaign when you're dead?"

"I won't die. You worry too much." I spot Mama heading back to the table. "I haven't told her, so keep quiet."

After lunch, we head back to the house. It still doesn't feel like home and I'm not sure if it ever will, but Zarina is so enthusiastic about the large, cold rooms and flashy decor. She didn't have a chance to really be nosy when Vinn was here before, so she takes full advantage and rushes off with Mama to check out some of the other rooms.

I bite my lower lip as a stupid idea enters my head. There doesn't seem to be many staff hanging around, and I can hear Josey banging around in the kitchen, so I know she's busy. Ash has gone off to do whatever she does when she knows I'm safely locked away in the house, and since I apparently dreamt of Frazer, Vinn's had him moved to his mother's team of security.

I take a tentative step towards Vinn's office. I've only ever been in once, and he was here. I tap lightly on the door and press my ear against the thick, dark wood. There's no answer and I can't hear movement inside, so I push the door and huff in annoyance. It's locked. Taking a step back, I stand on my tiptoes so I can reach the top of the door frame and run my fingers across it. Nothing. My eyes fall to the group of three small flowerpots hanging on the wall with beautiful flowers cascading over the sides. I check each one, digging my fingers into the soil until I feel the key. Smiling triumphantly, I pull it free and insert it in the lock. I glance around to make sure the coast is clear before sneaking inside and closing the door behind me.

I take a second to steady my breathing, leaning against the back of the door and looking around the large office. It's an old man's kind of place, and I guess he hasn't bothered to redecorate since his father passed. I make my way over to the desk, closing the blinds so patrolling security outside can't spot me. Vinn's desk is one of those oversized, dark wood things that you imagine a lawyers to sit at. Pulling the top drawer open, there's nothing but a half-drank bottle of whiskey and two glasses. I feel around the back and pull out a pair of silk knickers. They aren't mine, so I drop them like I've been burnt, screwing up my face in disgust.

PLAYING VINN

The next drawer has some paper files inside. The first has my father's name on it, so I open it and find bank statements and other financial paperwork. I guess after what I told him, he's dug deeper. It doesn't surprise me to see Papa's not as wealthy as he pretends to be. I slam it closed, not wanting to know the extent of his mess.

The next file is about me. Inside has my personal bank details, where I went to school, and my doctor's details. There's an open envelope and I peek inside, finding the doctor's report from after my attack, along with pictures. I stuff them back inside because I don't need reminders of what I went through. I work hard to keep it locked away, which isn't difficult seeing as I spent most of it drugged so the memories aren't vivid. But seeing those might bring it all back.

There's a gun laying at the bottom of the drawer, standard in Vinn's world. I sigh. There's nothing in here that the Spy would be interested in. As I put everything back, I notice a file splayed open on his desk. It shows the plans for some buildings, and when I take a closer look, I realise this must be the new project he's been working on. It's small apartments, lots of them, being built on green space. I grab a piece of paper from his notepad and scribble down the address. This is what he had the council pass through without the public knowing. Maybe the Spy could expose it. I'm pretty sure people will be furious that they'll lose a green space to a bunch of apartments. London is already full of buildings.

I'm locking the door when Mama and Zarina return. "We found a lot of bedrooms and they're all decorated the same," complains Zarina.

"Let me guess, white?"

"Yeah." She laughs. "What have you been up to?"

NICOLA JANE

Mama heads for the kitchen, saying something about an espresso, so I grab Zarina by the arm and pull her into the sitting room. "I found something for a story."

She groans. "No, Sofia. No."

"It's not big, but I think they'll like it."

"What exactly do you get out of this?"

"Apart from my dream to work for a newspaper?" I ask, rolling my eyes. "I can make something out of this, Zee. I could be an undercover reporter. Think of the things I could expose."

She laughs like I've lost my mind. "Listen to yourself," she hisses. "Most women would love this life," she adds, looking around the living room in awe. "He's sexy, powerful, and he's got a great home and a nice family. Why can't you just be happy?"

"Because I want more," I snap. "And maybe that sounds spoiled and bratty, but this isn't enough for me. I don't want to wake up one day and realise I'm trapped here forever. My mama did that and look at her, desperate to get home to beg forgiveness from the man who's spent years mistreating her."

Zarina looks concerned. Maybe because we never speak about my parents and what happens behind closed doors. "Does Vinn hurt you?"

I shake my head. He's scary in a dominant kind of way, and although he's pinned me down and held my throat, I've never felt threatened. Images of his head buried between my legs assault my mind and I shake my head to remove them. "No, but it doesn't mean he won't. We don't know each other, and he's got a temper. He's ruthless. You saw how he knocked the plates from the table in the cafe."

"So, you want to punish him just in case he hurts you?" she asks sceptically. "Because I have to say, that's crazy. What if he turns out to be the most loving husband ever? What if he makes the best father to your children?"

I shake my head. "It won't happen. He doesn't like me in that way. I've seen how he looks at his assistant. He doesn't look at me like that, in fact, he barely looks at me because he's never here. He'll have other women on the side. He probably already has."

Zarina takes my hand and smiles sadly. "It's almost like you're trying to prevent the hurt by dismissing the idea that he could actually be a nice guy. You're pre-empting something that might never happen. You can't live life like that or it's not living."

"Why should I sit around and play the good wife while he's out there doing God knows what with God knows who? If this job works out, I can earn money and save, just in case something bad does happen. I can be financially independent. That's a good thing. Planning ahead for every eventuality."

She sighs, nodding. "Right, well, don't say I didn't warn you."

I tap away on the laptop, smiling to myself. This is gonna be a good story. Suddenly, the library door crashes open and Gerry stands there, looking annoyed. He takes in my pyjamas and messy bun and his eyes bug out of his head. "Why aren't you dressed?" I stare back, bewildered. "The dinner?" he snaps. "Vinn's already at the gala waiting, and he sent me to collect you."

I slam the laptop closed, jumping up in panic. "Fuck, I forgot."

He buries his face in his hands. "At least say you have a dress."

NICOLA JANE

My heart slams hard in my chest. Vinn's gonna be pissed. I shake my head, and Gerry groans, muttering something behind his hands that's inaudible. "It's fine. I have dresses, I'll just grab anything."

"It's a gala. You can't rock up in one of those ugly summer dresses you wear," he hisses.

My mouth falls open. "I didn't choose those," I snap. "They were already in the wardrobe. Besides, I have some of my own clothes."

"Vinn specifically asked you to have your hair done today ." At the reminder of Vinn's rude words this morning, I smirk. This is another opportunity to go against the grain. "Don't give me that smirk," warns Gerry. "I'm not in the mood for games. Dress now, you have ten minutes before he loses his shit and starts blowing up my phone."

All the way to the gala, Gerry glances at me in the rear-view mirror, shaking his head in annoyance. He wasn't impressed when I came down to the car, but we were out of time and Vinn was already calling Gerry. We stop outside a large country manor. It's lit up and there are other sleek black cars parked out front in a neat row. Ash gets out the front passenger and opens my door, smirking. I think she finds my rebellion amusing. "He's waiting over there," she points out quietly.

Vinn's staring down at his mobile. As I approach, he glances up, and as he takes in my short, low-cut red dress, anger passes over his face. "What the fuck?" he hisses.

"You don't like it?" I ask, slowly spinning to show off the back that cuts so low, I couldn't wear underwear.

"It's a gala. You wear cocktail dresses to galas," he mutters, glancing around like he's expecting this to be one big joke.

Raven steps out of the grand building and comes to an abrupt halt when she spots me. "Oh," she gasps. Of course, she's in a floor-length, fitted black dress that clings to her curves perfectly. Her hair is neatly plaited to one side and her diamond earrings glisten.

"Oh indeed," repeats Vinn.

"I was just coming to tell you we're being seated for dinner."

VINN

I follow Raven inside, Sofia trailing behind me. "I'm sure there's an explanation," Raven whispers.

"I'm not interested in explanations."

"Give her a break. Besides, the dress does look good on her."

"Yes, if she was a hooker, the dress would be perfect for this evening," I snap, storming ahead.

"I hate this bullshit," complains Blu when I reach our table. Gia pats his hand, smiling. He hates being part of this life, but since marrying my sister, he doesn't have a choice.

I sit beside Gia, who stands to kiss Sofia's cheeks in greeting. "You look amazing," she gushes, glancing at me with confusion as she embraces her.

"Thanks." Sofia suddenly doesn't look as confident as she did when she first spotted me. Maybe it's because the entire room looked her way as she entered. Being the only person to wear red to a black-tie event is gonna have that effect.

Raven sits opposite me, alongside her husband, Mac. I inwardly curse, like I do every time I see her. She's wearing a long black dress that shows her tiny baby bump. That could have been us. Why the fuck did I mess it up? I sigh heavily, getting everyone's attention around the table. "What?" I snap, and they look away.

NICOLA JANE

Dinner gets underway and I eat in silence, too annoyed that Sofia defied me again to bother engaging as Blu and Mac make jokes about club life. After dinner, Sofia mutters something about the bathroom and marches off with Ash close behind her. Raven moves to the vacated seat. "Christ, get over the dress," she says.

"It's not about the fucking dress," I snap. "It's about her doing as she likes, not listening, not doing as she's . . ." I trail off. Raven's the wrong person to speak to about this.

She arches her brow. "Told?" she finishes. "She isn't a dog."

"You don't get it," I mutter.

"She's your wife. Treat her with respect and she'll do the same." Raven's phone buzzes and she opens an email "Great," she utters. "Another story is hitting the Daily Spy tomorrow."

I pinch the bridge of my nose, willing the dull thumping in my head to go. "It'll be another pile of shit. Ignore it."

"Maybe we should meet with the editor," she suggests, but I shake my head. I've done my research—the editor has no family, no one close, and nothing for me to threaten. She screams about women's rights and animal cruelty. I have no doubt she burns her bra at conventions condemning men. She's not the kind of person to listen and the sort of person who will smile at my threats before printing them all in her cheap rag of a paper, causing me more harm than good.

Sofia is heading back so Raven returns to her seat. The dress is sexy, and I'd appreciate it if it was on my bedroom floor rather than in a place like this, where rich men offer girls dressed like that good money for a night of pleasure. As she sits, the dress rides up higher. If she was to bend over, it would reveal everything. My cock twitches, and I'm reminded why I can't shift my shitty mood or the thumping head—I need sex. It's been months and I'm not sure how much willpower I have left.

"Sorry for—" she begins, and I stand abruptly, cutting her off.

"I should mingle," I mutter, walking away.

SOFIA

Vinn's been gone ages, mingling with the rich arseholes filling this room. Gia has spent the last twenty minutes eating Blu's face off while they whisper and giggle together like horny teenagers, and Raven and Mac have disappeared. I still have Vinn's bank card, so I make my way to the bar. It's not busy, as most people have table service, so I grab a stool and order a white wine and soda. Not being a big drinker, I never know what to order, so I stick to safety. I'm halfway through my drink when a man takes the seat beside me. He smiles, and Ash steps forward. "You can't sit there," she says.

I'm embarrassed and my face shows it. "Ash, it's fine," I hiss. "Honestly, I'm okay."

She steps back, and the man smiles wider. "Are you sure? I can move."

"It's fine."

He looks around. "I hate these events and I felt suffocated sitting over there. Thought a walk over here might help, and then I spotted you and thought you must be feeling the same."

I smile, nodding. "Something like that."

He holds out his hand. "Raymond," he introduces.

"Sofia," I say, shaking it.

"How come you're sitting here alone?"

"Same as you, needed a bit of space."

"Not surprising in that dress," he says, grinning. "You made quite a statement."

"I didn't mean to. I didn't get the memo."

He laughs. "I'm sure Vincent was happy about that."

"You know him?"

NICOLA JANE

He laughs again. "Everyone knows him." The barman comes to take his order. "I'll take a whiskey, neat. Sofia?"

"I'm fine. I can't drink much without making a fool of myself," I say, smiling.

"In that case, let's have some shots." He proceeds to order drinks I've never heard of and hands over his card. "What's a party without making a fool of yourself? Maybe you can top the dress incident," he jokes, and I laugh, feeling at ease.

"I really shouldn't." I glance around, but there's no sign of Vinn.

"I'm a forty-eight-year-old man, not after anything but company. What's the worst that can happen?"

A tray of different coloured shots is placed before us and Raymond smiles. "Let's drink the first to a happy marriage," he says, taking a green one. I do the same, and we clink glasses before knocking the drinks back. I wince at the taste of bitter apples coating my tongue. "Okay, that wasn't the best one. Try this," he suggests, chuckling. I take the pink shot. "This time, you choose."

I think for a moment. "Good company at boring events." This one goes down easier.

"So, how is married life?" he asks.

"Different," I mutter. "London is much busier than where I come from."

"I bet." He hands me a blue shot, and we drink to Italy. "My wife moved here from Canada. She took a few months to settle. She hated it at first."

"Does she like it now?" I ask, desperate to cling to the hope I might settle here and feel happier.

"She wouldn't leave."

He points to the empty tray, and the bartender tops up the glasses. "Let's do one after the other."

PLAYING VINN

"That's definitely not a good idea." I smirk. "I'll be carried out of here."

"I bet Vincent likes you to stay prim and proper," he sniggers.

"I'm my own person," I mutter, frowning.

"I hear he likes his women to be compliant and well behaved."

"I don't think that's true." I suddenly feel like I need to defend the husband I hate.

"Really? Does he listen to your opinions? Do you get to do what you wish?" I take a shot and swallow it, followed by another, and Raymond smiles. "I stand corrected."

"Vincent Romano doesn't tell me what to do!" I say bravely, holding up my empty glass.

"Is that right?" Vinn's voice rumbles from behind me, and I almost fall off the stool. Raymond grabs my hand to steady me. He looks amused.

"Vincent," he greets, smirking.

Vinn's eyes linger where Raymond's hand touches mine. "Let's go," he says firmly, ignoring Raymond.

"I'm not finished," I spit, lifting another shot from the tray. Vinn's hand wraps around my wrist, halting me just as it touches my lip.

"Now, Sofia."

Raymond arches his brow in an 'I told you so' way and stands. "Maybe I should go."

"You'll be seeing me soon, Raymond. Make no mistake," mutters Vinn in a deadly voice, and I shiver.

"Look forward to it," Raymond responds as he walks away.

Vinn pushes his face to mine. "Too far, Sofia," he whispers, his eyes dark and dangerous. His hand runs along my shoulder, and I freeze as he places it calmly around the back of my neck. "Drink the shot," he orders. My hand shakes, causing the blue liquid to run over my lower lip, where it's still positioned. "Now," he growls, and I jump with fright, spilling some of it down my chin. I slowly tip the glass, swallowing it. "Are you feeling the warm buzz?" he whispers, spreading my legs and standing between them. He reaches behind me and produces another full shot glass. He must have ordered more, and I wince, my stomach rolling at the thought of another. "Next," he says, smirking.

"I don't want any more."

"So, you'll drink for Raymond Clay but not your husband?"

"I've had enough."

"You'd had enough when I told you we were leaving, but you were insistent on finishing your little party." He squeezes my throat a little tighter, and I grasp the edge of the stool. "You ask me if I trust you and then drink cheap shots with my enemy."

"I didn't know," I croak, my eyes beginning to water as he applies more pressure.

"Is that how you met the Colombian, *puttana?*"

It's too much, the word 'whore' and then him daring to bring up Dante after I opened up and he saw the doctor's report with the disgusting pictures. I see in his eyes he regrets it the second the words leave his lips, but it's too late. I release a frustrated cry and shove him hard. He only stumbles back a step, but it's enough for me to stand. My hand hits his cheek, and the sound seems to echo as we both glare at each other, processing what just happened.

"I am not a whore!" I hiss, clenching my fists. "I'm not a whore," I repeat, tears stinging my eyes as I rush past him and head for the exit.

Gerry catches me in his arms as I fly down the stone steps, sobbing angrily. He holds me for a second until he spots Vinn and releases me. "Let's get you home," he whispers kindly.

PLAYING VINN

"It's not my home," I sniffle, sliding into the back seat of the car.

Vinn joins me, and we stare out of opposite windows in silence as Gerry pulls away from the house. I remember the underwear in his draw. "Do you love Raven?" I ask, my throat hoarse from crying. He doesn't answer. "You look at her like you do," I whisper.

We get home and I head straight for my own room. We need distance, which is a joke considering we're never together.

Chapter Eight

VINN

I scan my office. "Gerry!" I call, and he appears. "Someone's been in here."

He frowns. "Is something missing?"

I shake my head. "No."

"Maybe Sofia had a wander around?"

"It was locked," I say, and he shrugs.

"No one could have walked in off the street, Boss, but I'll check the cameras."

I settle behind my desk and open the drawers. Nothing is missing, but things have been moved. I hook the knickers on my finger and hold them up. I forgot about these. I drop them in the rubbish bin as memories of Raven spread on my desk assault my already horny brain. Sophia's question plays over in my mind. Do I still love Raven? I scrub my face and let out a loud groan. Fuck, why is it so complicated? I don't love Raven. Of course, I don't. I don't love anyone. But do I still want her? Every fucking second of every day. My body craves her. She was my last decent fuck, and now, I've had to resort to sorting myself out in the shower because I'm married. And the most interesting thing about that is even though Sofia drives me nuts, it was her I thought about this morning when I couldn't concentrate at work and needed to relieve myself. It was her

NICOLA JANE

taste on my tongue and her scent burnt into my brain. I slam my hand on the desk in frustration. Seeing her chatting with that piece of shit, Raymond, like he was a long-lost friend tipped me over the edge. I didn't like it . . . not one bit.

SOFIA

I clean the makeup from my face and stare at myself in the mirror. I don't smile anymore, not like before. Vinn didn't answer me when I asked about Raven, and it hurt. Why the hell did it hurt when I hate him? Maybe because I know I'm tied to him. Maybe because I'm a little jealous. I sigh. Raven is beautiful and elegant. She walks into a room and people stare. And yes, they looked my way this evening, but only because I was half naked. Who the fuck did I think I was, dressing in red to a black-tie event? I groan. Why do I even care?

The shots are making my brain fuzzy and it's making me think I'm hurt, but maybe I'm not. Maybe it's just the drink. I pat my face dry with a towel while making my way to the drawers, then I rummage through to find comfortable underwear. I laugh to myself. It's all new stuff—lace, silk, sexy, thongs—but nothing remotely comfortable. I pull out a lace bodice and grin. Christ, I've never worn anything so revealing and sexy. I hold it against my torso and stare in the mirror. It won't hurt to try it on. After Vinn's recent remarks about my appearance, it might be the boost I need.

I stumble around, trying to get the thing on, and then stare at my reflection. I look good, hot even. The alcohol makes me brave, and I pull a pose fit for Instagram, laughing to myself. I turn to check out the back as the bedroom door opens. I let out a squeak of panic as Vinn glares at me. His expression is dark, but it's not anger for once. No, this look is full of desire. He likes what he sees.

PLAYING VINN

"We're married, we should be in the same bed all the time," he says, not taking his eyes from me.

"Right," I mutter. I follow him like this is what I always wear for bed, and I don't even bother to put up a fight. Why aren't I putting up a fight? We get into his room, and I stand awkwardly while he loosens his tie, still watching me through hooded eyes.

Vinn begins to unbutton his crisp white shirt, and I bite my lower lip as he peels it from his body. My gaze follows his hands as he unfastens his belt, ripping it from the loops so it makes a snapping sound that causes me to jump in fright. He opens the button on his trousers. "I want to," I blurt out, and my cheeks instantly burn with embarrassment.

He slowly moves towards me, his eyes fixed to mine. "You want to what?"

My breathing is heavy as he gets closer. "I want to . . . I want . . ."

He stops so close, my breasts brush against his chest. "Show me," he whispers, taking my hands and guiding them to his zipper.

I slowly pull it down. I can feel his erection desperate to be released. I keep looking up into his eyes as I lower to my knees. I'm not experienced, but Zarina and I once watched a porn film for a laugh. Pulling down his trousers and shorts, I stare at his hard cock. It's big. I don't have much to compare it to, but it looks too big. I tentatively run my tongue over the tip, and he hisses as it jerks. "I'm not sure . . ." I begin.

"You're doing great, baby," he whispers, stroking a hand down my hair. It's pathetic that this one kind word has me smiling, and yet I know he's only saying it because I'm on my knees, about to suck his cock. How shallow does that make me?

NICOLA JANE

I hold the base, wrapping my hand around it, and lick him again. He continues stroking my hair as I carefully run my tongue underneath and along his shaft. He's breathing deeply, and I revel in the fact I'm the cause of that. I open my mouth and suck it in like a giant lollipop. Vinn moans and it spurs me on. I suck, moving my head back and forth, careful not to scrape him with my teeth. My jaw aches from his sheer size and there's no way I can get him all in my mouth, but I keep going until he pulls me back and crouches to my level. He kisses me hard, slowly pulling me to stand.

"The first time I come, I need it to be inside of you," he murmurs, leading me to the bed, but I shake my head.

"No," I mutter, and he frowns. "I don't want you to be soft and slow. Fuck me." This needs to feel like what it is, a fuck, a means to an end. We're not making love. I peel the straps from the bodice until my breasts are revealed, distracting him from overthinking my last statement. It works because he sweeps me up in his arms and slams me against the wall, sucking my breast into his mouth. I arch my back, desperate for him to ease the ache between my legs. He reads my mind, moving the piece of fabric between my legs to one side and lining himself up.

"You're sure?" he asks. I nod, gripping his shoulders, and he doesn't double check. Instead, he slams into me, and I cry out, shocked by the intrusion. He pauses, resting his head on my shoulder. "Fuck," he whispers. After a minute, it starts to feel more comfortable. "Are you okay?" he asks, and I nod. He kisses me, distracting me as he withdraws to the tip and slams in again. This time, he doesn't pause, just repeats it. His hands squeeze my arse as he pumps into me, grunting with each forceful movement. I can feel a warm tingle in the pit of my stomach, and he senses it too because he sucks my nipple into his mouth and the feeling intensifies. "Hang on, Sofia, don't come yet," he pants. He moves us over to the bed and withdraws, laying me on my front. He rubs my arse, then slaps his hand against it and rubs it again. I flinch, but it doesn't feel like a bad pain, and when he does it a few more times, I have to clench my legs together because the ache is worse.

VINN

I slap her perfect, tanned arse a few more times, rubbing between each strike. Her skin turns a peachy red, and I run my finger between her legs. She's drenched. I lick her juices from my fingers and line myself back up with her pussy. Gripping her shoulders, I ease back into her. She feels so fucking good, I'm barely hanging on. I push her arse cheeks together to give more friction even though she's already gripping my cock like a damn vice. She buries her face into the sheets and moans. It's sexy as fuck, and I slam harder, slapping her thigh. It sends her over, and I feel her pussy clenching around me as she quivers. Her body shakes as her orgasm washes over her and her tiny fists grip the sheets, screwing them up.

I could watch her all night, but she's too much and too new to this to go the distance. I pull out and turn her over, wanting to see her face when I come. I place one of her legs over my shoulder and guide my cock back to her wet pussy. She watches me as I strain to hold back. I wrap her hair around my fist and tug gently, pushing harder with each thrust. I close my eyes, growling when I release into her. My legs go weak, but I keep moving until I'm completely empty.

I brace myself over her while we stare at each other and try to catch our breath. Sofia was better than I'd imagined, and as I take in her dark eyes and rosy cheeks, I feel a flicker somewhere deep inside my chest.

SOFIA

NICOLA JANE

Vinn is distant again. It came suddenly, right after we'd done what we did. He doesn't make it obvious, though. Instead, he kisses me on the head and removes the bodice from my aching body. He discards it and pulls the sheets back, guiding me into bed. I wonder if it's a part he plays, the gentleman, but his eyes tell the truth, and right now, they're full of regret. "I have some things to finish in the office," he mutters, then places another kiss on my head. "Goodnight, *bellissima*."

Once he's gone, I wrap the sheet around my body. I need to delete the email I was going to send to the Daily Spy. Mama is right—I should make this work, and there's no reason why I can't. Seeing the kind, caring side of Vinn is nice, and maybe it's just because I gave in to him, maybe it's because he might finally get his child, but I want more of it. I want more of him.

I creep back to my bedroom and sit on the bed with my laptop open. I have a private file stored under the name 'coursework' but before I get a chance to open it to delete the articles I've written so far, an email pops up from the Spy. I stare in disbelief as I read it. It's confirmation that my story will appear in tomorrow's paper. Front page! But I didn't send it . . . unless . . . I open my sent items and groan. I must have hit 'send' when Gerry stormed into the library earlier today and made me jump. *Fuck.*

When I wake, the bed is empty. I don't know if Vinn even bothered coming back at all. I dress and head down for breakfast. Vinn's pacing as Gia reads something aloud. I recognise it as the article straight away.

". . . the planning permission was seemingly passed through without public input. The space is currently a green space

PLAYING VINN

used by many locals and even includes a children's play area. With so many properties already crowding the estate, it's no wonder residents in the area will be angered by Mr. Romano's latest business venture. People may also question the integrity of the local councillors and not for the first time. Jones has been investigated previously for—"

"Stop," snaps Vinn, and she places the paper down.

"That's not good," she mutters.

"We need to call a meeting," says Blu, standing and pulling his mobile from his pocket.

"Everything okay?" I ask, taking a seat.

"Ask me again if I make it home alive," mutters Vinn as he storms from the room and Blu follows.

"What happened?" I ask.

Gia glances at the door to make sure they're both out of earshot. "That Revenge person wrote another story. Vinn's got a project to build apartments on the Dale estate. He's got a lot of investors and if it falls through, it's his neck on the line."

"He can't help if it falls through," I say.

"They won't see it like that, Sofia. You know what these men are like. It mentions dirty money being invested and suggests a backhander to the council." "That's kind of true," I point out.

"These investors will not want to be outed like that. It puts them at risk of the cops looking more closely at where their money is coming from. They trusted Vinn to protect their names as well as their investments. They're gonna be coming for Vinn. Plus, these apartments were to help house women escaping violent relationships. He came up with it after his meeting with some woman who raises money for women's shelters. His heart was in the right place." I remember that woman because I was at the meeting. She told us some harrowing stories of women who have now made something of themselves after suffering many years of abuse. I feel a stab of guilt. Maybe he does have a heart after all.

Mama and my mother-in-law enter the kitchen, laughing about something. They've really hit it off and it's nice to see her laughing again. "Who died?" asks Rose, taking a seat beside Gia.

"Another story," explains Gia, pushing the newspaper towards her. She glances over it, then passes it to Mama.

"Who would want to make up those lies?"

"Vinn will sort it, Mum. Don't worry," Gia reassures her.

"I know he isn't innocent, but he does some good from the bad."

VINN

"Get me the editor on the phone," I order Raven.

"Is that a good idea?" she asks. She's trying to help, but I'm too wound up. When I glare at her, she nods, picking up the phone. She puts the call through to my office.

"Mr. Romano, I've been expecting you." The editor sounds smug, which only adds to my bad mood.

"You know I can have you for slander?"

"You could if it were lies."

"It is lies!" I yell. "That's why real newspapers won't print it. It's bullshit."

"Other newspapers won't print it because you scared them with threats. Editors talk, Mr. Romano."

"I'll speak with my solicitor, and I suggest you do the same!"

"I'll require proof to make a retraction," she says coolly.

"I don't need to prove shit."

"Fine, but my solicitor will tell you the same thing."

I disconnect, muttering in Italian. "We've gotta take this Revenge fool more seriously," snaps Blu. "We underestimated him."

PLAYING VINN

"Damn right."

"The council might retract the permission if residents question it. They can put it on hold while an investigation takes place."

"I can't put it on hold," I growl. "There's too much riding on it."

"I know but keep your head. We've got to meet with the investors and explain what's happened."

I stand, pulling my jacket on. "Fuck that. I'm Vinn Romano, I don't have to explain shit. I want to pay Raymond Clay a visit."

"Raymond?" he repeats, following me.

"He hates me since I cut his lover's fingers off. It makes sense."

"You can't go in there," yells the secretary stationed outside Raymond's office. I ignore her, marching in and coming to an abrupt stop at the sight of his fingerless lover on his knees sucking Raymond's cock. Blu sniggers.

"Don't let us stop you," I drawl.

Martyn James tries to stand, but Raymond places a hand on his head and keeps him there. "I won't," he snaps, jerking himself off. I roll my eyes and move towards the couch. Gerry keeps watch at the door, while Blu stays in the corner. Seconds later, Raymond tucks himself away and pours himself a drink. "I'd offer you one, but I don't like you so . . ."

I smirk. "Are you writing stories about me, Raymond?"

He laughs. "Do I look like I have time to write stories?"

"Honestly, yes. You must have plenty of time on your hands, seeing as I just caught you getting your cock sucked."

NICOLA JANE

"Everyone has time for sex, it's a stress reliever. Clearly, it's not something you have a lot of. Is that why your new wife looks miserable and drinks with strangers in bars?" He sits at his desk. "Have you tried looking closer to home?"

I glance at Gerry, giving him the signal. He moves to Martyn and wraps an arm around his neck. "Yah see, the thing is, I keep my circle tight, Raymond." Martyn panics, his feet sliding over the floor, trying to relieve the pressure on his neck. Raymond doesn't bat an eyelid. "So, I don't need to look closer to home."

"It was just a suggestion, no need to get upset."

"If I find out it's you, Raymond. I'm going to kill you, your wife, your children, and Martyn." Gerry drops Martyn, and he falls to the ground, coughing violently. "If I was you, I'd find a new lover. This one keeps getting you into bother," I say to him as I head for the door.

I spend hours placating the investors, assuring them I'm on top of this deal and they won't lose out. By the time I find my local councillor, I'm even more than pissed.

I take in the large house with four cars on the driveway and shake my head. I must have paid for most of this with the amount I put into his back pocket. I ring the doorbell and a young woman in her twenties answers. She blushes when I smile. "Helen, right?"

"Yes."

"Aren't you stunning," I admire, and she blushes deeper. "Is your father around?"

PLAYING VINN

She nods, opening the door wider and letting us in. She disappears and returns with Damien Jones. He pales. "Gentlemen, let's go into my office."

"Blu, keep Helen company," I order, and Damien shifts uncomfortably. I slap him hard on the back and smile. "Relax, Jones, she'll be fine. Blu's a gentleman . . . most of the time."

I follow him to his office with Gerry close behind me. "We have an emergency meeting first thing to discuss your project," he explains, pouring a drink with a shaky hand.

"I don't want to hear that, Damien. I want to hear that there's no problems."

"Vinn, we've been getting complaints all day. This can't be brushed under the carpet. You'll be lucky if they let it go ahead at all now." I pick up a silver pen and admire the intricate pattern before casually slamming it into Damien's shoulder. It pierces the skin like a butter knife, ripping his pale blue shirt. He screams out, reaching for it. Gerry shoves some material into his mouth to muffle his cries, and I grip his hand that's holding the pen. "Don't pull it out, Damien. That's the worst thing to do when you impale yourself on a sharp object. Now, you let your little friends on the council know that I'll come for each and every one of them until this project gets the go-ahead." Sweat beads on his head and he makes a muffled attempt to agree. "I don't want to have to go to all the trouble of fucking your daughter and having her involved with me, because honestly, I'm a fucking mess. Just ask my wife. But I will, Damien, if I have to. I'll fuck her and have little Vinns with her so we can be one big, happy family. Imagine that, me joining you for Christmas. Now, just so we're clear, the planning is to stay and I'm going to start the build next week. If anything goes wrong, I'm coming for you and all your little jumped-up friends on the council. I won't stop until I get what I want." He nods, and I pat him on the back. "Good man." I

NICOLA JANE

pull the pen from the wound in a swift movement and drop it on the desk. "Oops, you'd better get that seen. We don't want you to die before the meeting, and blood loss is a savage way to go."

Sofia is asleep when I get back, so I kick off my shoes and pull the sheets from her. She wakes, sitting too fast and looking around disorientated. "You're alive," she whispers sleepily.

I wrap her hair around my hand and tilt her head back towards me so I can get access to her mouth. "You're not naked enough," I growl, pinching her nipple. The pink lace panties are sexy but not needed right now.

"You have blood on your shirt," she points out.

"It's been a bad day." I gently tug her hair until she stands. "Now, get naked."

She shimmies out of the knickers, and I release her hair, taking a seat by the window and watching as she pours me a whiskey. She brings it to me and kisses me before crouching before me and pulling my belt open. I watch through hooded eyes as she releases my erection from my pants. She takes me into her mouth, and I suck in a breath, tipping my head back and closing my eyes as I revel in the feel of her wet tongue lapping at my cock. Seems Raymond was right—it does relieve stress.

Chapter Nine

SOFIA

The noises Vinn makes spur me on to take him as deep as I can to the back of my throat. There's something sexy about a strong man groaning because I'm driving him wild. He grips my head and stills me, then a long, low moan escapes him, and I feel his cock swell before he coats my tongue with his cum. He flops back in the chair, his arms hanging limply and his eyes closed. I wince as the taste in my mouth threatens to make me throw up. I stand and head for the bathroom, then use my hand to scoop water into my mouth. When I return, Vinn is in the same position in the chair, so I climb back into bed.

"Sorry," he murmurs, "I should have warned you."

"Did you sort business out?" I ask, staring up at the ceiling.

He gives a light laugh before rising from the chair and crawling up the bed until he's staring down at me. "Marriage, sex, and now small talk."

"You were so mad this morning, I was checking you're okay."

He places a kiss on my nose. "Careful, *bellissima*, I might think you care." His mouth slams over mine before I can respond, surprising me with a toe-curling kiss. He trails kisses back down my body, stopping with his head between my legs.

NICOLA JANE

He cups my arse in his hands, angling me towards his mouth before taking his time to taste me. Every lick, every suck, takes me a step closer to that delicious feeling I'm quickly becoming addicted to. He doesn't let up until I'm panting through an intense orgasm. He gives a satisfied smile, slapping my thigh and getting up from the bed. "Sleep."

"Where are you going?" I ask.

"Business," he says, fastening his trousers.

I'm woken a few hours later by Vinn's intrusion. I'm flat on my stomach, and he's spreading my legs and easing into me before I've realised what's happening. The man is insatiable. He doesn't go easy, slamming into me with force and grunting like a caveman. It's hungry and animalistic, exactly how I imagined him to fuck. I orgasm within minutes, and as I come down from the high, he pulls me against him, sitting back on his heels. Guiding my legs either side of his, he gently pushes between my shoulder blades until I'm leaning forward and supporting my weight on my hands. He leans back on his hands.

"Fuck me, *bellissima*," he pants. I'm a little self-conscious, knowing he's got a good view of my arse, but his hand crashes against my thigh, shocking me into movement. "*Sai quanto fa caldo?*" he growls. *Do you know how hot that is?* His words of encouragement boost my confidence and I move faster. He grips my hips, thrusting up to meet my movements. "Fuck, fuck, fuck," he cries, coming hard. He falls beside me on the bed, his arm laying over his eyes while he catches his breath. I crawl beside him and tentatively rest my head on his chest. I feel the way he stiffens slightly, and he makes no move to touch me. After a few seconds, he kisses me on the head and stands. "I need a shower."

Breakfast is much quieter today. Gia and Blu are at the clubhouse. With Blu being a Kings Reaper, he splits his time between them and Vinn. Gia explained that even though Blu—or Azure Rossi, as he's known in our world—is part of the mafioso, he only got back into it to save Gia, but before that, he'd walked away, which is unusual. Once you're in, you're in, and the only way out is death. Mama and Rose are planning a shopping trip, and I sit beside Vinn, quietly eating some toast. For once, he isn't staring at his mobile, but he isn't speaking either. I'm quickly learning he doesn't like intimacy after sex, and he hates small talk. I can't complain, I did, after all, tell him to fuck me, because the thought of him making love was too scary. I laugh to myself, earning an eyebrow raise from Vinn.

"What are your plans today?" he suddenly asks.

"Oh, erm, I thought I'd look for work." Our mothers fall silent, and I feel their eyes on me too. "I just thought it would be nice to do something," I add, shrugging.

"No," says Vinn firmly.

"Just something local," I add, ignoring him. "Maybe some office work."

"No."

"It would be helpful to have my phone back so I can make calls." "Which part didn't you understand?" he suddenly bellows, glaring at me. "You're my wife, what will people say if they see you working? They'll think I can't look after my family. They'll think I'm having money problems."

"I don't think anyone will take much notice, actually," I mutter. "Nobody has to know."

"I'll know. My answer is final." He stands, heading for the door.

"I wasn't asking your permission," I mutter, and he freezes, spinning around and marching back towards me.

"Leave!" he yells to our mothers, and they do as asked. His hand wraps in my hair, but it isn't gentle like before and I wince. He pushes his face into mine and holds a bunch of cash next to my cheek. "You want money, take it," he hisses, slamming it on the table. "I'll pay you for sucking my cock with that pretty little mouth and laying on your back while I fuck you. How about that?"

"I'm not your whore," I snap, trying to get free.

His grip gets tighter. "You think because you're in my bed, you suddenly have power?" He laughs coldly. "Nothing changes because I crave your damn pussy."

I grin. "Who are you trying to convince, me or yourself?"

"It's just sex," he snaps, "a means to an end. A way to get a son."

"What are you scared of, Vinn?"

"Nothing!" he snaps, releasing me. "I'm not scared of anything."

"Except feelings. It scares the shit out of you that you might actually like me." The realisation makes me smile, but he narrows his eyes.

"You asked me before if I still loved Raven."

I shake my head. "Don't say it, Vinn, because you'll regret it and you can't take the words back. You're lashing out because it scares the shit out of you, so you're trying to convince yourself that you feel nothing. Is it because she hurt you?"

"Listen to yourself," he sniggers. "You think having sex makes us real?"

PLAYING VINN

I scoff. "No. I think we're both making the best of a bad situation. Sex is sex, you're nothing special." I stand. "Just because I don't have your experience, doesn't mean I can't go anywhere to have sex. You're just convenient."

I race up the stairs, and he's behind me within seconds. I try to slam the bedroom door in his face, but he gets his hand in there and pushes it open with ease. He uses his large body to push me against the wall. "Convenient?" he repeats, shoving my shorts down my legs. "I'll show you fucking convenient."

VINN

It's hard and fast. Over in minutes. A fuck. Just a fuck. We dress in silence, the sound of our heavy breathing filling the air. She's right in some ways, it's convenient because we're married, and even though we're clearly not happy in this marriage, I can't cheat. The vows meant something, but I'm also a red-blooded male and I need that release.

"You'll come with me today," I say firmly, leaving no room for argument. It's so I can make sure she doesn't do anything silly, like get a job. Fuck, if my mysterious revenge stalker discovers my wife is working, it'll feed his gossip page. "Meet me downstairs in two minutes." I leave, slamming the door behind me.

We reach the office just as my mobile rings. I smile when I see Damien Jones's name flash on my screen. "Good morning, Damien. How's the shoulder?"

"Fine. I'm just letting you know the meeting went well and nothing has changed. Go ahead."

NICOLA JANE

"That's fantastic news. Glad we sorted that out." I disconnect and relay the news to Gerry. "Now, I can concentrate on finding out who the hell keeps trying to ruin my name."

"I'm sure they'll get bored soon enough," says Sofia.

"I'm not waiting around for that to happen."

"What will you do?" she asks.

"What I do best . . . ruin them."

SOFIA

"Can I use that laptop?" I ask Vinn as he settles behind his desk and eyes the laptop perched on a small shelf. "I'm bored, and I can amuse myself with the internet." He nods, and I smile, taking it and curling up on the couch. I open my emails and see there's another from the editor of the Daily Spy. I glance at Vinn occupied with his computer. There's a mobile number to call her urgently and my heart races in my chest. What could she possibly want? I can't call her without my own mobile, but I grab a pen from Vinn's desk and make note of her number.

I wander through to Raven, closing Vinn's office door. She watches suspiciously as I take a seat. "Can I ask something personal?"

She shrugs. "Sure."

"It's about you and Vinn."

Regret passes over her face. "I'm not sure it's appropriate. We've all moved on." "Did he ever lay with you, yah know, after . . ."

"Like did we cuddle and talk into the night?" she asks, adding a laugh. I nod. "Then no. I don't even think we did it in a bed. Vinn and I were hooking up, it was nothing serious and there was certainly no lovemaking with cute cuddles." She pauses. "Why are you asking?"

"No reason. Any chance I can borrow your mobile?"

"You don't have one?" she asks, surprised.

PLAYING VINN

"Vinn took it. I just wanna check in with my mama. She's out shopping with Rose, and I need some things picked up."

Raven fishes it from her handbag and hands it to me. "Don't tell Vinn. I don't want to get it in the neck."

I smile gratefully. "I'll just go to the bathroom and make the call, in case he comes out of his office."

I lock the door and dial the number, making sure to withhold this number. A woman answers on the second ring. "Hello, Jessica Cole speaking."

"Hi, you emailed me and asked me to call."

"Revenge? Nice to put a voice to the name. I wanted to arrange to meet you."

"That's not a good idea."

"I have an interesting offer for you."

"And you can't make that over the telephone?"

She laughs. "I could, yes, but I like to know who I'm working with."

"It doesn't matter. I can't write anything else about Vincent Romano, so whatever your offer is, I can't accept."

"Has he threatened you?" she asks, suddenly sounding interested.

"No, he doesn't know me," I lie.

"Right. So, what's your problem?"

"If he finds out who I am, he'll come for me. You know who he is and what he does, right?"

"Not exactly, I know everyone is scared of him, but I thought you were different. I finally thought I'd found someone to expose him. He hides behind this facade of a businessman, but I have a feeling you know the real man behind the suit."

"I can't go there, I'm sorry."

NICOLA JANE

"Okay, listen, forget meeting. Let's just stick to how things are. You get me something good on Vinn Romano, and I'll pay you."

"I can't, I'm sorry."

"I'll pay a thousand per story. The bigger the story, the more I'll pay."

"I don't need your money."

"What do you want?" she asks. "Everyone wants something. Why did you write the article in the first place?"

It's a loaded question. Why the hell did I? Revenge, anger towards him or maybe my father. Somehow, they all seem like stupid reasons now. "I guess I wanted to write. I always wanted to be a journalist, but I wasn't allowed to."

She pauses. "Then be a journalist. You're perfect for the Spy."

I laugh. "You want me to write from behind my mask?"

"Yes, why not?"

"Do all my stories have to be about Vincent?"

"For now. Get me something big and I'll consider sending you the names of people I'm interested in."

"Why the fixation on him?"

She laughs. "He tried to threaten me. No man threatens me."

Chapter Ten

VINN

"Where is she?" I ask.

Raven glances up from her computer. "You took her phone?" she asks accusingly.

"Where is she?" I repeat.

"And you treat her like a cheap fuck?" she adds.

I glare angrily. Why the hell is Sofia talking to Raven about us? "I'm gonna ask one more time."

"She's your wife. You can't fuck and run, Vinn."

The door opens and Sofia walks in, and upon seeing me, she shoves her hand behind her back innocently. She smiles awkwardly. "What's behind your back?" I ask.

She rolls her eyes and hands Raven a mobile phone. "Thanks."

"Who did you call?"

"My mama. I needed some things picked up."

"Like?" he demands to know.

"Women's things," she snaps, pushing past me to go into my office.

I follow her. "You might be pregnant," I suggest.

"I doubt it. We missed my fertile days, remember?"

NICOLA JANE

"Still, we'll get a pregnancy test just in case." Something about the thought of her being pregnant makes me happy, an emotion I'm not used to. "You spoke with Raven about us?"

"I spoke with Raven about you and her," she corrects.

"Why?"

She shrugs. "I guess I wanted to know if you fucked all whores the same."

I narrow my eyes at the way she implies I'm treating her like a whore. "And did you get the answer you wanted?"

"Yes."

I sigh. "I'm trying, Sofia."

"You don't need to. There's no point." I watch as she pulls a book from the shelf and sits on the couch.

"No point?"

"We're making the best of a bad situation, right? Sex is natural and we shouldn't look elsewhere in case your stalker finds out and sells the story. We wouldn't want the world to know about this sham."

"I'm interested to know why you think you have such a bad deal in all this?" I ask.

"I'm not in love," she says simply. I feel a twinge where my heart should be. "And now, because of you and my papa, I'll never know what that feels like."

"That's not true, Sofia," I murmur. "You'll feel it when you have our child."

"It's not what I meant, and you know it," she mutters, going back to reading the book.

I send Sofia home with Gerry and head to the Kings Reapers clubhouse. I don't have friends, but Riggs, the president of the club, is the closest fit. There's Blu, who I trust to advise me and protect my life, but I can't talk to him at the risk of him relaying things to Gia. I've never been in this situation before, where I've felt the need to discuss my private life or get advice. I keep things simple and focus on business and keeping the mafioso happy. I know how to do that.

Riggs looks up from his desk when I knock on his office door. "Did we have a meeting?" he asks, frowning. I shake my head and take a seat. "So, you're here because?"

"Remember when you were dealing with shit and you turned up at Enzo's? I gave you a bottle of Jack and sat quietly while you consumed the whole thing. Then, I sent for my driver to deliver you safely to your own bed, next to your wife, so you wouldn't wake up with regrets." He nods. "I'm there, at that point."

Realisation passes over his face, and he pulls a bottle of Scotch from his drawer. "This to do with the story in the newspaper yesterday?" he asks.

I sigh with irritation because he clearly didn't hear the part about sitting quietly. "No. I sorted that."

"So, if business is good," he says, pouring two glasses, "it must be a woman on your mind."

He slides a glass to me. "I thought it would be simple," I admit.

Riggs laughs. "There ain't nothing simple about women, and just when you think you got it all figured out, they switch it up and you're back on your arse again, wondering what the fuck happened."

"It was for my father, a last request from him to help his friend. I underestimated her."

"Did she do something wrong?"

I shake my head and drain my glass, holding it out for a refill. "I don't know how to do relationships. I thought we could get married and things would just carry on as normal. I didn't expect to want to abide by the vows I made or that I'd feel this overpowering need to keep her to myself."

Riggs gives a knowing smile. "It hits you out of nowhere. I swear, it's voodoo magic, brother."

"How do I stop it?"

"Stop it?" he repeats. "Why would you want to?"

"It's impossible to be happy in my position. There will always be someone waiting to fuck it up, and she's at risk from my enemies."

"So is Gia, so is Rose. If your enemies wanted to target you, they'd go for anyone you love. It's a risk we take."

"If it was Gia, I could kill Blu for not protecting her. Who do I blame when it's Sofia?"

"Brother, you can't live life waiting for something bad to happen. You're gonna have a kid, right, that's the reason you agreed to this whole thing? Don't you think your kid will be the biggest target?"

I rub my tired face. "You don't get it," I mutter.

"It's not her safety you're worried about, Vinn. It's your heart."

"Bullshit," I spit. "I don't have one."

He smirks. "You being here, just talking about this, tells me otherwise."

SOFIA

Vinn gave me my mobile back. He's put a tracker on it, but I can live with that. The second I get home, I go to my room and call Zarina. I know she disagrees with what I'm doing, but she's the only person I've talked to about it and I desperately need to get this off my chest. I relay what Jessica said. After a long pause, she laughs. "That's the funniest story you've ever told me."

PLAYING VINN

"I'm serious, Zee."

"You can't be, because if you were, I'd have to think you'd gone mad. Maybe the marriage was all too much, and now you've gone insane."

"What have I got to lose?"

"You mean apart from your limbs, or worse, your life?"

"Stop being dramatic. I need honesty here."

She growls angrily. "You don't want honesty because you're choosing to ignore my advice. If you don't want Vinn, just say, and I'll happily slide into his bed." Her words bother me, but I shrug them off. I know she doesn't mean it.

"He's using me for a son. He treats me as his personal whore. He's a complete, controlling dick," I list.

"You seem to think these are bad things," she cuts in.

"Zee, be on my side with this," I beg.

"I'm sorry, Sofia, but I can't. You're making a mockery of marriage and the wishes of the mafioso. Your father was right when he told you the families would treat you like a spy. If Vinn doesn't kill you, they might."

"They won't find out it's me."

"Look, you wanted my support, and I can't give it to you. Don't tell me anything else about the Daily Spy or I'll have to tell Vinn the truth. Not because I don't love you, I do, but I can't sit back while you ruin his name."

"Why are you so invested in him, Zarina?" I demand, angry at her words.

"Maybe I see what you don't. You're lucky, Sofia, and you're wasting the chance to make a real go of it. Do you know how many girls want to get away from our village? You got to move to London with a well-respected man. You're stupid for wasting it. Grow up." She disconnects, and I stare wide-eyed at the phone. Zarina's been like a sister to me. I can't believe how she's just spoken to me.

NICOLA JANE

VINN

Blu pulls out his iPad. "Sofia is right, her papa is deep in the shit," he begins. "I've been through every account he owns because, trust me, there were some hidden ones. He's been sending money to this account," he says, turning the screen to me. "It's overseas and connects to the following accounts." He clicks a screen and several more accounts appear. "This is why it's taken so long to trace, because every time we find an account, it's a cover for a different one. The trail stops with Angelo Diaz, an accountant in Colombia."

"So, Sofia was telling the truth, he's being blackmailed?"

"Blackmail is a possibility, but these sums of money are regular payments of around the same amount. Look . . ." He shows me another screen which breaks down the payments. "The hidden accounts I told you about," he adds, showing another screen, "one in particular stood out. It's in Mario Greco's name, and I balance is one-point-six million."

"He's working with them?" I state, and Blu shrugs. "Did you trace Mario?"

"No. This account hasn't been touched. There's another account that's accessed a lot but in Italy and London, which tells me it's Diego using it."

"Why is he letting Sofia and Angela think he has no money?"

"To hide what's really going on."

"I need to question Angela about Mario."

"I've already got Rose on it. Why do you think they're so close lately?" I smile, liking the fact he's thinking ahead. "Someone's gotta run shit around here while you're chasing Sofia," he jokes with a laugh.

"My mind has been taken with her and Revenge. Apologies. Thanks for stepping up, although I pay you well for exactly that."

PLAYING VINN

SOFIA

Ash delivered a message from Vinn two hours ago instructing me to be ready by eight. We're attending another black-tie event, and after last time, I decide I'm going to stick to the rules and dress appropriately. If I want information on Vinn, I need to play the doting wife and gain trust.

As I descend the stairs in my ankle-length designer dress and matching heels, the appreciation shows on Vinn's face. He crooks his arm for me to slip my hand in and leads me out to the waiting car. "You look stunning," he says as Gerry drives us. I stare out the window so he can't see my smile. It shouldn't warm my heart, but it does.

The council house is huge. I hadn't paid much attention before, but as we step inside, I'm amazed at its beauty. The stained-glass windows and lavish decorations set the scene for an exclusive event held by local councillors. Apparently, the place will be crawling with top police chiefs, which is why Vinn wanted to attend. My papa is the opposite to Vinn—he'd avoid events like this so as not to throw himself in their path. But Vinn almost taunts them. They must know who he is and what he does, but they still nod in greeting as he passes them, sometimes even stopping to shake his hand.

We find a quiet table and sit, just the two of us. We've never done this, and I look around uncomfortably, trying to think of conversation that might interest him. "Sofia, what job did you do back home?" he asks.

"I wanted to write, but Papa wasn't a fan, so I helped Mama around the house. Sometimes I was allowed to help in his office, filing or answering calls, but as the business got quieter, there was less need for me to help out."

"What would you do if you could choose?"

NICOLA JANE

I smile. "I'd like to be a journalist." His brow furrows, and I realise I've made a mistake, letting my mouth run away. "Just so I could write good stories," I rush to explain. "The news is full of bad things. I want to report the good in the world. There's a lot of it."

He smiles. "You want to lift people's spirits?"

I shrug. "I guess. If someone is feeling low and they pick up a newspaper, they're not gonna go away feeling happier. Maybe filling the stories with good things will spread hope."

He gives me an admiring look, nodding. "I never thought of it like that."

"What did you always want to be?" I ask, thanking the waitress as she sets two drinks down.

"Like my father," he answers quietly.

My heart melts a little. "You never dreamed of anything else, outside of this?"

He nods, taking a drink. "Of course, but I knew this would be my life, so what's the point in thinking about it?"

"It's not fair, is it? We never asked to be born into this life, and yet here we are, carrying out the sins of our fathers."

"It's just the way it is. What would you rather, work a nine to five, then fall asleep in front of the television surrounded by kids and a man who's barely providing?"

I smile, shrugging. "It doesn't sound so bad, if he loved me."

A look passes over Vinn's face, and I'm reminded of our situation. "Love gets you hurt."

"Well, I wouldn't know about that."

He finishes his drink. "Have you tried contacting Mario?"

I'm thrown by his sudden change in subject. "Of course, in the early days, but he never picked up the phone."

"And did you question your father?"

I nod. "Yes. He said he was working the oil rigs and couldn't be reached."

PLAYING VINN

"I don't think he's working the rigs, Sofia."

I bite my lip. I knew deep down it was lies, but in our life, you learn to trust things get sorted, and asking questions never gets any real answers. "Will you tell me when you find him?"

He nods once.

Suddenly, a female approaches. She's tall, almost Vinn's height, and pretty, like really pretty. Her skin is tanned to perfection and she's thin, way slimmer than me. I subconsciously place my hands around my waist to hide the slight period swell of my stomach. Vinn stands to greet her with a kiss on each cheek. They speak another language, French I think, but either way, I don't understand. He eventually turns to me and smiles. "This is Sofia, my wife."

The woman proceeds to speak in French, and Vinn laughs, shaking his head. "Sofia doesn't speak French. Italian and English only."

"Oh," she says smugly. "I don't often meet people who don't speak a variety of languages. What school did you go to?"

"She was schooled in Italy," Vinn replies.

They go back to speaking in French, occasionally laughing, and it pisses me off. I stand, getting Vinn's attention. "Bathroom," I mutter, marching off.

On my way back, a hand catches my own and I stare into the eyes of Raymond, the man Vinn warned was his enemy. He smiles kindly. "Sofia, how are you?"

I glance to where Vinn is still talking to the rude woman, seeing she's got her hand on his arm. "I'm great. How are you?" This man was nice to me, so why the hell should I be rude?

"Are you really great or pretending?"

I suppress a smile. "Okay, I'm getting there."

"Your husband is making waves with these new apartments," he goes on to tell me, taking my elbow and guiding me towards the bar. "Pushing it through and threatening council members."

"I don't know anything about—"

"Of course, you don't," he scoffs. "You're his pretty little wife. You don't get told all that."

I resent the label he's placing on me, and I narrow my eyes. "So, why are you talking about it to me?"

"Because I can see you're not stupid. You hate being the controlled little wifey and you want to rebel."

I start to move away, making eye contact with Ash, who steps forward. "I should go."

"Back to your husband who's talking to his former lover?" I hold my hand up to signal Ash to wait. She stands nearby. "Oh, you didn't know? He occasionally uses her when he needs things pushing through quietly. Bars, strip clubs, night clubs . . . she's the head of licensing. But that's Vinn all over—if he can fuck his way out of something, he will, and if he can't," he points to another man nearby, "he'll threaten them, their families, and anyone else who gets in his way. Poor Councillor Jones has sent his daughter into hiding after a visit from your husband."

I swallow, my mouth suddenly dry. "Why?"

"He didn't like the way Vinn flirted with her, suggesting he'd hurt her if Jones didn't pass the planning for the apartments."

"Hurt her how?"

Raymond shrugs. "Who knows? Rape, murder . . . nothing is past Vincent Romano. He said he'd get her pregnant so he's in their life forever. The lengths he'd go to for power is crazy."

"Why are you telling me this?" I croak.

"Because you deserve better. You're a nice girl, and he's a thug." Vinn spots me and his face morphs into anger. He says something to the woman and then moves around her, making his way towards me. I need time to process what Raymond

PLAYING VINN

said, so I head to the bathroom, almost running to put some distance between us.

I slam the door, then lean against it and close my eyes. "Are you okay?" asks a woman watching me through the reflection of the mirror.

"Yes, sorry, I'm not feeling well."

"It's stuffy out there."

I recognise her voice, but before I can place it, the door is shoved hard, and I stumble forwards. Vinn fills the doorway looking more pissed than ever. "What the fuck, Sofia?" he growls.

"I was saying hello, being polite."

"Vincent Romano," the woman says with a smile, and I roll my eyes. Of course, she knows him. She smirks when he fails to recognise her. "Jessica Cole, the Daily Spy," she adds, holding out her hand. Vinn stares at it coldly, and I stare at it in shock. That's how I knew her voice. Fuck, what if she knew mine? She eventually retracts her hand, laughing. "Enjoy the rest of your evening."

Once she's gone, I sag against the sink. Panic fills me at the thought of her knowing who I am. For a second, I forget Vinn's even here until he appears behind me, watching me through the mirror. "I don't like you talking to other men."

"Who was that woman?" I snap.

"The editor of—"

"Not Jessica! The other woman, the French-talking rude woman."

"An old contact."

"Have you got any bars waiting to be licensed?" I demand and watch as realisation that I know about her passes over his face.

"Christ, how long were you talking to Clay for?"

"Long enough to know you and she fuck."

NICOLA JANE

"Not anymore. There's been no one since I married you." Vinn runs his hands over my shoulders and stares into my eyes through the mirror. "I didn't like the way it felt, seeing you speaking to Raymond." He rests his forehead on my shoulder. "I was jealous," he admits quietly.

I hold his stare. "I was just being polite," I whisper.

"You don't need to be polite to men like him, *tesoro*."

I like the way he calls me sweetheart. After months of hurtful names, this one word makes me want to throw myself into his arms and reassure him that he doesn't need to be jealous because my heart is slowly beginning to beat solely for him. That realisation hits me hard, and my eyes burn with more tears. He turns me to face him and brushes his fingers along my jaw and into my hair. "Do we have to keep on hating one another? Couldn't we just try it, yah know, the other way?"

"Other way?" I repeat.

He brushes our lips. "Yes, enjoying each other." He cups my face and pulls me in for a soft, slow kiss.

Chapter Eleven

VINN

I take Sofia by the hand and lead her from the bathroom. Something's changed between us. We've reached a truce and it feels good. Maybe now I can get back to business and focus ... starting with Raymond Clay. As I pass Gerry, I lean into his ear. "Cause a scene. I need everyone to be distracted."

"Clay?" he asks, and I nod.

"Sofia, take a seat at our table, I'll get us a drink," I tell her. She nods, releasing my hand. Gerry speaks briefly with Ash, who nods and moves into the crowd, pulling a hood over her head.

Gerry suddenly pulls me to the side, yelling about a man with a knife. Nearby, someone screams, and panic descends over the room. People grab for their partners and rush for the exit. Gerry makes a show of guiding me as far as the doors before I yell at him to get to Sofia. He heads back, and I make my way out as the hired security runs inside yelling into their radios.

Gerry appears shortly after with Sofia, and I pull her against me. "I think Ash is inside," she says, panicking.

"Ash will be fine, she's trained."

Minutes later, Ash steps out with another man who I recognise as Clay's security. Her hands have blood on them, but the other guy still shakes her hand and thanks her before heading back inside with a paramedic.

"What happened?" Sofia gasps.

"A man's on the ground. I tried to give first aid, but it didn't look good," Ash explains, her expression grave.

"Let's go," I suggest, keeping my arm around Sofia's shoulders.

"Interesting," comes a female voice from behind, and I turn to where Jessica Cole stands. "Raymond Clay has been stabbed." I feel Sofia tense, but her face remains impassive.

"What a shame. Is he alive?" I ask dryly.

"At the moment, but wasn't he just speaking with your wife?"

I glance at Sofia, who nods. "Yes, I hope he makes it," she says.

"If you don't mind, I need to get my wife home."

"Won't the police need to speak to everyone?" she asks, smirking.

"I'm sure you'll inform them who was here," I mutter, guiding Sofia away.

The car ride is silent. We get into the house and Sofia mutters something about bed, but I snatch her wrist, halting her from escaping. "Not so fast."

I pull her to my office and lock the door. "Talk."

"Did you do that because he spoke to me?"

"Yes."

She covers her mouth, her expression horrified. "It's my fault?"

"No. We have a long history. He'll live, don't worry."

PLAYING VINN

"How can you be sure?"

"Because I didn't order his murder, just a wake-up call." I pull Sofia against me and close my eyes. I like the feel of her body against mine and my cock reacts immediately.

I run my hands over her arse, squeezing the flesh before pulling her skirt up inch by inch until my hands are full of the material. "This is a pretty dress," I mutter, pulling the material hard so it splits. She gasps, her eyes wide. "I'll buy you another."

I push her over my desk and admire her perfect arse, slapping my hand against it and rubbing the redness. I waste no time sinking into her, fisting her hair and flanking her body with mine, using the jealousy I felt earlier to fuck her hard. Maybe this marriage won't be so bad after all.

SOFIA

We fuck . . . it's primal and urgent, exactly what I needed after watching him with that French bitch earlier. The need to claim him burns in my blood, and when I drop to my knees and take him in my mouth, his eyes light with admiration. It doesn't take him long to come, and as he calls out my name, shuddering and growling, I feel a sense of pride. I can make this powerful man come undone and it feels good.

He kisses me on the head as I straighten my clothing. "Go to bed. I'll be up soon."

My heart twists and I hook a finger around his. "Actually, why don't we go together?"

He hesitates, and I can see his mind running overtime, but we've both admitted jealous feelings for one another, and we've had sex more than once. What's so hard about coming to bed with me? He seems to reach the same conclusion as he leads me upstairs.

NICOLA JANE

I lie on my side, watching as he undresses and climbs in beside me. "I like this truce," he admits, lying on his back with his arms behind his head, staring up at the ceiling.

"It's much easier and a lot less stressful," I add. "Tell me something about you," he says. "Something nobody knows."

I bite my lower lip, thinking about his question. "I don't have anything," I mutter.

He glances my way. "There must be something."

I shake my head. "I led a quiet life and was never allowed out. Not without Mario, anyway. What about you?"

He sighs. "I have so many secrets, *bellissima*, it's hard to choose just one."

"How many women have there been?"

He laughs. "Too many to count."

His admission stings a little. "How many times have you been in love?"

"How long has your father been mistreating your mother?"

I feel disappointed he ignored my question. "As long as I can remember. It's always been that way. I thought everyone's parents were like mine until Zarina came to stay once when they were fighting. She told me her parents never argued let alone fight physically."

"You and she are close, no?"

I smile. "Yes. She's like my sister."

"Your uncle wants her to marry into the mafioso too." He says it as a statement rather than a question. "Maybe we can find her someone and she can stay here in London."

"Vinn, how long is Mama staying?" It's been playing on my mind, and I know Papa will be going out of his mind without her.

"As long as you want her here."

"I've never seen her so relaxed. She's happy, but I know given the option, she'll choose him."

PLAYING VINN

"Then don't give her the option. How does that make you feel?" Vinn turns onto his side and watches me closely.

"Sad. Angry. Since being here, I'm starting to wonder who Papa really is. He never used to be like this. He's changed so much recently."

"In what way?"

Maybe I shouldn't tell Vinn about my papa, he'd be so angry if he ever found out. Family business is private, but while we're here, getting along, I feel the urge to let the words tumble out, so I do. "He has become much angrier. More distracted, less tolerant. When I told him I didn't want to marry you, he threatened to call the Colombians and have me sent there."

"You didn't want to marry me?" he repeats with a playful smile. I find myself smiling too. He kisses me, slow and almost loving, and when he pulls back, he smiles again. "Sleep now."

When I wake the next morning, I hear the shower. Feeling beside me, I note the bed is still warm and I smile to myself. Vinn stayed all night. I pick up my mobile and see an email from Jessica Cole. I open it, sitting up and wrapping the sheets around me.

Hi, Revenge. It was great to finally meet you. Tell me, when will I get my next story?

I feel sick. It burns the back of my throat, so I rush to the toilet, falling to my knees and vomiting. Vinn steps from the shower, wrapping a towel around his waist. "Are you okay?"

I nod, flushing away the evidence and trying desperately to hide my embarrassment. "Yeah, it must have been something I ate."

"Or you're pregnant?"

NICOLA JANE

Those words chill me to the bone. "No, honestly, it's just an upset stomach."

He reaches into the drawer and produces a pregnancy test. I glare at him. "I had some brought in."

"I'll do it later," I mutter.

He smiles, but I see the dangerous glint in his eye warning me to do as he says. I snatch the box and push to my feet. He won't let me out of here until I do it, and I have to speak to Jessica. I pee on the stick with Vinn watching. I'm past being embarrassed—he just saw me vomit, and not for the first time. I place the test on the sink unit and go back into the bedroom.

"You don't want to wait for the result?" he asks, frowning.

I snatch my phone from the bed. "I'm sure you'll tell me."

"Suddenly, it feels like the truce is on hold."

"Because I can't even vomit without you questioning my state. Everything comes back to the baby. Everything," I snap, then take a calming breath. "Sorry," I mutter, "I know that's the whole point." He stares at me for a few seconds before going back into the bathroom to brush his teeth. My heart sinks. A part of me desperately wanted him to reassure me it's not the only reason I'm here.

When Vinn returns, I'm half dressed. He throws the test down beside me on the bed. "Negative."

Relief floods me, though I'm not sure why. I'm not against giving Vinn a baby, not like I was in the beginning, but now we have a reason to keep our truce. He still needs me, and while he's being kind, I'm going to drag it out as long as I can.

VINN

I take breakfast into work. I couldn't stand the thought of sitting with Sofia this morning. I can't hide the fact I'm disappointed she's not pregnant. After the news story, I need to set records straight. I hand Raven a coffee and pastry, and she smiles gratefully but is busy on the phone, so I go straight into my office. There's a scribbled note about a video conference call with Benedetto at lunch today. I frown just as Raven pops her head in. "He called and left a message to say he'd be video calling you at noon and he expects you to answer."

I nod. Why the hell does he want to speak to me? He'd never email, as it was drummed into us that the 'e' stands for 'evidence' and so video calling is the favoured form of contact when you can't get face-to-face meetings.

The morning drags. My mind is stuck on this damn conference call, and Blu arrives to join me just as I'm connecting my laptop. He takes a seat in the corner, out of view.

Benedetto's name flashes on my screen, and I accept, leaning back in my chair like I'm totally relaxed. "Benedetto," I greet, smiling.

"Apologies for the last-minute arrangement. It's important. Are you alone?"

"Yes." "You're looking into Diego. Why?"

Of course, he'd know, I'm not even surprised. "I have my reasons." "Vincent, now isn't the time for vague bullshit. He's in my organisation, and I want to know why you're searching in his financial dealings."

"I'm suspicious," I admit. "He pushed for the wedding between me and Sofia, and I haven't seen Mario for a long time. I feel like you're both keeping things from me."

He narrows his eyes. "Mario is dead."

I try not to look too shocked, but I wasn't expecting that, and I glance at Blu. "Sofia doesn't know," I say.

"Nobody does, but I thought Diego would tell you." I shake my head, anger bubbling inside at being told this information by Benedetto. He must think I have no control. "Look, I think we should come together on this," he begins, and I lean closer.

"I have my suspicions about Diego and I'm keeping an eye on him."

"You didn't mention that when I saw you in Italy."

"Why would I? You know as well as me, it's not in our nature to share that sort of information. But your men are running checks and it's flagging up to Diego. He came to see me to say he thinks someone is watching him."

"I think you need to start being honest," I snap.

"I know about Sofia," he says. "I know she was attacked. I think the Colombians also killed Mario."

I shake my head. "Why?"

"Because Diego made a deal with them and didn't pay up. I don't know exactly what the deal was, but I'm working on it."

"Working on it?" I growl. "You're supposed to know what your men are doing!"

"It was before me, when my father was in charge. I had my suspicions before, but my father wouldn't hear of it."

"Have you tried reaching out to the Colombians?"

He nods. "It's a slow process. To talk to me, they want to make deals."

"Maybe I should go there and make deals. Maybe I should kill them . . . starting with Dante Arias, who raped Sofia while she was under your care."

He shifts uncomfortably. "Again, it was months before me. I'm tidying up my men. Starting with Diego. If I was you, I'd keep Angela there in the UK."

"Technically, Diego is part of my family now. Any new findings should be run by me and any plans to tidy up will also come through me."

Benedetto nods once before disconnecting. I slam my laptop closed. "What the fuck?"

"Mario is dead?" repeats Blu, just as shocked as me.

"That stays between us," I say. "There're only two things the Colombians would fight for—power and money. Dante had to have made some kind of fuck-up that involved one or both of those." "We're gonna have to bring him in, Boss. Before Benedetto gets to him and feeds us some bullshit."

I pull out my phone and call Diego. He wasn't happy when I took his wife from under his nose, only calling him once she was in London. He answers on the first ring. "Vinn."

"You're coming to London," I tell him. "I'll have Raven book the flight and send the details. It's important for your safety that you don't tell anyone, including Benedetto."

"Is Angela okay?"

"Yes. If you tell anyone about the flight or you don't get on it, she might not be."

SOFIA

I lost Ash in the centre of London. I feel bad, and even worse, my phone is stuffed between the seats in the back of the car, which means Vinn will be more than pissed. I couldn't risk bringing it with me and him tracking me here to Jessica.

I push the button to the second floor like she instructed me, and when I get to the hotel room, I knock on the door. She answers with a bright smile and invites me in like I'm her best friend. As soon as the door closes, I spin to face her. "Are you trying to get me killed?"

She laughs. "I'm not the one writing stories about Vincent Romano."

"And you didn't think you could just keep it to yourself? Sending that email was stupid. He could have seen it."

"But he didn't, and that's why you're here."

"I'm here to tell you I can't write anything else. Especially now you know who I am."

"That's disappointing, Sofia. I thought you were stronger than that."

"Stronger?" I repeat, laughing angrily. "You know enough to know what I did was stupid and dangerous. Things have changed. I can't write anymore."

"You're giving up on your dreams for a man?" she asks, arching her brow. "Wow."

"It's not like that."

"You told me you wanted to be a journalist. To do that, you need to take risks."

"I wanted to write pieces that would make a difference, that would help make people smile," I argue. "I didn't want to be the person who upset everyone."

"Vinn has thick skin, he can take it."

I shake my head and slowly walk back to the door. "I'm sorry, I can't be involved. Please don't contact me again."

"Actually," she says, and I pause, "it won't be as simple as that unfortunately."

"What do you mean?"

"I don't like Vincent Romano. I don't like what he stands for or how he behaves. I especially don't like the way he tried to threaten me. So, I need more on him, and you're going to get that for me."

"But . . . I just told you . . ."

She tips her head to one side and pouts mockingly. "I know you did, sweet pea, but that's not gonna work for me so—"

"If he finds out, he'll kill me."

"And that would make a great headline, but I'd rather keep it low key, maybe something about how he manages to get people to do exactly what he wants. How exactly did he get the permission for those apartments even after we exposed him?" I shrug, too shocked to reply. "Get me something and

PLAYING VINN

then we'll talk again about you giving up your dreams for a man like him."

Chapter Twelve

VINN

I meet Angela outside the cafe right across from where I intend to build luxury apartments for women trying to escape abusive relationships. She glances at me nervously while I pour us each a cup of tea from the china pot the waitress brought over. "I wanted to talk to you today about a couple of things," I begin. "Firstly, Mario." Her face stays blank, and I smile. She's got a good poker face. "I need to know if you know the truth, because if you don't, then what I'm about to say may sting a little."

"I know he isn't coming back to me, if that's what you're asking."

I nod. "But you didn't tell Sofia?" She shakes her head. "Because?"

"I didn't know for certain. Diego didn't tell me. I just guessed when he made no contact. It wasn't like my son to not check in with me for so long. And when you're a mother, you know if your child is no longer on the same planet."

"I also needed to tell you that you won't be going home anytime soon." She visibly swallows but chooses not to question me. Why isn't Sofia this compliant? "Benedetto wouldn't keep you safe there, and as I am now your family, it's up to me."

"Will Dante be joining me?"

NICOLA JANE

I shake my head and from my expression she knows what that ultimately means. "He's flying into London soon. If you'd like to see him, I will arrange it."

"Are you going to tell Sofia?"

I shake my head. "Not yet. And you won't either." I open a brochure showing what the apartments will eventually look like. "You're welcome to stay in my home with Sofia, I think my mother loves having you around, but if you want your own place, there will be an apartment spare for you." I slide a credit card across the table. "This is yours. Raven will send you details of the account and your allowance. I'm sure it will meet your requirements, but should you need more, please let me know."

She nods, slipping the card into her bag. "You're a good man, Vinn. I know my daughter is having a hard time settling down, but she will, eventually."

I nod. "As will you."

My mobile rings and I pull it out to see Ash's name. "What?"

"I can't find Sofia, Boss. She gave me the slip."

I stand abruptly. "Where was she last?"

"Central London."

SOFIA

I hand over my credit card to the barman. My vision is blurred, but it feels good. If I'm going to die, I may as well do it drunk. "Another one, please," I mutter, and he pours me a whiskey. It's foul-tasting, and when I took my first mouthful earlier, I almost threw straight up. It gets easier with each glass, but fuck knows why Vinn likes it so much.

It's a rowdy bar. Lots of office types are pouring in for after-work drinks, and I move towards the back of the bar. I watch the men and women laughing and talking loudly to be heard over everyone else. Why couldn't my life be normal like that? "Now, you look like a woman drinking to forget," says a smiling man as he takes a seat opposite me. I hold up my hand, showing him my wedding ring, and take another drink. "You're drinking to forget your marriage?" he asks.

I grin, shaking my head. "No, I'm telling you I'm married."

"Happily?"

I pause, my eyes flicking to my diamond wedding band. Am I? I think I could be, in time. "Yes."

"I used to be," he tells me, "until she left for someone else."

"Oh, sorry to hear that."

"Don't be, she was a bitch." We both smile, but when I look across the bar, it's into the eyes of Vinn.

"Oh shit," I hiss, pushing my drink towards the man. "You have to go."

"Did I say something?" he asks, looking around.

"No, but if you don't hurry, you may never talk again." I stand as my moody husband approaches looking pissed, with Blu and Ash at his back. "Hey," I mumble, giving a small wave.

Vinn glances at his watch. "Where have you been for the last hour?"

"Hour?" I gasp, gripping the table to steady myself. "It didn't seem that long."

His eyes narrow. "You're drunk?"

I hold my fingers up, showing a small gap between them. "Maybe just a little."

"Who's your friend?"

I glance at the guy still sitting at my table and shrug. "Who knows."

The man grins, holding out his hand to Vinn. "Clive, pleased to meet you." He's unaware of the dangerous man ready to rip the limb from his body. Vinn grabs it, twisting it up the man's back. He cries out, and I wince, unsure of how to make this better.

"Vinn, stop!"

"Clive, you should gather your things together and leave the bar," he hisses. Clive nods, looking ready to piss himself in a panic. Vinn shoves him towards the exit, and Clive practically runs. "Gerry is waiting in the car," he adds without looking at me, then he takes me by the hand.

"Wait, you're not mad?" I ask.

He stares straight ahead, leading me from the bar. "Oh, very mad, Sofia, but I can't do what I want with a hundred witnesses." I swallow, hoping it was a sexual innuendo.

Outside, it's begun to rain. I tip my head back and smile. I love the feel of it on my skin. I break free of Vinn's grip, and he glances back. "What are you doing?"

"I want to walk in the rain," I say, spinning and almost crashing into someone. I laugh, grabbing Vinn's arm. "Let's walk."

"Sofia, get in the car," he snaps.

Blu and Ash watch on as I continue to walk, Vinn following me. "Come on, don't you ever get fed up with being so fucking boring?"

He looks taken aback. "Boring?"

"Always bossing everyone around and scowling. You know, when you smile, you actually look handsome." I skip, keeping my arms out for balance. "You never laugh."

"Sofia, you'll get the flu. Let's go home."

"See, boring. When was the last time you skipped in the rain?"

"Nobody over the age of three skips in the fucking rain, Sofia," he snaps impatiently, and I laugh.

"Maybe they should."

He continues to follow me, and when we get to the end of the road, I spot a park and head that way. "Really?" he hisses in disbelief. "This suit cost a lot of money."

"Nobody ever melted from rainwater," she says, rolling her eyes. "Let yourself go for once."

VINN

I scowl. I'm fucking wet through, and she wants me to skip and dance through the park. It's empty, with everyone rushing off to find shelter as the rain gets harder, but she's lost her mind. "Live a little. Laugh a little," she continues. There's a patch of trees off to the left, and I grin to myself. She's still lecturing me as I scoop her up in my arms, taking her by surprise. She squeals as I march towards the trees, dumping her on her feet once we're out of view and pushing her up against the nearest trunk. I tug her hair so she's looking up at me and close my mouth over hers. Peace . . . that's more like it.

"You want me to live a little, Sofia?" I whisper against her mouth. She nods. "You want me to relax and laugh more?" She nods again. I shove my hand down her trousers and find her already wet. She hisses, jerking as I roughly rub my hand over her pussy. "Is this more like it, Sofia?" She closes her eyes, her small hands holding onto my shoulders as I push my fingers into her. "You went off radar today," I hiss. "I was worried."

"Sorry," she mumbles. She's so wet, it's hard to pull away, but I do, just as she's about to come apart. Her eyes shoot open. "What are you doing?"

"I thought you wanted to dance in the rain?"

She follows me back into the park. "I'd prefer to—" I arch a brow, daring her to say it out loud. "Oh, that was punishment for going off?"

"No, *bellissima*, that will come later. That was me shutting you up for five minutes."

NICOLA JANE

SOFIA

The second we get home, Vinn takes me upstairs and works on my punishment. If you can call a shower with a sexy man followed by hours of fucking a punishment.

By morning, I'm tired and hungover. Vinn wakes me with breakfast in bed, which surprises me. He's not usually so attentive. "I'm very busy today. Call if you need me, but only in an emergency. Ash will be right outside," he says, kissing me on the forehead.

I frown. "Outside?" I query.

"The door," he says, smiling.

"I don't understand."

He straightens his tie. "She'll be right outside the door," he repeats, pointing to the bedroom door.

"Why is she waiting for me?"

"She isn't. That's where I've told her to stay until I return this evening."

I laugh, taking a bite from my toast. "You're talking in riddles." He leans closer to me again, taking a bite of the toast and winking playfully. I smile because I like this side of him. Then, suddenly, his eyes darken, and his grin turns cruel. "Remember yesterday, when you decided to take yourself off on a little detour of London?" I nod, slowly realising where this is going. "Well, that won't be happening today."

I watch as he heads for the door. "Vinn, what are you doing?"

He holds up a key and pushes it into the lock on the other side. Panic takes over and I scramble from the bed, my plate crashing to the floor and shattering. Just as I get to the door, he closes it, and I hear the lock click in place. "Vinn!" I yell, slamming my hands against the thick wood. "Vinn, you can't lock me away!"

"Oh, *tesoro*, there's still so much you don't know about me," he says through the door. "I told you there would be a punishment."

"I'm your fucking wife," I scream, stamping my foot. A sharp piece of pottery slices the skin underneath and I cry out, dropping to the floor and gripping it. "Shit," I hiss as blood rushes to the surface.

"Which is why I have to keep you safe. I can't trust you out there when you're always slipping off. Why were you at the Parkfield Hotel?"

My breath catches in my throat. "Sorry?"

"You heard me, *tesoro*. Don't make me repeat myself."

"I wasn't."

His hand slams against the door, and I jump with fright. "Don't fucking lie to me." "I was in the bar, having a drink." "Who bought it?"

"Me."

"More lies!" he yells. "I found you yesterday because I traced your fucking credit card, Sofia. You didn't buy a drink in the hotel."

"Because it was busy. I went in and left straightaway." I hear him laugh. It's low and menacing. "I have to go. When I return, you will be here, waiting, exactly where I left you. Preferably naked."

"Fuck you, Vinn," I mutter angrily.

"You will, when I return."

My foot aches. I wrap it with one of Vinn's expensive white cotton shirts to stem the bleeding, but I'm pretty sure it needs medical intervention. I prop it up on Vinn's pillow and pull my laptop onto my knee. He isn't the only one who can dish out punishments. If he wants to end our truce, that's fine by me.

NICOLA JANE

VINN

Raven goes to lunch, and the second she disappears, the door buzzer rings. Why the hell does it always do that when she isn't at her desk?

"What?" I bark into the intercom.

"Mr. Romano, you wanted to see me?" It's Sofia's cousin, Zarina.

I buzz her in and sit back at my desk. She arrives looking fresh, like she's just had a workout. "Thank you for coming on such short notice." It was Blu's idea—Seduce the cousin and see what she knows. "Please, take a seat," I say, pointing to the chair opposite me.

"Is Sofia okay?" she asks, looking around the office.

"She's fine. Haven't you spoken with her?" She shakes her head, and a sad expression passes over her. "What's wrong?"

"Nothing. We just . . . had a slight disagreement. It happens." She shrugs.

"Look, Zarina, I asked you here because I need your help."

"Oh?"

"I'm worried about Sofia. I think her father is involved in things he shouldn't be and," I pause for effect, "I'm worried." She fidgets and avoids eye contact, so I move around to her side of the desk. "Zarina, it's very important that you tell me if you know something."

"I don't," she insists, "not really. Only what I've heard."

I rest my hand on her knee, crouching before her to make eye contact. She blushes. "Go on," I push.

"I heard her papa on the telephone. I think it was with Mario. He told him not to come back to Italy because he was ashamed of him. I don't know what he meant by that, but he was yelling, saying he disowned him."

"Have you told Sofia or anyone else about this?"

She shakes her head. "No. I shouldn't have been listening in."

I kiss her cheek. "Thank you. If you ever need anything, let me know."

"Actually," she begins, and I inwardly kick myself for being too polite, "my papa has arranged for me to meet a man here in London. My mama's uncle will escort me tomorrow. His name is Darias Marino. Do you know him?"

I try to keep a straight face. The guy's an arse, overweight, useless, and far too rich for his own good. "Yes, I do."

"Is he a good man?"

"I'm sure if your father chose him, it was for a good reason."

She sighs. "How did Sofia get so lucky?" she whispers.

"I'll see if I can find any eligible Italian men. There's plenty in London better than Darias Marino."

She stands, smiling. "Thank you." On her tiptoes, she presses her lips against mine. I instantly pull away, staring at her wide-eyed. "I appreciate your help," she adds, turning to leave. I know she and Sofia are close, but I don't think Sofia would be happy to share me with her cousin. I laugh to myself thinking about how mad she was this morning and I already have a punishment in mind if she isn't naked when I get back.

SOFIA

I admire Vinn's blood-soaked shirt and pillowcase. That will teach him for having white. Josey brought lunch and made such a fuss about my foot that I let her clean and bandage it, even though I wanted to leave it for Vinn to see what he made me do. I stare bitterly at the email right before I hit send. Fuck Vinn Romano.

It's a few hours later when I hear the key in the lock, and I straighten my woolly jumper. Vinn wanted naked, but I've given him fully clothed with at least three layers. I smile smugly when he sets eyes on me. "Josey said you hurt yourself."

"It was your fault, actually," I snap, and when he hears my tone, his face hardens.

He sniggers, marching over to my wardrobe and pulling it open. He removes the clothes, gathering one big armful and carrying it from the room. I don't need them anyway, I have layers. He then removes the contents of my underwear drawer. He returns looking pleased with himself. "Are you going to take the clothes off or should I remove them for you?"

"You wouldn't dare," I hiss, glaring at him. He takes my wrist, bending and throwing me over his shoulder. "Vinn, I swear, stop this. You're being stupid."

"I gave an order, and you didn't follow it."

"I am not one of your men!" I yell, hitting his back, but it doesn't bother him. He takes me into the bathroom and turns on the shower.

"It would be so much easier if you were, Sofia, because I could just kill you."

He dumps me in the shower, and I gasp as freezing water hits my face. "You're crazy." "Thank you." He smiles. "Now, take off the clothes."

"I'm not having sex with you," I snap angrily.

He laughs. "Firstly, I don't want you to, trust me. Secondly, I call the shots."

I pull the wet jumper over my head and throw it at him. He catches it, grinning. "The truce didn't last long," I mutter.

"All you had to do was play nice."

"All you had to do was let me live a little."

"In hotels, picking up guys in bars?" he yells.

I remove the next layer and drop it on the floor. "That's not what happened."

"Clive seemed to think so."

PLAYING VINN

I remove the final shirt and drop it. "I'm so sick of this."

He waits until I'm completely naked and shivering before turning the shower off.

"I am sick of you giving my men the run-around. I am sick of having my day interrupted with tales of your insolence and your immature behaviour. If I give you an order, you follow it, do you understand yet?" His teeth are gritted and his face angry. I suck in a deep breath and nod once. "Good. Get dried. I will leave you clothes for dinner. We're eating alone this evening. You have ten minutes." He marches out the bathroom, slamming the door.

When I exit the bathroom, there's a dress on the bed. It's flowy and short, ideal for dinner, but there's no underwear. I glance at myself in the mirror. I like my body. It's not too thin or too fat, but just right, with womanly curves where they should be. My size C-cup breasts are perky, and I've never thought about surgery or Botox.

I take a deep breath. He told me to be naked, right? I pull the bedroom door open. Ash isn't there. In fact, it sounds unusually quiet. As I make my way along the hall, I hear pots and pans banging and smell the irresistible scent of Lorenzo's homemade pasta and secret sauce.

My wet bandage leaves a print as I descend the stairs. The office door opens and Gerry steps out. His mouth falls open and he quickly turns his back to me. "Sofia, what are you doing?"

"Vinn told me to follow his orders, and his orders were to be naked."

"Something tells me you're about to piss him off."

I grin, passing him. "Oh, I really hope so, Gerry. It's my most favourite thing to do."

Connor is heading my way but turns and rushes into the kitchen when he spots me. I smirk. Why are they all acting like they've never seen a naked woman before? "Mrs. Romano," hisses Ash as I approach the dining room door, "what are you doing?"

"Relax, Ash, I'm proving a point."

Vinn has his head down, reading something on his phone. I'm almost at my seat by the time he looks up. His nostrils flare and he glances around the room, spotting his two security men already leaving. "What are you doing?" he hisses.

"Following your orders," I say, smiling sweetly.

"This is not funny," he growls, unbuttoning his shirt. He shrugs it off and holds it out to me.

"But you said—"

"Put the fucking shirt on now, Sofia," he yells, slamming his hand on the table.

I take it, struggling to keep the smirk from my face. "Careful, you'll hurt your hand."

"Why does it have to be so difficult with you?" he asks, slapping my hands away and taking over the buttons. "What do I have to do to make you behave?"

"Stop telling me to behave, for a start. I'm not a dog."

He fastens the last button just above my cleavage and keeps his hands there. He stares into my eyes. "You push every damn button in me," he mutters. "And I tell myself every day to ignore you, to let you have your tantrum, but then you step it up until I can't."

"Mama always said I was hard work."

His hand cups my cheek. "You certainly don't know how to follow orders."

"Careful, Vinn, it sounds like you're starting to warm to me."

His mouth crashes against mine in a desperate kiss. "I'll deny it if anyone asks," he whispers, spinning me away from him and bending me over the table.

Chapter Thirteen

VINN

Suddenly, Zarina is everywhere I turn. I told Sofia to call her and sort things out, mainly because I need to keep her close right now to build trust. I feel like she knows more than she's letting on. Once Zarina trusts me, she'll open up more because she's desperate to be liked. More than that, she's desperate for me to find her a better husband than who her father suggested. So, when Sofia announced her cousin was staying with us for the rest of her trip, I wasn't surprised. Apparently, she managed to convince her mama's uncle that my home was a better option than his.

It's been two nights since my men saw my wife walking naked through the house. Every single one of them has avoided eye contact with me, in fear I might gauge them out. I smirk at the thought of her boldness. It's highly irritating but also addictive, and I find myself excited to see what she'll do next.

I'm in my office when there's a light knock on the door and Gia steps in. She's holding Alfie, my nephew. I take him from her, and she sits. "I want you to stay calm," she begins.

"Gia, you can't start a sentence like that. Is this why you brought Alfie in here?" She knows he's the light of my life.

"Maybe," she shrugs, smiling. "Listen, Revenge has struck again." She produces a newspaper.

NICOLA JANE

"What? How did I not know about this? Raven usually gets a heads up."

"When you hear it, you'll understand why it was kept quiet."

I brace myself as she holds the paper. "Front page?" I snap, and she nods.

"Vincent Romano, sex predator or businessman?" she reads before diverting her eyes to her son as if to remind me he's here. "When I wrote my first article all those months back exposing Vinn Romano and his overpriced club, little did I know how right I was. I told you about his glitzy nightclub and all it had to offer, provided you were young and gorgeous. I've spent months uncovering the seedy tales behind the bright, white smile. I wasn't short of people ready to spill their guts about the businessman who has been linked to the Italian mafia—"

I grip one fist on the chair, and Gia eyes me cautiously. "That's never been mentioned before," I grit out.

"It gets worse," she mutters before continuing. "They wanted to remain anonymous. All from fear that the great Vincent will come for them. What exactly does that mean? I hear you ask. Well, for starters, he has links everywhere—the police, the court system, even our local councillors. Vivian Blackwell will dazzle us with her fake smile and tell us that new nightlife is just what London needs as she signs off another bar license. She forgets to tell us just how big a payment Vincent Romano slipped her—think inches, not cash—and when I approached her secretary, Blackwell wasn't available for comment. Silence speaks volumes, Ms Blackwell.

"And let's not forget his latest project. I recently exposed his plans to build in an already over-populated area. The planning permission was withdrawn pending investigation. Seems less than a day later, it was pushed back through. Would that have anything to do with Vincent's threat towards Councillor

Jones's twenty-year-old daughter? Or could it have been the injury Jones received and attended hospital for?

"Vincent Romano is a powerful man, in that there is no doubt. It's time we stood up to bullies who use sex and violence to get what they want. As women, we spend our lives fighting to be heard against people like this, it's time you listened."

I stare for a good minute, processing what she's just read to me. "It's a woman."

Gia nods. "Seems like it."

"Jesus."

"Make a list of all the women you've hurt and start there." She takes Alfie from me. "Well done for staying calm."

I wait until she's left the office before grabbing the nearest empty whiskey glass and throwing it across the room. It shatters against the wall, but I don't feel any better.

Blu comes in and takes in the broken glass. "Gia said you'd taken it well."

"This is well," I snap. "I haven't killed anyone. I want to find this piece of shit who's writing about me. My father spent years building that club up and this arsehole might bring it all down, not to mention the fact they brought up the mafioso!"

"I'm working on it, but it's hard. I asked Vivian, and she swears she hasn't spoken to anyone recently from the press. This is an inside person."

"If you start banging on about Raven again, I'll hurt you."

"What about the cousin?"

"Zarina? No, she's not the type. She's too quiet."

"She's suddenly hanging around a lot."

I sigh. "I'll bring her in and see how she reacts."

SOFIA

"What's going on?" asks Zarina, closing her bedroom door.

NICOLA JANE

I sit on her bed. "I'm not sure."

"I mean this," she snaps, throwing a newspaper on the bed. I glance at the article and wince. I didn't write those exact words. Jessica changed it, but I gave her the information.

"You told me not to talk about it with you," I point out.

"Now isn't the time to be a childish dick, Sofia. I thought things seemed good between the two of you."

I nod, my guilt showing clearly on my face. "It is. I feel terrible. But that's the last one, I swear."

"This could ruin his businesses. He might get investigated by the police."

The door opens and I spin around to find Vinn. "I need you," he mumbles, and it's the first time he's ever looked vulnerable. He takes my hand and leads me to our own room, where he kicks the door shut before wrapping his arms around me. "I need you so much, Sofia."

"Okay," I mumble against his chest.

He kisses me, but it's not like any of the other times. He's slow and gentle, caressing my cheeks with his thumbs with each swipe of his tongue. He slowly walks me back until my knees hit the bed, then before he lays me down, he peels off my dress. "You make it feel less crazy in my head," he mutters, trailing kisses over my shoulder and back up my neck. "No one's ever done that for me." My heart dances as he climbs over me. "I don't know what you've done to me, but I like it," he adds, lining his erection up at my entrance.

He rests his weight on his elbows and gently pushes inside, taking his time to make sure I feel every inch of his cock. He kisses me as he withdraws and then repeats it. His long, drawn-out movements are like heaven, causing my body to come alive with warmth. I feel like electricity dances between us, zapping back and forth. This time, when he comes, it's not hard and fast. His neck strains and a sound so primal and

PLAYING VINN

satisfied leaves his throat in a growl. It's a turn-on, and I follow him over the edge, gripping his arms and crying out into his chest.

Afterwards, Vinn pulls me into bed, wrapping his arms around me and holding me tightly. "I know neither of us wanted this marriage," he begins, "but lately, I've started to realise it isn't so bad." I run my fingers back and forth over his arm that circles my chest protectively. "Me too."

"I've asked your mother to stay here in the U.K. Benedetto may not welcome her back in Italy, and I don't think she'll be safe. She's part of my family now, and we all know Benedetto and the other families barely tolerate me. I've offered an apartment, or she has the option of staying here with us."

"With Papa?"

He kisses my head, inhaling my scent. "No, *bellissima*."

"What's he done wrong, Vinn?"

He sighs heavily. "I don't know exactly, but I don't think it's good." And for once, I don't argue or ask him for more, because deep down, I have my own suspicions about Papa.

We sleep wrapped around each other, and when I wake, it's with Vinn nuzzling my neck and pushing inside of me. We make love for a second time, and even though I have a dread in the pit of my stomach, part of me hopes this will last. Maybe over the next few days, he'll forget about the news story. These sorts of things blow over, and now Jessica has her big story, maybe she'll leave me alone?

VINN

I rub my brow, trying hard to remove the stress. "Fine, whatever," I mutter, dismissing Raven's concerns over the declining VIP bookings in the club. "It'll go quiet for a short time until this blows over and then they'll be back."

NICOLA JANE

"Maybe," mutters Raven, not looking confident. I brought Zarina into the office with me today. She's shadowing Raven for some office experience. Her plans to stay in London are looking more likely, which means she's looking for work until she finds a suitable husband. "What exactly do you need me to show Zarina? Does she know about the other businesses?"

"Stick to legit things. Just general office admin."

"Also, Dave Cline from a local news station wants to speak to you about an interview."

"Absolutely not," I snap. "I've had enough of fucking journalists."

"Actually, I thought maybe we could put a spin on it to work in your favour. I did some research, and Dave has history with Jessica. He was her editor when she was training. She accused him of sexual harassment, which turned out not to be true. He's got his own axe to grind."

I grab her and kiss her on the head, relief flooding me that we finally have something. "This is why I love you," I blurt, and she laughs, pushing me away.

"Behave or I'll tell Mac you're hitting on me."

Later, when I get home, Sofia is in the kitchen cooking. I lift the lid on a pan and inhale the smell of chilis and garlic. "What's all this? Is Lorenzo sick?"

"No," she says with a smile, "I gave him the night off so I could cook for you."

I smirk. "You can cook?"

She swats me with a towel. "Yes, I'm actually very good at it. How many times have you cooked in this kitchen?" she asks, stirring a sauce that looks amazing.

I take a seat. "Never. I have people for that."

"Don't you get sick of people running around for you?"

I laugh, loosening my tie. "No. But you look good in my kitchen. Sexier than Lorenzo."

"How was your day?"

I laugh harder. "Really? We're at that stage already?"

"You know, you should do that more . . . laugh. It looks good on you."

"Well, if you'd had a day like I've had, you wouldn't feel like smiling either."

I watch with interest as she moves around the kitchen, occasionally humming along to the radio. I find myself smiling. Somehow, I've grown to like Sofia. "At the risk of sounding like a real wife, why have you had a bad day?" she asks with a grin.

She passes me to go to the fridge, and I grab her hand, pulling her to stand between my legs. I tuck her hair behind her ears and stare into her large brown eyes. She's beautiful. Natural and perfect. "I don't think I ever told you," I whisper, placing a gentle kiss on her nose, "you're stunning."

She blushes. "Thank you."

"I hate we wasted time being so angry with each other. This is way better."

"It took you a while to see how amazing I am," she jokes, and I grin, kissing her on the lips.

"It did," I admit. "But now I know, we can stop wasting time pretending to hate each other and admit how we really feel." She breaks eye contact. Maybe I'm moving too fast. "It's okay if you're not sure how you feel. We'll take it slow. I'm just happy we're getting along."

SOFIA

NICOLA JANE

Vinn causes pain in my chest with each word. He's right, we're heading in the right direction and becoming more amicable every day. Last night showed me what it could be like if we keep this up, and I want to keep it up, desperately.

I serve dinner, a homemade pasta with Mama's amazing sauce. I'm aware I'm doing this to ease my own guilt, but as we tuck in and he groans in pleasure, a stab of happiness hits me. I realise I want to make him smile . . . all the damn time.

Zarina steps into the kitchen and halts at the sight of us eating at the worktop. "Oh, sorry," she mutters.

"Join us," I say lightly. It's rude to send her away.

"No, I shouldn't," she says, smiling awkwardly.

"It's fine," says Vinn. "This is amazing, try it." She glows under his words and smiles brightly, pulling up a chair as I go to grab a bowl. Vinn watches her as she tries the pasta. "It's good, right?"

She nods. "I'll have to make my specialty for you," she says, and Vinn glances at me. She blushes. "For you both," she corrects. It's not surprising she's developed a crush on him, he's been kind to her, so I laugh it off. I'm just glad she's talking to me, and I want her to find a nice husband. I'm pleased Vinn's finding someone for her. Maybe coming to London isn't such a bad idea for all of us, Mama included. She's been much happier here than with Papa in Italy.

"Where have you gone, *bellissima*?" asks Vinn, lightly touching my cheek.

I blink, grinning. "Sorry, I was thinking about London and Mama." I shrug. "How maybe it's the right move for us all." He leans over and kisses me on the head.

"Did you get any further investigating the Revenge person?" asks Zarina, and I glare at her. She shrugs like she doesn't get what I'm pissed about.

PLAYING VINN

Vinn groans. "No, although I might have a way to discredit Jessica Cole."

"Oh?" I sit up, paying close attention.

"Raven secured an interview tomorrow with a journalist she falsely accused of harassment. I hate to think what lengths she'd go to for a story."

"But you're still trying to find the identity of Revenge?" Zarina asks.

"Yes. Unfortunately, I can't let that one go. She is causing me some real issues with investors and people are cancelling bookings with the club. I can't let it slide."

I almost choke on my pasta, grabbing my water and gulping. Vinn rubs my back with concern. "What will happen to her?" pushes Zarina, and I will her to shut the fuck up.

Vinn grins. "What usually happens to people when they cross the capo of the mafioso?"

"You think it's a woman," I say. "You can't hurt a woman."

"Don't worry about it, it's not your problem." He stands. "Thank you for an amazing dinner. I have work in the office to finish up. I'll find you at bedtime," he says with a wink, and I nod.

The second he leaves, I glare at Zarina. "What the hell was that?" I hiss in a whisper.

"Don't you want to know if he's looking for you?"

"No, I want him to forget. I told you already, I'm not writing anything else. I've seen a different side to Vinn."

"You're deluded if you think this Jessica woman won't want to repay him for whatever he is planning. She won't go down without a fight and she's got you exactly where she wants you."

The sickness in my stomach returns. "Maybe I should just come clean."

"Maybe you should just run."

"Run?"

"Yes. Take some money and make a run for it before he finds out."

I shake my head. "I can't. I don't want to."

"It was only a few months ago you hated his guts and refused to marry him," she reminds me.

"Like I said, things are better between us. We're learning to get along, and I know I've made it harder on myself, but actually, I really like him, Zee. I can't just walk away."

She rolls her eyes. "You can if it's a choice between life and death. He's going to find out, Sofia, and then what?"

"Maybe I can come to an arrangement with Jessica, make her see I can write better stories, ones that make people smile instead of tear them down."

Zarina stands, shaking her head. "This is going to end in a mess. You should run."

Chapter Fourteen

VINN

I wake with Sofia in my arms. It's becoming my favourite way to start the day. I decide to work from home today. I have a surprise for Sofia, and I know she's going to be really excited, so Raven's organised for Dave Cline to interview me here. It seemed more appropriate to give the impression of a relaxed family man.

There's more good news when Blu tells me Diego is booked onto a flight. He'd been dragging his feet and making excuses as to why he was delaying. I regret not flying to Italy and sorting this out there, but there's no way I could have forced information out of him in another boss's territory.

I take Sofia's hand and lead her into my office. "I have a surprise," I announce, pulling her to sit on my knee. She looks worried, and I laugh. "Relax, it's a good surprise."

"I'm not used to this," she reminds me, and I kiss her, hoping that will relax her since she seems on edge lately.

"You said you wanted something for you, like a job," I say, and she nods. "So, I picked these up and thought you could maybe enrol." I point to the university brochures on my desk. "Journalism or whatever course you'd like to take." She stares at the colourful brochures, lost for words. "If you don't want

NICOLA JANE

to, it's fine. We can look for something else." I'm learning to accept she wants a life outside of us.

"You want me to go to university?" she whispers.

"If that's what you want."

She nods, tears forming in her eyes. "Yes, I'd love that. I thought being a journalist was out of the question."

"I never said that, your father did. I don't have a problem, despite hating journalists," I say with a wink. "I liked what you said about making a good difference. The world of news needs someone like you. And if you're still serious about it after you graduate, we'll get you a great role with a respectable newspaper."

She throws her arms around my neck. "I don't know what to say," she whispers. "I'm so grateful. I can't believe you listened to me when I told you my dreams."

"I've always listened to you, Sofia. It was you who never listened." She giggles, placing kisses along my jaw.

Dave Cline is in his fifties. He has two grown children with his ex-wife, and he explains how he hired Jessica Cole as his junior a few years ago. "She was always too big for her boots," he mutters. "Had big ideas she'd change the world. I was happy to encourage her, but then she started writing trash. I couldn't print that shit, I'd have been sued. She didn't get that and accused me of being sexist. Anyway, in the end, I let her go. I couldn't put up with her crazy accusations and bad attitude. Next thing I know, the cops are banging on my door and arresting me for sexual assault. She told them I'd touched her inappropriately several times. I told them that was impossible, that I'd left my wife the year before for my

PLAYING VINN

gay lover, and I wasn't bloody interested in her. She eventually admitted she was lying but not before having me arrested and putting me through a trial for unfair dismissal."

I raise my eyebrows and take a deep breath. "That's quite a story."

"Yes, one she never writes about," he points out. "I hate her newspaper. It's not even a real newspaper, it's a gossip rag. So, I want to give you a chance to put your side forward."

I nod, giving him my best poker face.

"Jessica is an ex of mine," I say, and he gasps. "She's angry that I married Sofia and is hell bent on painting me as the villain, when in actual fact, my only crime was falling in love. Some people can't stand to see others happy, especially when they're successful."

He scribbles some notes down. "Right, let's screw the bitch over. We'll go over the questions and practise the answers, and then, if you're happy, I'll record the interview on my phone."

I nod, giving a satisfied smile. I have no choice but to discredit her stories. My club is suffering, and my apartments could go the same way if this carries on. Investors are getting itchy feet, wanting to pull out.

SOFIA

Vinn's story went on the newspaper's social media page. Jessica Cole's been emailing me since, demanding I call her, but I ignore her messages. Vinn's in a great mood and we're currently surrounded by his biker friends at the Kings Reapers clubhouse. Blu insisted we all watch the news here together, and I have to admit, Vinn was good. He came across like he was concerned for Jessica's mental health and insisted he was only speaking out so that other men with disgruntled exes harassing them would speak out too and seek help. Now, I just have to avoid Jessica and pray she doesn't tell Vinn what I've done. I want this all to go away so we can move on.

Anna hands me a glass of wine. "Tell us about university," she demands excitedly. The men are by the bar, and I catch Vinn's eye and smile.

"He surprised me with uni brochures. We're going to check some of them out next week."

"I knew he had a heart," she says, smiling.

"It took us a while to get to this point, and there were times I wanted to kill him, but I'm glad I didn't because when he's being like this, I think I could fall in love."

"Could?" Leia repeats. "I hate to break it to you, but you're already there. I can see it in your eyes." I blush. I'm most definitely falling for him, which is why I hate lying to him. "And he is too. Look how he keeps glancing over here."

"I'm happy for you both," says Anna, patting my hand. "You make a great couple, and I can see the change in him already. He's smiling more." "How is the baby-making going?" asks Leia, and Anna hits her in the arm. "Come on, we all want to know," she laughs.

"We did a pregnancy test not too long ago and it was negative."

Anna smirks. "I guess it means you can keep trying."

"Actually, I still haven't had my period. I didn't mention it to him because he was disappointed with the negative test. I'm going to do another test tomorrow."

"That's so exciting," Leia gushes. "He'll be so happy if you are."

"Just keep it between us for now. He's a private person," I say, and they agree.

Chapter Fifteen

VINN

Sofia touches my arm. "I think we should go home. Zarina is drunk," she whispers, and I nod. Zarina is dancing on the table with Raven and Gia. I go over and hold out a hand to help her down. She takes it, smiling seductively. I'm pretty sure Sofia's noticed the way her cousin is around me, but the way she's looking at me now has me worried she's going to hit on me, so I call Gerry over to take over.

We get home and I head to the office, telling Sofia I'll be with her soon. I have emails to catch up on and I've also got a location on the Colombian that hurt Sofia, so I need to do my research.

An hour later, I'm lost looking at maps of Colombia when the office door opens and Zarina enters. I inwardly groan. This isn't going to end well. "Everything okay?" I ask.

She stands before me, resting her hands on the desk and making sure her arms push her breasts up over the silk slip she's wearing. "I was wondering if you managed to find me a husband yet?"

"Maybe we can talk about that tomorrow." She bites her lower lip and stares at me from under her lashes. She's pretty and sexy. If I wasn't obsessed with Sofia, I might be tempted to go there. "Goodnight, Zarina," I add sternly."Yah know, I told Sofia how lucky she is to have a guy like you."

"Thank you," I mutter, going back to my laptop.

"I don't know why she caused you so much trouble.""Well, we're all good now. We've moved forward."

"Have you?" she asks, wobbling as she moves around to my side of the desk and rests her arse against it. "Because if you weren't one hundred percent happy, there's always another option."

I smile, wincing slightly and feeling embarrassed for her. "That's great but totally inappropriate. You've had a lot to drink, Zarina. Go to bed." She runs a finger over my arm, and I pull away. "Please."

"Fine," she mutters. "Could you help me? I'm not very steady on my feet."

I hesitate but close my laptop and stand. She hooks her arm through mine, and I lead her upstairs. "Why do you have to be so perfect?" she whispers.

We stop outside her door. "Believe me, I'm not. Far from it, in fact."

"To me, you are," she says, and then unexpectedly, she throws herself at me. I stumble back and turn my head away to avoid her lips. She hisses angrily. "She doesn't fucking deserve you."

"I don't deserve her, and I don't want to do anything that will ruin what we've finally got. You can't behave like this in my home."

Zarina stamps her foot like a spoiled brat. "She's lying to you!"

I pause, working out if this is the drink talking. She keeps her eyes locked to mine. "Her whole family fucking lie. Her papa is the master at it."

PLAYING VINN

I grab her upper arm, marching her into her room and closing the door. "You told me you didn't know anything about him!"

She swallows, looking away. "I don't, not really, just what my papa says about him always lying. But I know about Sofia."

"What about Sofia?"

"Maybe I shouldn't say," she murmurs.

I'm losing patience. I grip her chin hard and glare at her. "You have five seconds before I lose my shit."

"It's her. She's the one lying about you."

"What are you talking about?"

She tries to remove my hand, but I pinch tighter. "Revenge," she cries, and I instantly release her, stepping away like she's punched me. "She's Revenge."

I stare open-mouthed, then shake my head. "You're lying."

"I'm not. Check her emails. I told her not to get involved."

"She wouldn't."

"I'm sorry. I told her I'd tell you if she carried on. I'd never have done that to you. She really doesn't deserve you."

I grab her again, "Don't breathe a word of this conversation to anyone, especially her, or you'll be at the bottom of the Thames. Am I clear?" She nods, and I storm out.

I take a deep breath before opening the bedroom door. Sofia is naked in bed, fast asleep on top of the sheets. I stare down at her with my heart aching. Zarina must be lying. Maybe she thought I'd give in to her advances. I carefully take Sofia's laptop from the nightstand and go back to my office.

I open it and check the inbox. There's nothing but junk mail, just as I suspected. I go to the sent box and it's empty. I relax a little. Opening her address book, I scroll down and pause when I see Jessica's name. My heart rate picks up again and I close my eyes briefly, the realisation hitting me that she could be Revenge. The pain that follows is like a fire in my chest.

NICOLA JANE

I open some of her files, finding nothing of interest, until I stumble across a file labelled 'coursework'. I keep the cursor hovered over the file, knowing that this could well be a turning point because Sofia doesn't do coursework.

I glimpse at my father's picture and shake my head. I can't ignore this. If Sofia has betrayed me, I need to know.

SOFIA

I stretch out and open my eyes. The space next to me is still empty and cold, which means Vinn didn't come to bed. I sit up and almost scream in fright when I see him sitting at the end of the bed watching me. I laugh. "You scared me." He doesn't speak but gives a small laugh. "Are you okay?" He nods. "Are we playing a game?" I ask, grinning. I get on all fours and slowly crawl towards him. "Should I guess what you're doing here in last night's clothes, watching me sleep naked?" I kneel beside him and run a hand over his thigh. When he still doesn't speak, I lean closer, placing a kiss next to his mouth. "Were you thinking of all the ways you were gonna fuck me?" I throw a leg over him so I'm sitting on his lap facing him and I rub against him.

"Something like that," he mutters.

I smile. "I like the sound of that."

He takes me by the waist and lifts me from him, practically dumping me on the bed. "Shower. We have things to do today."

"Oh?"

"University, remember?"

"Today?" I ask, excitement building.

He heads into the bathroom, and I dive up to follow him. He undresses quickly. "Can we both get in there?" I ask, wiggling my brows. He shakes his head, and I frown. "Are you okay?"

"Yep, just got a lot on my mind."

PLAYING VINN

I smirk and step into the shower. "Well, let me help you."

I make a grab for his cock, but he snatches my wrist and holds it tightly. "No, Sofia. Not right now."

I step out like a wounded puppy he's just kicked and wrap a towel around myself. He hasn't been this cold in a long time, and I hate it. He washes quickly and gets out. "Meet me downstairs when you're ready."

I wait for him to leave and shut the door. Taking a pregnancy test from the cabinet, I sit to pee on it, then I get in the shower.

VINN

"What's wrong with you this morning?" snaps Gia.

"Nothing. I just want to eat in peace." I feel Sofia's eyes on me. My mood clouds the entire room, and it's obvious to everyone I'm pissed about something. "I think I'm closer to finding out the identity of Revenge," I add, and Sofia tenses.

"Good, kill them and move on, I'm sick of it already," says Gia, and I scoff. Would she say that if she knew the truth? Zarina keeps her head lowered, not speaking or making eye contact with anyone.

"You're very quiet this morning," I point out. "Nothing to say?" She shakes her head. "Hangovers are a real bitch," I mutter. I don't know why I'm so pissed at her. Maybe a part of me wishes she'd never told me.

After breakfast, I tell Gerry to stay at the house to keep an eye on Zarina. He knows me too well and he'll spot my turmoil. I'm not ready to answer questions yet and could do without him hanging around me, so I drive us to the university with my usual security tailing us from a distance.

I was going to cancel the visits, but I want her to remember what she almost had, so I'm going to show her the university and get the enrolment forms because having hope and losing it is soul-crushing. I smile to myself. I can't wait to crush her.

NICOLA JANE

We look around and it's obvious Sofia loves it. She grabs my hand and practically drags me to the huge library. I never really saw the appeal of university. I got where I am through hard work, so it's possible to be successful without a degree and a shitload of debt for the privilege. "I love it," she gushes, kissing my cheek. "Thank you so much for this." I take the enrolment forms from the office assistant and fold them.

"There's a deadline," she tells us. "Those forms will need to be in by the end of the week." I nod. It's not a problem because Sofia won't be filling in any forms.

On the way back to the car, she slips her hand in mine, and I resist the urge to let go. When she touches me now, it burns. "You're really quiet today, Vinn. Is everything okay?"

I nod. "If you've changed your mind about this, it's fine," she continues.

"I haven't."

"Did I do something wrong?"

I meet her eyes across the top of the car. "I don't know, Sofia, did you?" Her eyes linger on mine for a second too long before she ducks into the car and I follow.

"I don't think I did," she continues. She's got fucking nerve lying to my face again and again after everything I'm doing for her.

"Then don't look so worried."

I drop her back home, following her inside to get Zarina. I don't want to risk her confessing all to Sofia before I'm ready, so I insist she come with me for more work experience. Sofia grabs my hand, letting Zarina walk ahead to the car. "You know she likes you, right?" I nod, and she looks worried. "So, it's probably not a good idea to encourage her to spend time with you."

"Are you jealous?" I ask with a smirk.

PLAYING VINN

Her brow furrows. "I don't have to be jealous to not like it, Vinn, and I don't like it. What's going on with you today? Did something happen between you two?"

"Why would you think that?"

"Because you're acting weird. I don't understand."

I push my hands into her hair and stare down at her. Even now, after what she's done, she takes my breath away. Maybe that's why the betrayal stings that little bit more. "You don't have to worry, *bellissima*, I love you." The words leave my mouth so easily, I almost believe them myself. She gasps, and before she can answer, I kiss her. I take it slow so I can enjoy the taste of her one last time. Our final kiss needs to be perfect.

SOFIA

I watch Vinn drive away, still confused by his odd behaviour. I know he's dealing with a lot, but the way he's pushing me away while still holding me close is messing with my head. I tell myself it's the guilt of everything weighing me down, that I'm seeing things that aren't there.

I go back inside and head for the library. I need to make that call to Jessica before she does something stupid. A man answers her mobile, and I consider hanging up but find myself asking for her. "I'm sorry, she's unavailable," he says.

"Erm, it's actually really urgent I talk to her. She was trying to get hold of me yesterday."

I hear him speaking with someone else in a low whisper before he comes back on the line. "Are you a friend?"

"Yes," I lie.

"Can I take your name?"

"What's going on? Where is she?"

"I'm sorry to inform you that Jessica was found dead in her apartment this morning." I freeze, unsure of what to say.

NICOLA JANE

Thoughts race through my head so fast, I have to lower into a nearby seat. "I don't understand," I whisper.

"I shouldn't really say anything else," he whispers back.

"Was it accidental or was she ill?"

He hesitates. "They're saying she took her own life."

I disconnect the call. My hands are shaking so bad, I struggle to press the correct button on my phone. Vinn didn't come to bed last night and he's been acting weird, but it's not like I can ask him, or he'll wonder how I know before the rest of the world.

I sit for a while thinking over the last few hours. Vinn's odd behaviour. He's too clever to make it look so obvious, he only did the interview yesterday. Did she kill herself? She seemed so strong and ready to take on the world. It doesn't make sense.

Gia interrupts my thoughts. "I've been looking everywhere for you."

"Sorry, just processing the university and how huge a life-changing decision it is."

She smiles. "You're going to love it, I'm sure. Anyway, did you do the test?" she asks.

I nod. "I haven't spoken to Vinn yet. He didn't seem in the mood this morning."

"You mean—" I nod, and she squeals, rushing over to me and hugging me. "That's so exciting!"

"Please keep it to yourself. I'd like to make a big deal of the announcement, but I want to wait until he's in a better mood."

"Of course."

Chapter Sixteen

VINN

I get the call to say Diego has landed and Blu's taking him to the lockup underneath the house. It's something my dad had adapted when he originally bought the place. He had the cellar knocked through to make it bigger and then sectioned it into two areas. They're heavily soundproofed, so a gun could be fired down there and it wouldn't be heard in the house. There's also a separate entrance around the side of the house, away from prying eyes.

When I arrive, Gerry drives straight into the underground garage so I can go into the basement without being seen. Blu is with Diego, who's pacing back and forth. "Thank God," he says when he sees me. "Have you got somewhere safe for me?"

I hold my arms out and look around the space. "Is this not what you had in mind?"

"Benedetto will find me here."

"No one knows about this," I say dryly.

"Do you know why he was looking into me?" I used what Benedetto told me and twisted it to make it look as though I wanted Diego to come here so I could protect him.

I shake my head, shrugging out of my suit jacket and handing it to Gerry. "He doesn't trust you."

"Why?" Diego half laughs like he can't believe Benedetto wouldn't trust him.

"Maybe the money exchange between you and the Colombians?"

He stops pacing and his expression gives away the second he realises why he's here. "I don't know what you mean."

"You do."

"Look, let's talk this out. I can explain everything. It's simple, but I understand how it looks."

I unclip my cufflinks and hand those to Gerry too, then take my time to roll up the sleeves of my designer shirt. "I'm waiting."

His body language gives away the fact he's nervous and twitchy as he looks around, probably hoping for a way out. "I lost Benedetto's money. Half a mill on the tables. The guy who owned the casino offered me a way out. I sell some powder on my streets, and he clears my debt."

"What guy?" I ask, and he shrugs. I take the first punch and my stress eases slightly.

Diego stumbles back and cups his jaw. "I just wanted to pay the debt. He told me it would be simple."

"And you believed him?" Blu asks with a sarcastic laugh.

"I was desperate and not thinking straight. I knew I could shift the gear easily through my men, so I gave him shipping dates and locations. It was hidden amongst Benedetto's stuff."

"You used his ships?" I snap, my eyes wide. I glance at Blu, who looks just as amused by his audacity.

"It was easy. I was already in charge of what went on those boats. Look, it isn't too late, if you want in on the deal, I can make it work."

Blu punches him this time, and as Diego's head flies back, Blu growls deep in the back of his throat. "Don't fucking insult us," he hisses.

"So, if things are so fucking great, where's Mario?" I ask.

"He found out, got involved, and got himself killed."

I shake my head. "I'm not buying it. Bag him," I order. Gerry grabs him with Blu's help and they force him into a wooden seat. Gerry binds Diego's hands behind his back and then secures him to the chair with pull ties. I stand close, watching as he fights his restraints. Blu places a thick material bag over his head and grips a handful of hair, holding it back. Gerry gets a bucket of water, slowly tipping it over Diego's head. He gasps, trying desperately to catch a breath, but as his airways fill with water, he chokes.

I nod, and they stop. Blu pulls the bag, and Diego vomits down himself as he sucks in much needed oxygen. "The next time you lie to me, it'll be a minute, not twenty seconds."

"I caught him," he spits, his breathing heavy. "I fucking caught him with the dirty Colombian."

"From the beginning!" Blu yells.

"The casino was true. Mario was in on it. We were making good money, so we carried on. But then I walked in on him with Dante's brother. They were . . ." He trails off, looking uncomfortable.

"Should we try the bag again?" I snap.

"Fucking!" he yells angrily. "They were fucking!"

Having a gay son in a life like ours isn't good. It's seen as a weakness and that son would not be considered a leader to his family. He'd be an outcast. "So, what happened?" Blu pushes.

"I pulled my gun and shot him."

"Mario?" I clarify.

He shakes his head. "His lover."

"That doesn't tell me where Mario is," I growl.

"Dante found out. He knew about them, so he pulled Mario in and questioned him. He told him what had happened."

"Where the fuck is Mario, or I swear to God," I warn, snatching the bag and pushing it in his face.

"Dante killed him. He's on a mission to ruin my family."

"That's why he took Sofia?" I gasp. Diego nods, and I punch him, breaking his nose. "Have you seen the pictures?" I yell, hitting him again. He spits blood on the ground.

"It's not over. That's why I sent Sofia to you. He's coming for her."

"Why? He took his revenge."

"That was starters. He's coming for mains and he won't finish until he's had dessert. His words, not mine."

"Does he know where she is?" I ask.

He nods. "Yes. Recently, thanks to your little newspaper stories. He isn't scared of the Italians."

"You dragged me into your fucking war," I shout, hitting him over and over until my fist splits and I struggle to catch my breath. I stagger back as his head falls to the side. He's unconscious and unrecognisable. "We need more security," I mutter, heading for the exit. "Get me the best."

I storm into the house and head straight upstairs. I suck in a breath at the sight of Sofia sitting on my bed with her legs crossed, writing something. She looks up and a small smile tugs at her lips. "I was just filling the applications out." Her eyes fall to my bloodied fists. "You're hurt." She places the paperwork to one side and rushes over, taking my hands in hers and examining my knuckles. I allow myself a moment to enjoy her touch before snatching my hands away and heading into the bathroom. "Let me at least clean them up," she says, following me. It hurts to look at her, so I close the door, ignoring the shock on her face.

When I'm done, Sofia's nowhere to be seen, and I'm glad. I need space to breathe. As I go downstairs, Zarina is just coming through the door with Ash. "Stay in your room until dinner at seven," I tell her, and she nods, doing exactly as she's told without a question. Fuck, she's exactly how I expected Sofia to be. "Ash, keep her and Sofia apart."

Blu comes in, wiping his hands on a rag, and follows me into his office. "Are you gonna tell me what's going on?" he asks, pouring us each a drink.

"I've found Revenge." He stops pouring to stare at me. "It's Sofia."

He drinks his whiskey in one, then tops up before handing me mine. "What the fuck? Are you sure?" I narrow my eyes, and he nods. "Of course, you are, stupid question. Have you asked her why?"

I shake my head. "She isn't aware I know."

He takes a deep breath, his eyes full of questions. "What are you gonna do about it?"

"You know what I have to do, Azure," I snap bitterly, and his eyes widen. "Vinn, you can't." The Kings Reapers have rules and hurting women is against everything they believe in, not that I'd ever ask Blu to do it. There're some things only a capo should deal with.I drink my whiskey and slam the glass on the desk. "I don't have a choice. You know I don't. If this gets out, it will look like I can't handle my shit. If I can't keep my house in order, who the fuck's gonna do business with me? And then there's the whole disrespect she's shown. Defying stupid orders like what to wear is one thing, but trying to ruin me, telling people my business, I can't let that go. There are rules in this life and she fucking knows them all."

Silence stretches out between us as we come to terms with what needs to be done. "Since she came into your life, things have been crazy," Blu admits. "And with her father saying all that crap, it's about to get harder."

"Tell me about it," I mutter, sighing heavily.

NICOLA JANE

"We could always let the Colombian have her," he suggests, and my heart twists. It would be the easiest solution—let him think he's taken her from under my nose and he can deal with her. But I know what he'll do when he gets her, and it will be so much worse than what I have to do.

I shake my head. "No. It needs to be quick and clean." Even saying the words pains me.

Blu sighs. "Gerry?" he suggests.

I shake my head again. "It's gotta be me."

"Shit, Vinn. Have you thought about how that'll stay with you? You love her. It ain't gonna be simple." "It has to me so it sends a clear message out that I won't tolerate betrayal. Not even from my wife. And I should feel the pain, every part of it. It will remind me not to be so stupid again. But first, I have to clear the space in the lockup."

Blu checks his watch. "Honestly, he'll be dead by the morning. I'd leave him to bleed out if I was you."

"Just a heads up," I say as he gets up to leave, "Gerry took Jessica Cole out last night. He made it look like suicide. She left a note saying she saw my interview and was left devastated that we'd never get back together. The police will come knocking any time now."

"Have you got an alibi?" he asks.

I nod. "Yes, I was with Zarina."

He groans. "Not with her in that way though, right?"

"No, but no one else knows that, including my sister. It stays between us."

SOFIA

I checked every news site, every social media outlet, and there's nothing about Jessica on there. Surely, the media would report on that just because of who she was. I glance across the table at Zarina. She's got her head down and hasn't said a word, again. Vinn still looks angry, chewing his food like it's about to be stolen from him. Gerry appears and mutters, "Boss, we have company."

Vinn nods. "Send them through." A man in a suit walks in followed by two police officers. "Good evening." Vinn smiles, standing. "How can I help you?"

"We have some bad news. I'm afraid Jessica Cole was found dead this morning in her apartment." I grab my water with a shaky hand and take a sip to distract me. "That's terrible," says Vinn, looking genuinely upset.

"Did she make contact with you at all last night?"

Vinn shakes his head. "No, I haven't heard from her at all."

"While we wait for the post-mortem results, can you confirm where you were last night between the hours of eleven and six?"

Vinn hesitates, glancing at Zarina. "I can, but maybe we should go somewhere private." I glare between the two of them, a realisation dawning on me. "No, say it here," I demand.

Vinn glances at the floor before looking me in the eyes. "I was with Zarina last night." The officer looks at Zarina, who nods once to confirm. I suck in a breath. It hurts so bad, I don't quite fill my lungs. "Thank you, we'll be in touch if we need anything further."

Vinn nods, and Gerry shows them out. I stand, bracing my hands on the table, while Vinn takes his seat, leaning back with a smirk on his face. "Sit, we haven't eaten." I want to laugh. He seriously wants me to sit and eat dinner like they didn't just confess to shattering my heart? "You said—" I begin.

"Sit, Sofia."

I swipe my hand across the table, sending the plate skimming to the other side. It smashes to the ground and food splatters the wall. "I don't want to sit!" I scream. Vinn doesn't react, but Zarina silently sobs, her shoulders shaking. "How could you?" I whisper in her direction. I half expected it from Vinn, it's the reason I tried to keep my guard up, but I didn't think for a second Zarina would act on her feelings. We were close, like fucking sisters. "You told me you love—" I begin again, cutting myself off with a sob.

Vinn sips his wine like nothing out of the ordinary is currently happening. "We both said things."

"Why?" I ask, my voice choking. I hate being the girl who doubts herself, but was it me? *Wasn't I good enough?*

"Betrayal stings, doesn't it?" he asks thoughtfully.

"I can't do this," I whisper, turning to leave.

"You will do this, Sofia, and you'll do it now. SIT DOWN!" he yells. His voice is loud and commanding. I've never heard him so angry and I almost follow his instructions, but then I remember what he's done and I run, taking off out the front door and around the side of the house. I hear Vinn yelling my name and glance frantically for a place to hide while I work out a plan. There's a door ajar, so I slip inside, pulling it to and staring down a set of stone steps.

I creep down, careful not to let my shoes make a sound so as not to alert him to where I am. As I get to the bottom, there's another door. This one is steel, but again, it's ajar. I wait, listening for Vinn's footsteps and working to steady my breathing, but then I jump in fright when I hear a cry from somewhere behind the metal door. It's a man, there's no doubt about that. I wince, wondering if I should stay hiding here or risk going back up to find somewhere else.

"Jesus, Diego, you're a stubborn bastard. Just go already," I hear Blu say. "We need this space. You're not Jesus, we're not expecting a resurrection or anything spectacular. Just let go."

The moaning continues. That can't be Papa, but I have to know for sure, so I push the heavy door and step into the dully-lit room. Blu has his back to me, but there's no mistaking my papa tied to a chair with his head hanging limply to one side and blood pouring from his face. The sound of my gasp alerts Blu, and he spins to face me.

"Shit," he hisses. My foot barely touches the first step before Blu's arms are wrapped around me and I'm hauled against his body. "Calm," he whispers as I fight against his hold. "Sofia, it's okay."

"Get the fuck off me," I scream, struggling harder. The top door opens, letting a stream of cold air in. Vinn fills the doorway, his arms across his chest, watching with interest.

"Did you leave the door open?" he asks dryly, and Blu nods. "Let her go." He releases me, but I stay rooted to the spot, my fists balled at my sides and my breathing heavy. I don't want to be down here, involved in whatever the hell's going off, but I don't want to be near Vinn either. "Come, Sofia, don't be shy," he drawls. When I make no move towards him, he sighs impatiently. "Bring her," he orders. Blu grasps my arms and marches me forwards and up the steps. At the top, Vinn snatches my wrist and drags me stumbling back into the house. We go upstairs, and once I'm in the bedroom and he frees me, I pull out a large bag from under the bed. Vinn watches me with amusement. "Where exactly are you going?"

"Away from you," I hiss, throwing it on the bed and pulling open a drawer. "Why is Papa in there?" I begin to cry at the thought of him tied up, dying. Tears blur my vision as I sit on the edge of the bed, burying my face in my shaking hands.

"Poor Sofia," he murmurs, but his tone is mocking.

"Did you kill Jessica?"

"I couldn't have," he says, leaning against the bedroom door.

"Because you were fucking Zarina?"

"At what point did I say I fucked your cousin?"

NICOLA JANE

I pause, glancing over my hands at him. "You—"

"What I said was, I was with Zarina last night. I didn't mention fucking or anything else."

"So, you expect me to believe you sat talking all night? You've been acting weird all day, and she's been avoiding me."

"I expect you to believe me when I say I have an alibi. Don't get me wrong, given the chance, I think Zarina would definitely let me. She made it pretty clear last night, but I turned her away."

I stand, feeling hope in my chest, brushing my tears away. "So, you didn't cheat?"

He shakes his head.

VINN

Relief floods her face and she moves towards me. "I thought you'd cheated," she whispers, placing her hands on my chest. "So, she threw herself at you?" I nod. "I knew she liked you, but I never thought she'd do anything about it. I thought she was loyal to me." "No one is ever truly loyal these days, Sofia."

"I'm so relieved you didn't," she whispers. Her hands move to my face, and she cups my cheeks, pulling me down for a kiss. When I don't kiss her back, she pulls back, looking confused. "I'm sorry for flying off like that."

I take her wrists in my hands and lower them to her side. "I know what you did," I whisper calmly. Her brow furrows. "Zarina told me." She begins breathing faster, her eyes darting around, avoiding me, and when she tries to pull away, I tighten my grip. "So, I understand how you felt just then when you thought I'd betrayed you because it's exactly how I felt when I was told my wife had been lying and sneaking around with Jessica fucking Cole!" I yell the last bit, and she recoils.

Chapter Seventeen

VINN

I shove her from me, and she falls on the bed. "So, pack your shit, make it look like you've done a runner."

"It wasn't supposed to be like that."

"Don't tell me. I don't want to hear your bullshit lies. For once in your life, do as you're told and pack your bags."

I watch as she slowly begins to pack her clothes. She's going slow and it pisses me off, so I begin grabbing handfuls, angrily throwing them in. Once it's full, I zip it up and shove it back under the bed. "Now what?" she asks.

"Lucky for you, I have a second room out there. You can be with your papa."

"You won't kill me," she says, sounding sure.

I laugh, grabbing her upper arm and marching her back downstairs. Zarina appears in the kitchen doorway. "Say goodbye to your cousin," I snap, and Sofia smiles wide. She's hiding her fear well, and I admire her for that, but some sick part of me wants her to cry and beg for forgiveness. At least then I'd know she regretted fucking me over.

"Goodbye, Zarina. Look after him for me," she says sweetly, her voice dripping with sarcasm.

NICOLA JANE

I roll my eyes and shove her outside. We go back down the stone steps. "Why did you do it?" I ask, passing her dying father and proceeding to the next room.

"I was angry. I didn't want to live this life." I push her to sit on a stool, and without me asking, she places her hands out front for me to tie them. She's far too confident that I'm not going to do this, which makes me more determined. She's not fucking immune because she gave me her pussy. "At least Zarina is a virgin," she says with a grin. "It's what you wanted." I pull the ties extra tight, pinching her skin, but she doesn't flinch.

"Shut the fuck up," I snap.

"I'm impressed you turned her away," she adds.

"Trust me, if I knew then what I know now, I wouldn't have."

"Will you get with her next?"

I laugh sarcastically, annoyed by her easy chat. You wouldn't think she was facing death by the way she's acting. "She'd be easier to handle than you, more compliant and grateful."

"You know, without my dead body, you'll technically still be married. It could stop you moving on in the future."

"I've instructed the solicitor to draw up the divorce papers. I'll forge your signature."

She wriggles like she's getting comfortable. "Right, so how are we doing this?"

It's enough to send me over the edge. I pull out my gun from the back of my trousers and push it against her head. She closes her eyes, and I see a flicker of fear for the first time. Good, she needs to be scared. "I was gonna give you everything," I hiss.

"At the time, I didn't know that. I was angry and hurt, scared of what the future held with a man I didn't know."

"I can't ever forgive you," I growl.

She looks into my eyes, seemingly calm again, and she smiles. Tears balance on her lower lashes making her brown eyes glisten. "I'm so sorry for hurting you, Vinn. If I could take it back, I would, but I was a naïve girl scared of living a life like my parents."

I push my face to hers and sneer. "You didn't hurt me, *cagna*. You gave me a reason to get out of this marriage."

SOFIA

My palms are sweating, and my heart is hammering in my chest. The look in Vinn's eyes is dangerous and I don't know if he's going to pull the trigger any second. His mood is unpredictable, but I know I have to remain calm because that's what you do in this life, my papa's words running through my mind. *Stay calm, don't react.*

I suck in a deep breath and close my eyes, preparing myself in case he does it before I've had chance to make peace with the world. "I'm sorry. I can't say it any other way, and now I don't have time to make it up to you. But please know that I tried to stop, but Jessica blackmailed me to continue." He frowns, clicking off the safety. My words aren't enough, he wants me dead, so I press my lips together in a tight line. "Okay, I'm ready," I say with a nod.

"You think I won't do it?" he whispers, and the metal of the gun digs into my temple.

"I don't think you have a choice," I say. "I love you, Vinn. It took me a while, but I do."

Silence stretches out and the ringing in my head turns up a notch until it's deafening. I begin a silent count.

One . . . two . . .

Suddenly, footsteps come racing down the stone steps and the door crashes open. "Gia, get out," yells Vinn.

I turn my head and watch with hope as she runs into the room and grabs Vinn's arm, trying to move the gun from me. "You can't kill her," she yells.

NICOLA JANE

"Gia," I warn, "it's okay."

She ignores me, still clinging to Vinn's arm. "She's pregnant."

Vinn stares at me, shocked. "No, we did a test."

"She did another because her period didn't come. She's pregnant, Vinn. You can't kill her."

Vinn lowers the gun, putting the safety back on and tucking it away. His face is full of confusion and disappointment. After trying so hard for a baby, he's finally having one with the woman who hurt him. He takes a few steps back, and I growl angrily. I was ready. I accepted death and now he's pulling out. "I betrayed you. The families will expect you to kill me," I yell. "They'll say you're weak." Gia tries to cover my mouth, but I move my head. "They'll send someone to do it, and they might kill you."

Vinn doesn't bother to look at me. Instead, he takes Gia's arm, pulling her towards the exit. I shiver as cold air wraps around me, and I jump when the door slams and let out an angry cry. "I was fucking ready!" I yell but I'm met with silence. *Great, now what?*

VINN

I go to my bathroom and grab a test kit. Gia thinks love conquers all, and I wouldn't put it past her to lie just to delay Sofia's death in the hope I'll change my mind. But if she's not lying and Sofia is pregnant, it will change everything.

Sofia is shivering when I return, but I ignore the overwhelming need to wrap her in my jacket and hold her. I cut the ties holding her hands, and she wiggles her fingers as the blood rushes back to them. Pulling a bucket into the centre of the room, I pass her the test. She unwraps the packaging before pulling her jeans down without so much as an eye roll. Pulling out my gun again, I decide if it's negative, I'll pull the trigger. If it isn't, I'm screwed.

PLAYING VINN

The sound of her pee hitting the metal makes her blush. She holds the stick there for a few seconds before passing it back. I place it on the side, watching as the results window changes colour. Sofia takes a seat back on the stool, wrapping her arms around herself. "Can I check Papa?" she whispers.

"No." He's still breathing, I can hear his gasps every so often.

"Can't you end him quickly? He's suffering."

"He deserves to." I groan when a faint line appears in the window, telling me she is in fact pregnant. I pick it up angrily and throw it across the room.

"Now what?"

"You just brought yourself nine months."

Sofia jumps up and runs from the room to her father. Rolling my eyes, I follow. She's on her knees, sobbing hard and grasping his limp hands in her own. "Oh, Papa, what did you do?" He groans, but he's too weak to respond. Sofia presses her hands over a wound on his leg. It's no good—there's too many holes in the guy for her to cover. I ordered Blu to give him a slow death and bleeding out is exactly that. "I hate you, Vinn Romano," she whispers.

I smirk. "The feeling is mutual, *cagna*."

"Papa," she murmurs, gently cupping his cheek. "I'm here. It's okay, you can go."

I roll my eyes. I hate drama. I pull out the gun I had loaded and ready to kill my wife and pull the trigger. Sofia screams, falling back into the pools of her father's blood. Diego's head flies backwards as the bullet penetrates his skull, spraying more blood and brain matter. Sofia keeps screaming until I place a hand over her mouth and haul her to her feet. I keep her back pressed against my front as I walk her from the room.

By the time we break out into the fresh night air, she's sobbing so hard, she's retching. I release her, and she falls to the ground, landing on all fours and coughing violently, then vomiting onto the trimmed lawn. I wait, letting her empty the contents of her stomach before grabbing her by the hair and pulling her to stand. In order for me to hate this woman, I have to treat her with the contempt she deserves.

SOFIA

I'm taken to the attic. I've never been up this far in the house because the stairs leading to it creep me the hell out. My limbs ache, and I'm so cold, my teeth are chattering together. It's the only sound that can be heard as Vinn unlocks the door and forces me inside. "What about my mama?" I ask hoarsely.

"I'll allow her to stay here and clean for me."

I nod. Mama will hate it, but once it gets out that I've betrayed Vinn, she'll never be accepted back in Italy, especially not without Papa. I see his broken skull in my mind and begin crying again. I can't stop the flow of tears no matter how hard I want to, because crying in front of Vinn makes me feel weak and vulnerable

"He deserved to die," says Vinn bluntly.

"According to you," I mumble, moving farther into the room and away from him.

It's a simple room with a double bed, cotton sheets, and a bedside table. There's a bucket in the corner, and when Vinn sees me staring, he smirks. "Your en-suite." I have nothing left for him, so I lie on the bed, keeping my back to him. "You can go now. I'll see you in nine months."

"You'll be seeing me before then, Sofia. I make the rules."

"From this moment on, I'll never respond to you again," I whisper, my heart cracking a little more. "And in nine months, when you take this child, I pray you see my dead, soulless eyes whenever you look at it."

When I hear the door close and the lock click, I cry harder. I never thought I'd feel disappointed to be alive. I bury my face into my pillow to muffle my sobs.

VINN

I stand outside Sofia's door, listening to her heart breaking, and rest my head against it. I close my eyes and take a deep, calming breath, building up the strength to walk away.

Gia's waiting with Blu in my office. He gives me a sympathetic smile, "Sorry, she insisted on waiting," he mutters, which earns him a glare from my sister.

"It's late, Gia. Go to bed.""What happened? Is Sofia okay?"

"She's alive, if that's what you're asking."

Gia sags with relief. "Can I see her, check if she's okay?"

I shake my head. "No. As far as this family is concerned, Sofia is dead."

Her eyes burn into me. "Where is she?"

"In the attic, safe and well."

"She's carrying my niece or nephew. I can't act like she's not a part of this family. You're married, for goodness' sake."

"Gia," mutters Blu in warning.

"Fuck off, Blu," she yells, and he raises his eyebrow in surprise. "This is between me and my brother, not your boss."

"Gia, it's best not to get too close to her. In nine months, it'll be like she never existed," I drawl, pouring a whiskey.

"Only that's not true, is it, Vinn? Because she will live on through your child and through here," she hisses, hitting me in the chest over my heart. "You don't stop loving someone."I smirk. "Who said I loved her? She was a pain in my arse. I'm glad to be rid of her."

Gia shakes her head and opens the office door to leave. "You stubborn men will never learn. You can tell yourself she's nothing and you can live without her, but we both know that's not true. She might have fucked up, but worse things happen in a marriage. If you kill Sofia after this, I'll walk away from this family forever."

"You can't just walk away!" I yell at her retreating back, and she spins to face me with a face full of rage. "You know the rules."

"What the fuck is that supposed to mean, big brother? Are you threatening me?"

"Gia!" yells Blu. "Enough!" She holds his stare for a defiant few seconds before leaving the room, slamming the door hard behind her. Blu lets out a breath. "Fuck, she could make me piss in my pants when she gets like that. Imagine her with a gun?"

"It's why women don't run shit," I mutter.

"Are you okay?"

"Better than okay. Put the word out that Sofia is dead along with her lying father. Make sure it reaches as far as Dante. And arrange for a video call with Benedetto tomorrow. If he wants to go to war with me over Diego, I need to prepare. Arrange for Josey to show Angela her new room first thing. She'll be sharing the staff quarters."

"Vinn—" he begins, and I know by his tone he's gonna give me a pep talk.

I open my laptop, interrupting him. "That'll be all, Azure."

He concedes with a nod and leaves.

Chapter Eighteen

SOFIA

Three days have passed and the only person I've seen in the whole time is Ash. She's been tasked with swapping my en-suite bucket twice a day and she also delivers me breakfast, dinner, and my evening meal. So far, I haven't touched any of them. I'm sick to my stomach and the thought of swallowing even the smallest amount of food makes me gag.

I hear the lock and open my eyes, not moving an inch from my foetal position on the bed. Vinn enters, filling the doorway with his huge, muscled body. It's wrong that after everything, he still makes my heart squeeze and butterflies take flight in the pit of my stomach. I remain still, staring back at his cruel eyes. It's the one thing I've noticed has changed since I saw him a few days ago. "Ash said you haven't eaten in days." He waits for a reply he won't be getting, then sighs. "Sofia, you need to eat something." He steps closer, pushing the door closed. "Think about the baby," he adds a little more softly.

I suck in a breath, the mention of my baby hitting me right in the chest. It's all I've thought about, that and the fact I'll never watch it grow up, that I'll have to hand it over to this monster. A lone tear falls from the corner of my eye and hits the pillow. Vinn crouches, and for a second, a look of regret passes over his expression before he remembers who he is and narrows his eyes. "It's not a polite request, Sofia. You will eat your next meal, or I will make you."

I stare past him to a spot on the wall. It's a scuff mark that I've spent hours wondering how it got there. Was someone else locked up here? Was it done when furniture was delivered here, and did the delivery driver know it would be used by a prisoner? "Sofia, are you listening to me?" Vinn waits a second before standing. "Your mother has been asking after you. Eat your next meal, and I'll let her visit." My eyes flicker, but I don't remove them from the scuff mark. *Mama.* She must be heartbroken to be cleaning for this piece of shit. Why did my Papa get involved with this man? What did he do so wrong to deserve a painful, drawn-out death? "Fine, Sofia, have it your way. I'll bring your dinner at seven. Be prepared."

VINN

"Would you like me to have a word?" asks Josey tentatively when I tell her to have Sofia's dinner ready by seven. "We got to know each other quite well, I think she might listen to me."

"No. She'll eat this evening."

"But . . ." She trails off when I glare at her.

"Seven," I repeat before going to my office.

I open my laptop to prepare for my second call with Benedetto. The first didn't go too well when I told him about Diego's betrayal to the mafioso. I should imagine most of his anger was because this went on under his nose and he knew nothing of it. It brings his leadership into question.

"Vincent," he greets, his face coming into view as the video call connects. I decided honesty was the best policy when it came to Sofia. I told him about her betrayal and her pregnancy, so he knew the reason for me not ending her just yet. However, he also knows what I plan to do once my child is here. It's expected. I don't need the Italians, I decided long

PLAYING VINN

ago I could be just as powerful here in London without their connections. And, ultimately, they need me more so they can do business here in the UK. But I told him out of courtesy, and I don't want to completely cut ties until I'm ready.

"Benedetto," I nod, "I trust you're ready to talk."

"Of course. Your news was not expected when I spoke to you last. I've done some checks and it seems you're right, Diego's dealings behind my back went deep. Shocking really, I misjudged him. I always thought he was stupid."

"He was," I mutter. "He crossed me."

"Vincent, I regret what happened, but the Grecos are your problem. You married their daughter."

"Dealings were done under your nose with an enemy," I snap. "You'll help me go to war with Dante."

"I made contact," he says, and I keep my face impassive even though I'm angry. I've been trying to make contact for days. "Diego's debt has been passed to you. The Colombians are not happy you took his life without speaking to them. You'll need to make a new deal with him directly."

"I'm not making a fucking deal with him," I growl. "Are you seriously going to brush this off like it isn't your debt?"

"I didn't marry the girl."

"Piece of fucking shit," I mutter.

"Careful, Vinn, you sound more and more British every day."

I laugh coldly. "Consider this fair warning, Benedetto. I don't take kindly to being screwed over, and I'll be looking at the deals we made just months ago after your father passed. As it stands, I have no choice but to freeze any boats you have coming into London, and I'll be disrupting your current distributions that my men are driving around as we speak." I disconnect and pick up my mobile. "Gerry," I snap the second he answers, "call the Italian's lorries back to the yard. Nothing moves until I say."

Blu walks in as I end my call, and I fill him in on my conversations. "That explains why we can't contact the Colombians. They'll be working on a new deal, new terms."

"They can come up with what the fuck they like, but I'll kill every single one of them before I pay a penny of that shithead's debt."

"Death is the only way to stop them," he agrees. "We need a plan."

Seven o'clock comes, and Josey presents me with a beef roast dinner. "It's her favourite," she announces proudly.

I climb the stairs and try to get my emotions in check because it's killing me to watch her so lifeless and broken. Gia was right, it's not easy to stop my feelings for her, and as soon as she's eating again, I can go back to pretending she isn't living in my house right above my bedroom. I've spent most of the day checking in on her using the camera I'd installed years ago. She hasn't moved from the bed.

When I open the door, she's staring blankly at the opposite wall. "Sit up," I bark, but she doesn't respond. "Sofia." I place the tray on the bedside table, hoping the smell will rouse something in her. "Please," I say, a little quieter, and her eyes flick to me. "Please, Sofia, don't make me force this food down your throat." I beg her with my eyes because I really don't want to make her eat like that. When she still doesn't make a move, I growl with frustration and snatch the tray. "Fine, have it your way."

PLAYING VINN

I storm back into the kitchen, taking Josey by surprise. "Blend it," I order. Josey closes her eyes in a brief moment of sadness before taking the dinner and pouring it into the blender. She blasts it for a few seconds at a time until the consistency is smooth. She grabs a tall metal cup used for milkshakes and empties the mixture into it.

"Are you sure I can't just speak to her," she asks again. I snatch the cup and head back up the stairs. This time, I don't have to give myself a pep talk about being firm or hard on her because I'm angry. Angry that she's making me do this and she'll still hate me for it. She won't see it's for the good of my child.

I fling the door open, and it crashes against the wall. She doesn't flinch, which only angers me more. I grab her chin, forcing her to look at me as I tower over her. A flicker of anger passes over her face. Good, she needs to start fighting. I stick my thumb in the side of her mouth, pushing it to the gum right at the back. She coughs, gagging.

SOFIA
His thumb brushes the back of my throat, and I gag, my eyes streaming as I cough violently. He kneels on the bed, pressing his knee on my hand to stop me grabbing him. I use my spare to hit out, but it doesn't deter him. Instead, he wedges his fingers into my mouth so I can't close it and then proceeds to pour something from a silver cup down my throat. I cough, covering us both in blended food. He switches his hold on my mouth, clamping it shut. "Swallow," he yells. He then pinches my nose until I have no choice but to swallow the disgusting food. When he's satisfied I've followed his order, he releases me, letting me suck in oxygen. "Now, do I have to do it again or will you eat?"

NICOLA JANE

I stare up at him defiantly, and he looks disappointed before beginning the process all over again. We must be halfway down the cup when the door opens and Gia rushes in. She seems to have a habit of rescuing me. "What the hell are you doing?" she screams, trying to pull Vinn from me. He releases me, and I roll onto my side and vomit all over the floor. We all stare at the undigested mush.

"Seven tomorrow morning," he hisses, storming from the room.

Gia bursts into tears, wiping my hair from my face. "I saw on the camera," she whispers. "I saw." I flop onto my back, suddenly feeling exhausted. "I don't know what to do," she adds. Any decent person would get me out of here or ring the police, but I know she can't, not without risking her own life. I stare at the ceiling while she strokes my hair. "Sofia, please eat something. I'll get anything you want, biscuits, fruit. I swear, ginger biscuits helped me with sickness during my pregnancy."

I roll onto my side so that my back is to her. I don't mean to be rude, but I'm done with this family, and if I died right now, I wouldn't care. In fact, I'd welcome it.

VINN

I sit at the dinner table, trying to regain control of myself. Gia storms in looking pissed. "What the fuck, Vinn?"

"Why were you watching the camera in my office?" I demand.

"You left the screen on, and I was looking for you. Do you think all this distress is good for the baby?" she yells.

Mother walks in with Zarina and they take their seats. I still haven't decided what to do with Zarina. She's everything I wanted in a wife, yet I can't get my head from Sofia. "Gia, either sit or leave," I say, shrugging.

"I'll leave. I won't sit here and pretend everything is okay."

PLAYING VINN

My meeting with Riggs goes well later that evening. I know he'll have my back against the Colombians, just like I had his when going to war with his enemies. An alliance with the MC was one of my best decisions. Once business is out of the way, he refills my glass. I shouldn't drink any more, my eyes are already blurring, but it helps to take my mind from Sofia, so I take it gratefully.

"What happens between you and Sofia now?" he asks.

"Do we have to discuss that? I'm so tired of it."

"We don't have to, but I thought you might want to speak to the king of dick decisions."

"Getting her out of my life isn't a dick decision."

"Tell your heart that." "If you're gonna get all sentimental on me, Riggs, I'm gonna go," I warn.

He grins. "Let me say one thing and then I'll leave it. You'll need her around once the kid is born. It ain't easy having a newborn who screams for its mother. I know you're a cold-hearted bastard, it's why I banned Leia from dating you, but do you honestly think you can hold a gun to her head once she's given you something so amazing?"

"Zarina will take care of the child. And yes, I will be able to pull the trigger. There are no feelings."

"You sat right there not so long ago," he says, pointing to where I'm currently sitting, "and you basically admitted to falling for her, so don't lie to my face and tell me you feel nothing. Even when Anna drove me nuts, I wouldn't have been able to put a bullet in her and especially not after she gave me a kid. With Benedetto out of the picture, surely you don't have to prove anything."

"It's not about proving anything. It's about her making a fool of me, laughing while I declared war on the person responsible for trying to damage my name. All that time, she was in my bed. She crossed me, and I can't walk away and pretend she didn't."

Riggs smirks. "Isn't it punishment enough that she's trapped with you forever?"

"You cross the mafia, you face death. She knew that and she didn't care. Zarina told her how it would end, and she still didn't care."

"Zarina," Riggs repeats. "Her name keeps cropping up."

"And why shouldn't it? She's loyal, respectful, and compliant."

Riggs shudders. "Doormat."

"Wife material," I correct him. "Something I should have looked for more closely before I married Sofia." "But I bet Zarina doesn't get your blood pumping like Sofia does. I bet she doesn't challenge you. Isn't that boring for a man like you? It's why you wanted Leia and why you had Raven. Sofia kept you on your toes. Admit it, you liked that about her."

I smirk, draining the last of my drink. "It was nice to catch up." I stand and head for the door as Riggs laughs.

"You know I'm right. Nothing is more addictive than a challenge."

"Goodnight, Riggs," I say over my shoulder.

SOFIA

I'm woken by the lock of the door clicking open. It's dark outside, but I have no way of knowing the time. I know it's Vinn by the way he hovers in the doorway, and when I open my eyes, he's closer than I thought, causing me to jump with fright. Moonlight streams in through the rooftop window. There are no drapes or blinds, so it lights the room enough for

PLAYING VINN

me to see the sad expression on his face. "Sorry," he utters. "I didn't mean to wake you."

He sits on the edge of the bed, staring at me. Ash provided me with cleaning products earlier, but I've yet to find the strength to clean up the vomit from the floor. The smell is intense, and after a few silent minutes, Vinn reaches for the bucket of water and begins to clean up the mess. "There's a doctor coming to see you tomorrow. He'll check you over." I watch him scrape the crusty mess into an empty bucket using tissue. "Ash said you refused to leave this room to shower or wash," he adds. The fear of running into Zarina and tearing her face off is enough to keep me in here until I feel less angry and more stable. "I'm going to take you for a shower," he continues, but I shake my head. There's no way I'm going anywhere with him.

"Well, at least I know you can hear me," he mutters. He finishes cleaning the vomit and places the two buckets outside the door. "Walk or I'll carry you." It's a threat I know he'll carry out, and I don't want him to touch me, so I push the sheets from my aching body and slowly sit up. The room spins from me because I've been lying down for too long. He holds out his hands, but I make no move to reach for them. Maybe I'm resisting the connection because I'm scared those butterflies are still there waiting to zap me, or maybe it's because I'm equally as scared they're not and I'll feel nothing. I don't know what's worse.

I finally stand, holding onto the wall until I'm ready to walk. Vinn walks ahead, leading the way down the stairs towards his room. I stop at the room before, my old room. I push the door open, because I'd rather use this shower than his. "Sofia, no," hisses Vinn, trying to pull me from the room, but it's too late. I lock eyes with Zarina. She's in my bed. Right next to Vinn's room.

NICOLA JANE

I thought I'd want to hurt her. I imagined ripping her hair from her head while screaming profanities. Instead, I simply stare, then my eyes fill with tears, which only embarrasses me. "Sofia," whispers Vinn, his voice full of regret, "it's not how it looks." I step back, taking a few shaky breaths. My heart twists and I wince. Why does heartache hurt so much?

I turn and slowly make my way back to the safety of the attic room. It hurts less there, where I can't see them or smell his scent. A choked sob leaves my throat and I curse, not wanting him to see me like this again. "You did this yourself," he says from behind me. "This was you. We could have had something so good."

I crawl into bed and wrap the sheets around me without bothering to respond.

Chapter Nineteen

VINN

When morning comes, I am in no mood to deal with Sofia, but I climb the stairs regardless and present her with a bowl of porridge. She keeps her back to me. "You will eat," I say firmly.

"I hate you," she mutters. I shake my head, angry with myself for breaking her to the point she won't take care of my unborn child. I hate myself right now, but I also feel a sense of relief that she's spoken.

"Are you trying to kill the baby?" I ask. "Is that why you won't eat?" She doesn't answer and it infuriates me that I might be right. "Sofia!" I shout, hoping she'll react, even if it's in anger. I growl, running my hands through my already messed-up hair. "Okay," I relent, "I get why you're mad. I understand why you hate me, but please, for the baby, just fucking eat something."

"I want her to leave," she mutters so low, I barely catch it.

"Who?"

"Zarina. I want her to leave."

"Will you eat if she does?"

"Yes."

"Fine, consider it done."

NICOLA JANE

"It's a nice apartment with security," I tell Zarina as she fiddles with the key I just handed her. "Raven will take you."

Raven glares at me, her eyes burning holes into my head. Gia told her about Sofia, and now, all the women in my life hate me. "It's a great little fuck pad," she says with a fake smile. "Vinn takes all his women there."

I roll my eyes. "Just go."

"Right away, boss," she says, fluttering her eyelids and doing a little curtsy.

"Really, Raven? Yah know, I can sack you."

She scoffs, heading for the door. "And who would save your arse if I wasn't around?"

Gerry passes her as he heads into the office. "What's up with her?"

"The women in my life hate me right now, Gerry. Get used to it."

"Your day is about to get a lot worse. The Colombian's sent a message." He places a box on my desk, and I eye it warily. Gifts from enemies are never good news.

"Do I need to look inside?"

He nods, so I stand and lift the lid. A putrid smell assaults my nostrils and I scowl. Inside is a severed head. "Who the fuck is this?"

"Antonio. His body was left at the docks and his head was hand delivered to the front gate just now. He was on night watch at the container yard last night."

I close the box. "Any note?" He shakes his head. "Then I guess we'll wait and see what he's got for us next. The good thing is, we're drawing him out with our silence. Even if he isn't here himself, his men must be. Let's see if we can locate any of them, maybe pay a visit."

SOFIA

The doctor is a man. I guess they're easier to pay off than women, and he doesn't bat an eyelid when he sees me curled up on the bed. I smell, I know I do. It's also abundantly clear that I'm here against my will. Not only that, but I'm still covered in my father's blood. It's dried into my hair, my hands, and my clothes.

Vinn stands nearby, hovering like an annoying fly. Since I ate the porridge, I feel slightly better. I managed to keep it all down, which I'm surprised about.

The doctor checks my blood pressure, and Vinn hands him the sample bottle I was instructed to give right before the doctor arrived. He checks my pee, then feels my stomach. He sets about opening a bag and pulls out a portable scanner. "Any idea how far along you are?" he asks, and I shake my head. "When was your last period?" I shrug.

Vinn sighs impatiently. "Sofia, stop being awkward."

I ignore him. "I'm here against my will," I say as the doctor fiddles with the machine.

"I'm going to need you to lift your shirt."

I stare blankly at the ceiling, and Vinn mutters in Italian, calling me a stubborn cow before pulling my top up for him. "You're a doctor. You need to inform the police," I snap. "This man is forcing me to stay here. You have a duty of care for your patients."

The doctor squirts cold liquid on my stomach and presses the scanner to my abdomen. "If I were you, *cagna*, I'd pray this good doctor finds something growing in your womb or the police will be the last thing on your mind," Vinn whispers next to my ear. A thumping sound fills the room and we both stare at the doctor, waiting for him to speak.

"That's your baby's heartbeat. I'd say you're around six weeks, so still very early. I'm going to prescribe some folic acid and a multivitamin. You're very pale, maybe some fresh air each day would help," he says, looking at Vinn. "I'll also prescribe you an anti-sickness drug to help ease the nausea. That will be the reason you can't eat."

"The reason is because I am a prisoner here. I want to leave."

The doctor begins packing away his things. "I'll call back around twelve weeks for another scan to check growth."

"Is she gone?" I demand, and Vinn shakes the doctor's hand and asks Ash to show him out.

"Yes. She left this morning."

"For Italy?"

He frowns. "She's staying in London."

"No, you promised—"

"That she would leave this house but not London."

"Why is she staying here?" I hiss.

He smirks, tucking some of my matted hair behind my ear. "You're a mess, Sofia. Take a damn shower."

"Will she be your next victim?" He takes me by the hand, and I cry out. It surprises us both and he stares at me in shock. It shocked me when I felt the electricity between us, I thought it would be gone, but all it does is remind me that he isn't mine.

"Why did you kill him?" I sob. I can't get my papa's lifeless, bloodied face out of my head. It haunts me.

"I'll make a deal," he says, his face serious. "Shower and I'll tell you." I nod, and he gives me a satisfied smile. "Let's go."

Vinn takes me to one of the spare rooms and turns on the shower. He keeps his back to me, and I strip before stepping into the warm water. I groan in pleasure as it heats my skin. Vinn turns back, and I notice his dark expression and hooded eyes. He still wants me, and I'm thankful for the frosted glass of the shower screen. "Your father was involved with the Colombians."

I stare out through the top part of the glass, the part that isn't frosted. "No, he wouldn't have been—"

"He was. Heavily. He owed them money and found a good way to pay, but it involved working for them. Mario was involved too."

I think of all the times they were away on business. I never questioned them, even when they told me I couldn't tell Benedetto. "But that means Papa might have known—"

"Dante? Yes, he did."

VINN

Sofia stares at me for a long time. I can see her mind working overtime while she pieces it together. Then, a tear rolls down her cheek. "Was it because of him?" I nod. "Because he owed them?"

I shake my head. "No. It was revenge. Dante was getting your father back for killing his brother."

She goes quiet again. "It happens, doesn't it? Being in this life, we're all at risk," she asks quietly, like she's trying to make sense of it all. I nod. "So, you killed Papa because it was his fault I was attacked?" I shake my head, and she frowns. "Where's Mario now?"

"He's dead. Dante killed him."

Sofia cries harder, covering her face with her hands. She looks so helpless and exhausted, part of my feels bad for her. I sigh, moving to the shower and grabbing a sponge. "Your father and brother were in a mess. They played with fire knowing they'd get burned eventually. If Dante hadn't killed your brother, Benedetto would have." I run soap into her skin, and she remains still.

"Why did you kill Papa?"

"Did you know your brother was gay?" She nods. "He was in love with Dante's brother. That's what started the whole thing. Your father found them together and shot Mario's lover. Dante wanted revenge."

"Please, Vinn, tell me why you killed Papa."

I rinse the soap from her skin using the shower head, then turn it off. "He lied. He made me look like a fool. He used me to save you, and in turn, put me in the Colombian's firing line. He risked my family, my life, everything, for a daughter who's screwed me over."

"Send me back," she mutters as I wrap a towel around her. "Give me to Dante and he'll leave you alone." My heart squeezes. Why would she offer herself up for me? "Right before he sent me home, he told me he could easily fall in love with me. It's the only memory I have of that time. Maybe if you hand me over, all debts will be paid."

The thought of another man loving her causes me more pain in my chest. I'd rather her be dead than with another. "You're forgetting one thing," I say, leading her back to the attic. "For the next eight months, you're staying here with me. I'm not sure war can wait that long."

She nods, a sad look in her eyes. "Try not to get killed."

"Careful, I might start to think you like me," I say, using words we'd exchanged when we first began falling for each other. She recognises my reference, and her face hardens.

"If you're going to die, I want it to be on the blade I'm holding."

I laugh. "I'll make sure Josey cuts your food up so as not to give you a knife with your cutlery."

PLAYING VINN

"Don't worry, Ash checks it's there each time she collects my plate."

More days pass and Vinn's upgraded me to a notebook and some pens. It sounds ridiculous, but I was so happy when he handed them over, I almost hugged him. I've also been eating. I can't manage a lot of food, but small amounts more often are working for me, and the anti-sickness pills help.

I'm drawing when Vinn visits with my evening meal. He lays the tray on the bedside table and glances over to see what I'm doing. He snatches the notebook and holds it closer to his face. "You can draw," he says, sounding surprised.

He hands it back, and I continue shading the portrait I drew of Papa. He messed up, but I love him, and Mama does too, that's why I'm drawing this, for her. "Maybe one day you can draw me," he adds.

"I only draw things I like," I mutter.

He sniggers, used to my snipes of hate towards him. "Would you like to give it to her?" he asks, and my head snaps up to look at him. "I'm sure your mother would love to see you."

"What do I have to do?" I ask suspiciously. Nothing is for free when it comes to Vinn.

He laughs, shaking his head dismissively as he leaves.

A few hours later, I'm wrapped in Mama's arms, sobbing against her while she strokes my hair. "It's okay, *figlia*," she whispers.

NICOLA JANE

"Everything's such a mess," I sob.

She pulls back and wipes the hair from my face. "We'll work it out."

"How? Papa is dead, Mario is dead, and we're trapped here."

She smiles. "I know you don't see it right now, but we're safer here than in Italy. Your papa did some terrible things, and Benedetto would have sent us away."

"So, we should be grateful to Vinn?" I snap angrily. "He's a monster."

"He didn't have to let me stay. He could have sent me back, and I would have been killed. Cleaning might not be what I had planned, but at least I'm safe and I'm near you."

"Stop it," I hiss. "You're sounding grateful to be cleaning up after Vinn fucking Romano. I watched him kill Papa," I say, sobbing again. "I'm pregnant with his child."

Mama looks around, catching sight of the camera. She presses her lips to my ear like she's comforting me. "*Figlia*, it's so important you change his mind about you. Make him see what a good girl you are."

I shake my head, staring at her like she's lost her mind. "No."

"Don't you want to be here for your child? Don't you want to watch it grow? You can have that, just make him see it's worth keeping you alive."

"I can't do that, Mama."

"Do it for me," she begs, grabbing my hands. "I'll be alone."

"You'll have Zarina and this baby."

"None of it will be worth it without my beautiful girl." Her eyes fill with tears. "Please, Sofia. Fight to live."

The door opens and Vinn tells us our time is up. It angers me so much, I growl in frustration. Mama kisses me on the head. "Thank you, Vinn," she says politely as she leaves.

I scowl. I will not thank him for allowing me a measly few minutes with my own mother.

PLAYING VINN

"Problem?" he asks, looking amused.

"I hate you," I say. I make a point of saying it every single day.

"Old news," he mutters.

"Like our marriage," I retort.

"Speaking of which," he says, pulling some folded paperwork from his back pocket. "I have these for you to sign." I stare at the offered document but make no move to take it. "If you don't sign it, I'll forge your signature, but I thought you'd want to read over the divorce."

"Won't this look suspicious when you've begun to tell people I'm dead?"

"I backdated it to the day you left. It's the reason you walked out, and you being dead is purely a rumour. I haven't confirmed anything . . . yet."

"You've thought of everything."

"I'm organised."

"And when the divorce is finalised, will you be forcing Zarina into your bed?"

He smirks. "She doesn't need to be forced, *cagna*, she climbs in willingly."

I fly towards him. It shocks us both, but he catches my hand right before it meets his face. He twists my wrist and pulls my arm up my back, pushing me against the wall. I feel the warmth of his minty breath against my face as he nuzzles his nose into my hair. "Oh Sofia, you have no idea how much I want to fight you," he whispers, and I feel his erection pressing against my arse. The shirt I was wearing has ridden up and he trails his fingers over my lace panties. "You've gone very still, *cagna*, and that makes me think you want my hands on you." I shudder, breaking the spell he has me under, and I try to fight him off. He laughs, stepping back. "I'd never force you, Sofia, it's not my style. But if you ever need relief—"

NICOLA JANE

"Fuck you," I snap. "And get out."
He adjusts his trousers, amusement in his eyes. "Pity."

Chapter Twenty

VINN

Back in my office, I stare at the camera image of Sofia in bed. She's got that defiant look in her eyes and she's staring right back like she knows I'm watching. "Don't do it, princess," I whisper to myself as she kicks the sheets from her body. "You're poking the lion inside me."

She parts her legs and runs her hand over her inner thigh, all the while watching the camera. My erection strains painfully against my trousers. Her other hand gropes her breast over the material of her shirt. My shirt. I gave it her after she showered, and fuck, it looks good on her. She closes her eyes and her head falls back, her mouth parts slightly, and her tongue darts out to wet her lower lip. I begin to loosen my belt. Fuck, she makes it hard for me to resist her. A groan leaves her mouth and I pull my cock free. What I'd give right now to be buried inside of her. Her fingers brush over her panties and she whimpers. I grip my cock, closing my eyes briefly.

"Oh, Frazer," she whispers all breathy and relaxed, and my eyes shoot open. "Did that get your attention, Vinn?" she asks, sounding amused as she pulls the sheet over her body. "Stop watching me, you creep."

I slam the laptop shut and tuck my now flaccid cock back in my pants. *Stupid cagna*.

NICOLA JANE

At breakfast the next morning, I can't stand the thought of sparring back and forth with Sofia, so I send Josey up with her breakfast. Josey's been asking to see her, and since last night, I've done nothing but picture Sofia in various sexual positions. It's distracting and tiring.

I listen outside the door as they hug and whisper excitedly about how much they've missed each other. Am I the only one who sees this woman for the deceitful bitch she is? Everyone else seems to fucking love her.

Gia appears at the bottom of the stairs. I go down to where she stands, judging me with a raised brow. "Watching her from a camera, listening outside her room . . . I'm starting to think you're obsessed."

"Keeping an eye on the mother of my child isn't odd behaviour, Gia."

"It is when you proclaim to hate her so much. It's okay to love her, Vinn."

I scowl. "It's okay in a world where you don't lead a whole clan of dangerous men. Anyone who crosses me has to pay, Gia, you know that."

"You could change all that. Dad would never have killed a woman."

I roll my eyes at her naivety. She didn't know half the things my father got up to. He was a good capo, never letting the women in our family see the ugly side of this life. He sheltered them, something I try to do. Gia's married to Blu, so she sees too much these days, but that's his problem. "She made me look weak. Now, I have to work extra hard for the next few months to make sure men know I'm as strong as ever. When the time comes, they will know that even my own wife doesn't escape from my wrath."

"They'll see a cruel, cold bastard who killed the mother of his child."

"And they'll never cross me."

"Brilliant, and then what?" she asks, looking unimpressed. "You show them how big and bad you are so they never cross you, but they won't respect you. And what are you going to tell your son or daughter when they ask about their mother? Because they will, as they grow."

"They'll have Zarina. She's agreed to raise the child as its mother. Once Sofia is gone, Zarina will move back in."

Gia shakes her head. "I don't even know you anymore," she whispers. "No brother of mine would kill a woman over something so stupid."

"Stupid," I snap. "I have investors questioning if they should pull out of a multi-million-pound deal because they think I can't protect them from the law. If I keep Sofia around, they'll have no choice because they can't trust me with her writing that bullshit. My associates think she's corrupt, a spy for the cops, a snitch. You know how bad that is in our life. I've had to tell them she's already dead so they don't come to kill her with my fucking child inside of her."

"You're the boss. You have the say. You don't have to explain anything to them."

"Gia," I growl impatiently, "if you can't stay out of this, you'll have to leave."

She gasps. "You're kicking me out?"

"I'm saying you need to stop trying to save Sofia. It won't work. I've made up my mind. If you can't handle that, then leave."

NICOLA JANE

She presses her lips together in a tight line and nods. "You're right. I can't live with the man I used to look up to. Not when he's making a huge mistake. Alfie and I will move out."

I didn't expect that response, so I follow her as she storms across the landing. "Will you move into the clubhouse with the Kings?" I ask.

"Like you care," she retorts, slamming her bedroom door in my face.

I sigh heavily. "Of course, I care. What about my nephew?" She ignores me.

Everything's going to shit.

SOFIA

I lie on the bed staring at the ceiling. After seeing Josey and Mama all in one week, I'm slightly happier. Josey gave the same advice as Mama—make Vinn see I'm a good person who just did a stupid thing. She insisted he's got a good heart deep down and she believes I can bring it out of him. I have no intention of pretending I'm sorry because I'm not. He's proved what a monster he is by keeping me here, by killing Papa in front of me, and by being a bastard since. But I do have a plan—follow their advice, get Vinn to forgive me, and when he trusts me enough to let me out of this room, I'll run. I'd rather live on the streets than for a second longer with Vincent Romano.

Vinn brings me my evening meal. It's the only way to gage the time—my meals are never late, and so I know it's seven o'clock. I feel his eyes burning into my exposed arse. The second I heard him climb the stairs, I laid down on my front to pretend to draw in the book he gave me. I pulled the shirt around my waist so he'd see my pink lace knickers.

When I've let him stare a few seconds, I glance over my shoulder and make a show of pulling the shirt down. "Sorry," I mutter, "I was lost in my drawing." I've been drawing his portrait and I hold it up for him to see. He moves closer and takes the pad, placing my dinner tray to the side.

"It's good," he says. "Really good."

He heads for the door. "Actually," I say, sitting up and crossing my legs. His eyes fall to where my shirt rides up slightly. "Can't you eat up here with me?" He shakes his head. "Please, Vinn. I'm so tired of eating alone."

I watch as he battles with himself and smile when he closes the door and shrugs from his jacket. "I'll stay while you eat."

"Won't yours get cold?" He doesn't reply, but instead takes a seat on the end of the bed. I grab the tray. It's pasta. "I love Lorenzo's pasta," I whisper, taking a forkful and putting it in my mouth. I close my eyes in pleasure and moan. "That's so good."

Vinn smirks. "Josey suggested I get you some books on pregnancy," he says.

"She did?"

"She suggested one about babies too, but I don't suppose you'll be needing that."

He wants a reaction, but I don't give him one. Instead, I groan again over another mouthful of pasta. "I should have married Lorenzo. The man can cook."

We fall silent while I eat as much as I can before placing the tray back on the side. I make no move to straighten the shirt, and Vinn stares at the gap between my legs. "Maybe you can take me to shower tonight?" I ask.

He grins, shaking his head. "No."

NICOLA JANE

"But I'm too hot up here and you won't allow me to have the window open. Heat rises, so this must be the hottest room in the house." I give the shirt a shake as if to emphasise what I'm saying.

"Enjoy the rest of your night, Sofia." He stands and takes my tray. I watch as he leaves, angry he didn't fall for my flirting. I'll need to up my game.

***

It's dark outside and a few hours have passed since Vinn left me alone. I stare at the red light blinking in the top corner of the room. Vinn hasn't mentioned the camera, but I know it's how Gia saw him force-feeding me, which makes me think he watches me. He never mentioned me calling out Frazer's name either, and I definitely thought he'd react to that.

I take a deep breath. I have to do this if I want to get his interest again, but my nerves are crumbling with each passing second. I stand, making sure to face the camera as I unbutton the white shirt and drop it to the floor. I wasn't lying, it is hot up here, but my nipples still pebble as the air hits them. I lie back on the bed in just my panties and slide my arms behind my pillow. I need to remind him what he's missing.

VINN

She's perfect. Her breasts don't move, and if I didn't know better, I'd think she'd had plastic surgery to keep them so perfect. But I know they're real, I've felt them. That thought embeds inside my head and my fingers itch to touch them. She's doing this shit on purpose, I know she is. Asking me to stick around for dinner? She can't fucking stand me, so I know it's some sort of plan. But this teasing is taking it too far. I haven't fucked since she was in my bed and my cock is begging me to just go up there and sink into her.

I drink the whiskey I poured right before I opened my laptop to check on her. Part of me wishes I hadn't bothered. Sofia stirs, getting my attention. She moans, and I stare closer at the screen. Her hand is definitely under the sheet and she's moving it slowly. The sound of her breathing tells me she's touching herself, and I growl, she's making this hard. Her eyes are closed and she's moving subtly. Maybe she doesn't want me to see this. Maybe she's trying not to make it obvious. She stiffens, the outline of her body goes rigid, and she shudders, crying out as she brings herself to orgasm. It's too fucking much, and I slam the laptop closed and rush to her room.

When I unlock the door, Sofia is still on the bed with her cheeks rosy and her lips slightly apart. She watches as I move to her, and I see the sudden fear when I wrap my hand around her throat. I push my mouth close to her ear. "What are you trying to do, *cagna?*"

She bites her lower lip and blinks at me with innocent eyes. "I don't know what you mean," she whispers.

I apply more pressure, and she raises her hand to my face, brushing her fingers across my lips. Her scent hits me and I open my mouth automatically, tasting her sweet juices when she pushes them in. "Stop trying to entice me, Sofia," I whisper in a threatening tone. "It won't end well for you."

"I'm lonely," she mutters, wincing when I squeeze harder. "And bored."

"And you think showing off to the camera is a way to solve that?"

"You're here, aren't you?"

"No more," I hiss. "Fucking someone I hate always ends badly. Fucking you might end in your premature death."

"Sounds exciting." She smirks, reaching her hand out and brushing my cock through my trousers. "It's certainly got you going."

I push away from her. I've never had a woman behave like this and it's fucking with my head. She pops her fingers into her own mouth and hums in pleasure.

"And there I was thinking you were some shy virgin."

"I'm what you made me," she retorts.

It takes every inch of will power I have, but I leave the room, and for a fleeting second, I wish Zarina was still here. Maybe fucking someone else will make me forget about Sofia.

SOFIA

Vinn avoids me. Days pass and the only person I see is Ash. It's frustrating. How the hell am I supposed to get him to trust me if I never see him? The red blinking light on the camera has stopped flashing. He isn't watching me anymore.

I lose myself in writing, recording memories and remembering things from when I was younger. Playing with Mario, lounging in the pool, hanging out with Nono in his shed where he'd make little model trucks from wood. There are bad memories too. I can't stop them once they start, just like the tears that flow as I write them down. Papa yelling and hitting Mama until she could hardly stand. Me hiding under the dinner table, squeezing my innocent eyes shut and covering my ears. I hated it when they fought. Mario would often sit with me for hours because Mama would have to go and lie down and I hated to be alone.

Mario . . . poor Mario. I remember the day he told me he was gay. I was so angry because he'd been flirting with one of my best friends. We argued and he promised me it was all a show so Papa would stop getting at him. I was sixteen when

PLAYING VINN

he told me, and I didn't care. I loved him just the same, but I knew Papa would be angry, so we kept it a secret.

The door opens, interrupting my daydreams. I'm surprised to see Vinn. He looks agitated and there's blood splatters on his crisp white shirt. "Busy day at the office, dear?" I drawl.

He throws some trainers at my feet, and I stare at them. "Put them on," he orders.

I remind myself now is not the time to question him. I'm intrigued and possibly leaving this room, so I push my feet into them quickly. "You'll need a sweater." I grab it, pulling it over my head sharpish, then I follow him downstairs to the ground floor. He opens the front door, and I stare wide-eyed. "You want to go, right?" It has to be a trick, so I stay quiet. "That's your big plan?" I shake my head. How the fuck does he know all this? "I've spent days thinking about it, why you suddenly turned into this sex-crazed harlot. That's not you, Sofia. And then it dawned on me, you're trying to play me again. I'll trust you, and you'll leave."

I stare outside at the winding path. I'd never outrun him, and there's no way he'll let me go. Even if I was to reach beyond the gates, he'd have me brought straight back. So, I fold my arms over my chest and turn on my heel, heading back towards my room. Disappointment crushes my chest. "Wait," he barks, and I stop, keeping my back to him. "The doctor said you needed to take a walk each day. We haven't done that, so let's start."

I look back over my shoulder to where he's holding out his hand. Just to prove a point, I keep my arms folded over my chest and push past him, stepping out into the fresh air. I take in a lungful and close my eyes. I never thought I'd miss the cool British weather, but I have, so much.

We walk in silence for a good five minutes. The house is surrounded by a high wall topped with wire to stop intruders coming in or prisoners escaping, who knows. We do a continual loop around the house. "Was I wrong?" he asks. "About your little plan?"

"Yes," I lie.

"So the little show you put on?"

I shrug. "Maybe I'm losing my sanity locked away all day and night. I only ever see Ash, who isn't very talkative. Anyway, where would I go? And why would I leave Mama? It's not like I have family waiting for me. You don't give yourself enough credit, Vinn. Maybe you awakened something in me I never knew existed." We fall silent again, both thinking over my words. Maybe they aren't strictly a lie, because before Vinn, I'd never had an orgasm like that. I'd never felt a desire so strong towards someone. Those sorts of feelings don't just disappear, no matter how much you hate a person.

"You shouldn't try and pull me back in, Sofia. I'm not a good person, especially lately. Who knows what will happen if you distract me?"

"Who said I was looking for a good person?" I whisper, glancing at him.

He stops and assesses me with his dark eyes. "Sofia, stop."

I shake my head, a rush of emotions hitting my chest. I know this isn't real—it can't be because I hate him—but I step towards him anyway and slowly reach up, resting my hand against his cheek. "I hate you," I whisper.

He nods, his breathing shallow. "The feeling's mutual."

My lips are so close to his, I feel his every breath. "Glad we understand each other."

"If you kiss me, Sofia, it's an open invitation for me to fuck you right now."

Heat pools between my legs. Why does his dirty mouth make me feel so fucking turned on? I close the gap, gripping his face in my hands as our mouths crash together in a hungry kiss. He backs me against the wall behind a pillar so we're out of view, then he pulls away, turning me away from him and tugging at my leggings and panties. Once they're halfway down my thighs, he rubs his hand between my legs to check if I'm ready for him. I'm so fucking ready, it's embarrassing.

Vinn grips my hips and slams into me. I cry out, digging my nails into the wall as he continues a punishing onslaught. His fingers move down to my swollen clit, and he rubs circles while continuing to slam into me. I orgasm hard, so hard I almost collapse. Vinn catches me, wrapping his arm around my waist to hold me against him. His punishing pace continues until he slams one hand against the wall and buries his face into my neck, grunting through his release.

After catching our breath, we pull our clothes back into place in silence. He doesn't even look in my direction as he heads inside. I follow, trailing behind like a sad, lost puppy. Why the hell am I disappointed by his lack of affection? What did I expect? Inside, he stops at the bottom of the stairs, keeping his eyes downcast. "We shouldn't have done that," he mutters, and for some reason, his words cut me like a knife. "It was a mistake, and it won't be happening again. Would you like to shower?" His casual question throws me for a second, and I hesitate. He takes my pause as hurt and smiles sympathetically. "You know it can't go anywhere, Sofia."

I scoff, looking him up and down. "Christ, you're nothing to write home about, Vinn. I had an itch to scratch, that's all."

I storm up to the spare room to shower, not caring if he follows or not. When I step out, there's fresh clothes on the bed, his shirt and new leggings. On top of these is my notebook and pencils. I frown. I go to the door and try to open it, but it's locked. I smile to myself . . . I've been upgraded.

Chapter Twenty-One

VINN

Staying away from Sofia to break the pull I have towards her didn't work. I thought I was strong enough to see her again, but that went to shit the second she kissed me. I'm so fucked.

I sent Gerry to get Zarina, and she knocks on the office door before entering. "You wanted to see me?"

I nod. "I'd like you to stay here again."

She smiles, looking surprised. "And what about Sofia?"

"That's my business. Gerry will get your things. You'll be in my room."

Her eyes light up and something inside of me aches, forcing me to rub my chest, right over my heart. I need to do this to move on. I tried to stay away, but it didn't help. Zarina is the perfect woman to be a wife. "I'm not sure I should stay in your bed until we're married," she says quietly.

"What difference will it really make, Zarina? As soon as the divorce goes through, we can marry. It's being pushed through." It's a lie, because Sofia still has the paperwork.

Zarina nods. "I will stay in your bed, but we can't have sex."

"Of course," I say, smiling. Another lie. I need to fuck her to forget her cousin. "Go and get comfortable. I'll be there shortly."

NICOLA JANE

Zarina is lying in bed in a full nightdress. It reminds me of something my nona wore. She's on her back, stiff as a board and staring at the ceiling. "Relax, Zarina, nothing's going to happen unless you want it to."

"I was thinking about Sofia actually," she says, sadness passing over her face. "Maybe she should know about our plans for a wedding. If I'm going to raise her child, she should know that."

"And what would be the point?" I ask, stripping off. She watches me cautiously. "There's thirty-one weeks left of her pregnancy. That's a long time." I climb into bed, and she stiffens further. I roll my eyes and flop back into my pillows.

"She's still my cousin."

"If you want to tell her, be my guest. I just think it'll make things worse between you. She's hardly going to be happy about it. She's eating well and resting. You might stress her out again, then she'll starve herself." I take Zarina's hand in mine. "Let's do it my way first. At least get her to the half-way mark."

SOFIA

Vinn brings breakfast and my heart squeezes. I have to remind myself this is a plan, that I don't like Vinn. He sits by the window as I tuck into my toast. When I'm finished, I stand. "I want to show you something," I say proudly. I take his hand, and he stares at where our skin meets. I lift my shirt, and his eyes move to the bare skin underneath. "When I was naked in front of the mirror last night, I noticed this." I place his hand over my tiny bump and turn sideways. "See?" Vinn's expression softens as he gently rubs his hand over the smooth skin.

PLAYING VINN

"I'm practically a whale," I announce, laughing. Biting my lower lip, a sudden idea enters my head. "And these," I announce, lifting the top over my head in one swift movement. His eyes widen at my naked body, and I cup my breasts. "Are bigger, don't you think?" He nods instead of answering verbally. I move over to the mirror and pretend to admire my changing body. "I'm going to be huge. What if I get stretch marks and my breasts sag?"

Vinn suddenly shakes his head and blinks a few times, like he's trying to shake away the image in front of him. "What will it matter?" he asks coldly, and we both know the meaning behind his words.

"I don't want the only image of me that my child sees to be one of me covered in stretch marks."

"I hardly think he'll remember," he mutters.

I wince at his words and a look of guilt passes over his face. I force a smile. "You're right. I'll have so many more things to worry about after I've given birth. I was reading the book you got me. It says you can freeze breast milk. I thought after the birth, I could express some. They say it gives the baby the best start in life." He stares blankly, and I shrug, feeling stupid. "It was just an idea. I'm sure powdered milk is just as good, but I guess it's up to Zarina."

"No," he nods, "it's a good idea." I pick up the shirt and pull it over my head. "How long after I've given birth . . ." I begin.

"Sofia," he mumbles.

"I'd just like to know. And will I spend any time with the baby, or should I just hand it straight over?"

He stands, avoiding my eyes. "I haven't given it much thought. Have you signed the divorce papers?"

I shake my head. "The book says if you're giving up your baby, you should hand it directly to the new mother."

NICOLA JANE

He nods, pulling open the door. "I'll speak with Zarina. She'll be at the birth anyway, so I'm sure it will be fine."

I suck in a painful breath but paste another smile on my face and nod. "Good idea." I knew the answers and I pushed for them anyway, so why is it crushing my heart? I'm going to fight to change his mind so nothing he's just said is final. I still have time.

Ash brings my lunch, placing it on the bedside table. "Ash, is Vinn home today?" I ask casually.

"I think he and Zarina went to the office today," she says, heading for the door.

"Zarina?" I repeat, and Ash nods. "She stayed here last night?"

She nods again. "She's moved back in," she adds as she leaves.

The news makes me smile. My plan is working. He's trying to stop himself from wanting me by moving her back here. I still have time. Zarina is a good Italian girl and wouldn't dare to have sex before marriage.

It's early evening when Vinn enters my room. "Ash will take you for a walk this evening," he says firmly.

I frown. "No."

"What do you mean no? The doctor said—"

"I know what the doctor said, but I'm not a dog that needs walking around the yard. I'll walk on my own."

He laughs, shaking his head. "No."

"Then I'll stay here." I go back to writing in my notebook, but he remains in the doorway. "Goodbye," I add bluntly.

"Why do you always have to be so difficult?"

PLAYING VINN

"It's my prerogative. I'm on death row." He rolls his eyes like my statement is dramatic. "Speaking of which, I want to talk with Zarina."

"I don't think that's a good idea." "She's my cousin. She's in your bed. I want to speak to her." He looks momentarily flustered and is probably wondering how I know. I smile. "You look worried."

He stands straighter. "Not at all. Be ready in an hour and you can join her for dinner."

I didn't expect him to agree, but I nod to disguise the panic I feel. That backfired, I just wanted him to know that I knew she was here again.

Ash leads me downstairs and towards the dining room where Vinn is sitting at the table with Zarina to his side. I narrow my eyes. I assumed it would be me and her, but I should have known better. I take a seat and notice Zarina's hand on Vinn's. She keeps her head lowered, avoiding any eye contact with me.

"I expected you to pull a stunt," says Vinn. "It's so unlike you to follow instructions."

"Maybe I've changed."

"You wanted to speak with Zarina," he adds, smirking.

I take a sip of water, staring longingly at Vinn's wine. "I had a speech of sorts," I begin. "One where I begged you not to ruin my life, not to let Vinn take my child, and . . . well, yah know. But seeing you sitting here, in my seat, holding his hand, the hand that I once clung to, it hurts me, Zee. I can't lie." Our eyes finally meet and hers are filled with guilt. It's eating her alive. "I don't think you meant to take Vinn," I add. "I think you liked him, and I made it easy for you to turn his head because I fucked up." I move my eyes to Vinn. "I fucked up. I can't change that, but I'm the mother of your child. I know you love me, Vinn. I can see it when you look at me."

Vinn shifts uncomfortably. "Enough."

I lean closer towards him. "I know you do. You can't keep away from me. Your body craves mine, and you don't regret what we did the other day, I know you don't. You enjoyed it as much as me. We can have that all the time, Vinn. We can be together." I sound as desperate as I feel. "We can move forward together."

Vinn stands, grabbing me by the upper arm and hauling me to my feet. "Enough!" he yells. "Ash, take her back to her room."

"No!" I cry, grabbing onto his arm. "Just listen to me."

"Now, Ash," Vinn shouts. Ash steps forward, but I shove her back. I didn't plan this, and I'm being led completely by my feelings that decided to rush forward all at once to make me look like a fool.

"Zarina," I cry, "you're choosing him over me, over blood?"

"I'm sorry," she whispers, tears streaming down her cheeks.

Vinn tries to push me gently without hurting the baby. "Sofia, stop this. It's not good for the baby."

"Look me in the eyes and tell me it's over. Tell me I'm imagining it all and you don't love me."

Something cold switches in his expression, and I shiver. "I've made up my mind and this desperate behaviour is only pissing me off. We are done. Over," he says firmly.

"You didn't say it," I point out.

He sighs heavily before looking me in the eyes. "I don't love you."

I let the words settle between us before nodding. "I'd like to go for that walk now."

"Ash—"

"Alone," I add. "I can't go anywhere but around the house. You have men guarding the gates. I need some alone time."

"You're alone all goddamn day," he snaps.

VINN

I follow Sofia on her walk around the grounds. The agreement was I stay at least a metre away, but it's important she gets air, so I backed down. Choosing my battles with her is becoming a habit. I can still feel the way her hand gripped my arm so tight back in the house. She'd taken all of this well so far, but I knew a meltdown was coming. She's been in denial for weeks about how this is going to end. I'm surprised she went this long.

We do a couple of circuits before she sits on the front steps. "You can go inside. I'm just gonna sit out here for a while."

"No. You need to go back to your room."

"Why did you move me from the attic?" she asks.

I shrug. I don't know what made me do it, it just felt right. When we're getting along, I forget what she did and it's almost like we're okay again. But then I remember, and it hurts all over again. I sigh heavily. I'm Vinn fucking Romano . . . I don't hurt.

"Sofia—" I begin, but a popping sound behind me pulls my attention away and I glance back at the same time Sofia screams. Both my men are lying on the ground with blood spreading over the white stones. I pat my pocket, already knowing my gun isn't there because it's in the office. I growl, grabbing Sofia by the hand and dragging her towards the door.

"I wouldn't take another step if I was you, *escoria de la mafia*."

"Mafia scum?" I repeat, turning slowly with a smirk on my face. I gently pull Sofia behind me, keeping her hand tightly in my own. "I'm offended, Dante," I drawl, letting my capo mask slip into place.

"Imagine being so fucking arrogant that you left only two men on security."

"Imagine," I say dryly.

"Where's Blu and Gerry?" Sofia whispers.

"They left an hour ago, *mi pájaro hermoso*. Did you miss me?"

"Sofia, go inside, I'll be just a few minutes," I say, releasing her hand.

"I don't think so." Dante shakes his head. "She stays."

I run my eyes over the five men behind Dante. Sofia will never make it up the steps and be able to close the door without them killing her. Our last hope is that Zarina or one of the house staff is listening and will call for back-up. "What do you want, Dante? I have shit to do."

"I heard you were looking for me," he drawls.

"Yes," I say. "I'm going to kill you."

He grins. "Is that right? Firstly, I'm not as stupid as to leave myself unarmed and unguarded."

"Yes, that was a fuck-up on my part. I've been side-tracked lately." Distracting him with pointless conversation is my only option while I wait for someone to turn up and draw attention so I can get Sofia inside. "Women," I add.

"She is quite the distraction. It was hard for me to leave her on that boat looking so sun-kissed and goddess-like."

"I don't think it was as memorable for Sofia," I say dryly.

"Don't worry, she made all the right noises." He smirks. I bite my tongue to stop my reaction, and he sighs. "Anyway, this is going on for too long. I was planning on executing you right here on the steps of your beautiful home, but I have a better idea. Let's go."

PLAYING VINN

I begin to walk towards him, and two of his men move forward, grabbing an arm each. Another man heads for Sofia. "Run," I tell her, and she turns a little too quickly, tripping on the step and falling to the ground. I try to go to her, but I'm held back. Dante reaches her and takes her hand, gently helping her to stand.

"Don't be scared, *hermosa*. It was never personal."

"Please let me go. I won't tell anyone. I hate Vinn. He's kept me here against my will."

I narrow my eyes, and Dante grins in my direction. "Is that right? Well, let's talk about that on the way." He leads her away from the house, keeping a firm grip on her wrist.

We're bundled into a van with three goons between us. Sofia keeps her eyes to the ground. Would she really have gone off without giving me a second thought had Dante let her go?

The van eventually slows to a stop and one of the goons moves towards me. I head-butt him square in the face, and he falls to his knees like a bitch. I laugh when the other two dive on me, both jabbing punches into my sides. When the van doors open, Dante joins me, laughing. Then his hand dashes towards Sofia and he pulls her from the van by her hair. "If you want your wife to stay in one piece, I suggest you stop trying to be the hero," he hisses.

I glance around as we're dragged from the van. We're in some type of industrial yard, and I can here banging and machinery. No one will be able to hear us around here, but I guess that's why they chose it. We're forced into a small lock-up where there's only one chair and a large hanging meat hook above it. I smirk as I'm jostled towards it.

Chapter Twenty-Two

SOFIA

My worst nightmare is being tied to a man I am madly in love with but hate just as much, yet that's exactly where I find myself. I stare at my left wrist where the metal cuff connects me to Vinn. The worst part is, Vinn's hanging upside down from his ankles with blood pouring from the wounds Dante's men gave him when they beat him for a solid ten minutes. My right hand is cuffed to a rusty metal bolt in the wall.

Dante smiles at my bewildered face. "This isn't the end. I haven't quite decided what to do with you. But your husband," he bends at the waist slightly to try and get a glimpse of Vinn's bloodied face, "this motherfucker will bleed to death, and then, I will take his little empire piece by piece." He looks pensive for a second, then grins as he whispers in Vinn's ear, "And maybe I'll keep your wife also, she was a good fuck."

Vinn's eyes shoot open, and he grins, showing his crimson-covered teeth. "You're wrong," he hisses, crashing his forehead against Dante's and taking him by surprise. I wince and turn away. "This is my wife and my empire, and no fucking Colombian is taking shit."

NICOLA JANE

Dante punches him in the gut before storming from the lock-up. "What are you playing at?" I whisper. "Are you trying to get him to kill you now?"

"Maybe. Were you really gonna leave back there?"

I shake my head. "Of course not. I was hoping they'd let me run so I could get help. What do you take me for?"

"A desperate woman trying to save herself," he mutters.

"Unlike you, I have morals. I wouldn't sit by while my husband was being killed."

Vinn smiles. "Isn't a small part of you happy I took a beating?" I roll my eyes. "I did that for you."

"Because you had a choice?"

He winks, and my heart speeds up. "I'm going to kill every last one of them, *moglie*. I told you before, Colombia will burn for you."

I glance at the door, knowing they're all just outside. "And how do you plan to do that?"

"Remove my belt," he whispers, and I glare at him.

"Now isn't the time."

"Are you going to help me or not?"

I stand and the cuff on my right wrist clangs. "How? I'm cuffed!"

"Your teeth."

It's a task, but somehow, I manage to open his belt using my mouth and teeth. Biting the buckle, I'm able to tug it from the loops. I put it in Vinn's cuffed hands, and he feels along the leather. He uses his teeth to remove a small pin and holds it up with a grin. "Let's get these cuffs off." He wiggles the pin in the cuff we share and it frees me. "Now you take the pin and release me." I do the same and then I uncuff my right wrist. He takes the pin and swings himself up to grab an ankle. Within seconds, he's jumping to the floor.

The door swings open and Dante glares at us. "What the fuck?" he yells. The rest of his men rush to his side. "Gentlemen, join me. It's cosy in here," Vinn drawls, grabbing a metal pole they used to hit him with.

I watch as the men rush him and he begins swinging the metal pole like some kind of action hero. Within seconds, Dante's goons are laid out on the ground and Dante is moving in on Vinn. I glance at the open door, then back to the men who are exchanging threats. I look towards the door again. I have to take the opportunity to leave because staying will mean returning to that hell with Vinn, and yes, I love him—a small, stupid part of me wishes he'd change and be the man I want him to be, the man I know he can be—but we've done too much to each other. A scuffle breaks out and I realise Vinn's dropped the metal bar and they're fist fighting. I edge towards the door, slowly and carefully so as not to draw attention to myself.

"Don't do it, Sofia," Vinn says, and I freeze, looking back to where he's dodging hits.

My eyes fill with tears. "I don't have a choice."

"There's always a choice." He hisses when a fist connects with his chin. "Raven taught me that," he adds. "And I told her there wasn't. I told her I had no choice, that I had to marry you. I hated the idea, just like you."

"I have to leave. I can't let you kill me."

Vinn gets Dante under the eye and shifts his attention back to me. "I was never going to." I frown. "I decided to send you away."

"Lies," I yell as I move closer to the door.

"Not lies," he says calmly while dodging more hits from Dante. "No more fucking lies. Let's be honest for once, because let's face it, we haven't tried that since the moment we met." He hits Dante, causing him to stumble, giving Vinn the advantage. He pummels his fists into Dante's face until he's lying still on the ground. I turn to the exit and rush from the building. Seconds later, I hear a gunshot, followed by five more.

As I reach the end of the road, a lorry is pulling away from one of the factories. I wave my hands frantically and he slows to a stop. I climb into the large vehicle and slope down in the seat, hiding in case Vinn's behind me. "Drive," I hiss.

As he pulls away, looking confused and slightly worried, I see Vinn in the mirror, looking around in the middle of the road. It breaks my heart to see him so messed up. "Have you got a mobile I can borrow?" I ask. The driver nods, handing me his phone. I smile gratefully and dial Josey's number. I'd taken it from her when she came to see me before and I'd memorized it just in case. When she answers, I frantically ask for her to put Mama on. When I finally hear her voice, I break out into fresh sobs.

"Sofia, is that you?" she asks, sounding worried.

"Mama, you can't tell anyone I've called. You have to meet me. We're getting out of here."

"And going where? What happened? Where's Vinn?"

"He's alive. Don't worry about him. Mama, I need you. Please."

"Okay, where?"

I turn to the lorry driver. "Can we make a stop?" He nods. "Okay, Mama, go to the main road, we'll be there in five minutes."

She agrees, and I disconnect. "Where are you off to?" the driver asks.

"Wherever you're going," I say with a weak smile, and he laughs. "I just need to get away from here. There's a dangerous man who'll come looking for me."

"I'm heading to Ireland. Have you got a passport and money?"

I shake my head. "It's fine. Drop us at the ferry and we'll make our way somewhere."

"To be honest, at this time of night, they'll not be too vigilant. We can try hiding you in the trailer?" I nod eagerly. Anything is better than facing Vinn's wrath.

VINN

"Your face pisses me off," says Blu, and I drink the rest of my whiskey before refilling the glass. "It's been two weeks. She's gone. Let her go."

"With my fucking child!" I yell.

"You've had men scouring London. She's not here."

"She can't have left, she had no money and no passport."

"Because your psycho arse hid hers!"

"You're crossing the line," I warn.

"Well, someone needs to. I've had to watch your sister heartbroken because you basically pushed her out—"

"Not true."

"One hundred percent true. You loved Sofia and you treated her like shit."

"She lied to me!"

"It doesn't matter anymore because she's gone. Now, for the love of God, put the whiskey down and get a grip of things. You might have gotten rid of Dante, but that doesn't mean the war is over. The Colombians will come looking for him."

"And prove what? As far as I'm concerned, I never met the man. They'll spend eternity looking for him." We sent Dante and his little gang to the incinerator. They're ashes now. But Blu is right, I need to stop drinking and sort my shit out.

Zarina pops her head around the door. "I'm packed." I nod so she knows I heard her. Having her around is a reminder of

NICOLA JANE

the mess I made, so she's going home to Italy. I just want it all to be over and the world to go back to how it was before I met Sofia.

I watch from the office window as Zarina's car to the airport drives away and I feel a sense of relief already. Then, Riggs' bike pulls in, and I groan. Usually when he turns up here, it's bad news. I head out to meet him, and he's grinning like an idiot. "I have something for you," he says, handing me a piece of paper.

I stare at an address. "Is this what I think it is?"

Blu looks over my shoulder. "How the fuck did she get to Ireland?"

Chapter Twenty-Three

SOFIA

Ireland is beautiful, and I'll be sad when we have to leave here. Staring out at the busy town, I smile when I spot Mama crossing the road and heading into the cafe where I've been working since we arrived two weeks ago. "I thought I'd meet you to walk home," she announces. She's wary of our new surroundings, and I can't blame her. It's different to London—people here are friendly and kind, which makes her suspicious after being with Papa for so long.

"I told you, I'm fine."

"And I told you, it's my job to take care of you." She gives me a sad smile, and I know she's thinking of Papa and Mario.

"Sofia, get yourself home," says Charlotte, my new boss. She hands me fifty euros, and I stuff it in my pocket. She agreed to pay me cash in hand for temporary work. It's the holiday season and she's rushed off her feet, so she was willing to take me at any cost.

I hook arms with Mama and we step out into the cold. Charlotte said snow was forecast, and we're excited. We don't often get that in Italy. She also put us in touch with an elderly man who was looking for a housekeeper. Mama covers that, and he lets us both stay for hardly anything. I think he likes having company. He loves to cook, and I'm not surprised when we get back and there's two bowls of soup laid out. I hate that we have to move on soon, but I know Vinn will find me if we stay too long.

"Where will we go?" Mama asks as we climb into bed later that evening.

"One of the customers goes to France in his fishing boat. He'll take us in two days. That's when he's next sailing."

"And then what?"

I sigh. I know she's worried. We've never had to support ourselves because we've always had Papa. "I don't know, Mama."

"We can't run forever. He'll never stop because you're having his baby."

I run my hand over the now visible bump and my heart aches. I'd give anything to have a normal, loving husband. "What do you suggest we do?"

"Go back to Italy and beg Benedetto to forgive our family and take us in."

"He'd never risk a war with Vinn for us, Mama. You know that. Forget Benedetto and Vinn. Forget the mafioso. It's just us now." I turn my back and switch out the lamp.

VINN

"I don't know how this turned into a big trip," I mutter, moodily.

Blu shrugs, looking just as annoyed as me. "Are you kidding? We weren't going to let you stomp on in and scare the shit out of Sofia," says Gia.

"Besides, we care," adds Leia, giving my hand a squeeze. Chains mutters something, and she releases me with an eye roll in his direction.

When Gia turned up with Blue, Riggs, Anna, Leia, and Chains, I refused to get in the van they'd hired. Getting my pregnant wife back to London wasn't going to be easy, and now with this lot in tow, it'll be much harder. "You must take your time and be patient," says Anna. "No forcing her."

"And tell her how you feel," adds Gia. "If she can see you're being honest, she'll forgive you."

"I have rope," I say, holding up my bag, "and a gag. This isn't going to be a friendly reunion."

Gia gasps. "Vinn, you can't kidnap her."

"It's not kidnapping, she's my wife."

"If you talk to her, she'll come willingly. Isn't that better?" asks Leia.

"You're scared she'll reject you," states Chains with a smirk.

"I also have a gun," I warn, glaring at him in particular.

"Glad to see you've learned your lesson," he says, making reference to my lack of weapons which allowed Dante to take us. "Didn't you beat Blu for that same thing?"

"Blu let my sister get taken," I remind them all.

"Thanks for raising that again, Chains," Blu hisses.

I glance out the window at the dreary Irish weather. The grey clouds promise snow, and I pray we make it out of here before then. An hour later, Riggs stops outside a small cottage. "Just letting you all know, if I find another man in her bed, I'm going to kill them both," I warn.

"I think I should go in there first," says Gia. "You'll mess this up."

I roll my eyes and get out of the minivan. Gia rushes after me, trying to take the bag from my hand while hissing that I don't need rope. I knock loudly, and a few minutes later, an elderly man answers. "Where's Sofia?" I bark.

Gia nudges me. "Sorry," she cuts in politely. "We're friends of Sofia's and we were wondering if she's around?"

"Sofia?" he asks, looking confused.

NICOLA JANE

I pull out a photograph. He narrows his eyes to look at it, then smiles. "Jenna? She's over the road at The Horse and Cattle." He points to a small bar that's heaving with life. "I'll show you the way," he adds, and I stomp off before he can get his coat.

SOFIA

Mama isn't impressed by the noisy bar, but I can't help smiling at the loud chants of the local rugby team. It seems they won the cup and they're very happy about it. I duck down as beer sloshes out of glasses around us. "Let's finish up and go," I say, and she smiles at my suggestion to end her torture.

"Don't rush on my account, *Jenna*," comes a familiar stern voice. I slowly look into the eyes of my husband and my blood turns cold. Mama stares wide-eyed, looking at me for guidance. "Aren't you pleased to see me?" Vinn asks, pulling up a chair and joining us. "Maybe you're surprised I'm still alive after you left me to die?"

I glance over the faint bruising on his face. "I knew you'd be okay."

"Let's find somewhere to talk," suggests Mama, standing.

"I like it here," I say, wanting the safety of these people.

"Sofia, don't be naïve. I can kill you here too," he mutters.

Vinn stands and holds out his hand, which I ignore, pushing past him and making my own way outside, all the while my brain is racing to come up with an escape plan. "How did you find me?"

"You knew I would." I thought I'd have more time. My heart is beating so hard, I worry he'll hear it. "Riggs and the others are with the old guy," he says to Mama. "Join them." She nods, heading over the road, and I'm suddenly angry. He always gets his own way. He bosses everyone about, and they all just do it.

"I'm not coming back to London."

"You are." He grips my jacket and tugs me closer. He unzips it and places a hand over my bump. His eyes are warm and he almost smiles. "Zarina went home to Italy."

"Good for her." I step back and refasten my coat.

"We both messed up."

"Some more than others," I snap.

He nods. "Crossing me wasn't your best idea."

"I'm talking about you, Vinn!" I yell, and he looks surprised. "You kept me hostage. Locked me in a room."

"You could have gotten me killed. You tried to take me down."

"But I failed because you're still standing here with that smirk on your face, bossing everyone around like you're the king." I take a breath. "You pointed a gun at me. You planned to kill me and take my baby."

"When you say it out loud, it does sound bad. I guess I could have handled it better."

"We can't salvage this, Vinn."

He nods. "I know. But we can come to an arrangement. Come home." When he realises I'm standing firm, he sighs heavily. "Look, you have no one here but me and your mother, and however much you protest, you know you have to come back to London with me. So, why don't we call a truce and work something out so we're both happy?"

I shake my head. "How can I trust you not to lock me away again?"

He reaches into his pocket and pulls out a mobile phone and a set of keys. "This is your phone and the keys to my house. You're not a prisoner."

"You made my mama clean for you!" I remind him, and he looks at the ground. "You locked me away from her after you killed my papa! You made me pee in a bucket!"

"I was angry."

"And so was I!" I yell, causing a few passing people to glance our way. "Too much has happened. A key and a phone won't make it better.""Then what will?"

I shrug. "I don't know."

I spot Gia heading our way and smile. "Hey, you," she says, embracing me. "Is my brother being nice?" She rolls her eyes. "In fact, don't answer that."

"Gia, we're talking," says Vinn firmly.

She links arms with me and begins leading me back towards the house. "It's cold out here, Vinn. Talk tomorrow."

"Tomorrow?" he repeats, following us. "We're not staying here."

"Yes, we are," she sing-songs.

Chapter Twenty-Four

VINN

It's been two days since we arrived in this god-forsaken shithole. The Kings returned home, leaving me, Gia, and Blu. I'm no closer to talking Sofia around and I'm getting impatient, which is why I find myself on an early morning run. I wasn't prepared for the rush of feelings that hit me when I first laid eyes on her after arriving here. The relief I felt knowing she was safe. Her small bump is obvious now, which surprised me. There's also been a steely look in her eyes, and fuck, it turns me on. She isn't taking my shit anymore, and a dark side of me wants her to push the boundaries so I can throw her over my shoulder and fuck some sense into her.

I shake my head. She can't even stand to look at me. The only way I'm getting near her again is by force, and that's already proven to be a failure. My eyes hone in on the female jogging in front of me. I know that arse, so I pick up my speed to catch her. Falling in sync beside Sofia, she pulls out one of her ear buds and groans when she sees it's me. "Expecting someone else?" I ask dryly.

"When are you going home?"

"Whenever you're ready," I say, smiling.

"I've told you, I'm not going back with you, Vinn."

"But you are, Sofia. You really are."

NICOLA JANE

She slows to a stop. "I don't have time for this. Stop following me around."

She looks good, glowing in fact. Her small, rounded stomach shows under her Lycra vest. I place my hands on it and briefly close my eyes. "We're tied together forever, Sofia. That's a long time to hate each other."

"What happened to showing your enemies you can't be taken for a fool? You were more worried about them than me. Your reputation is so important, you'd kill me to save it. I can't have my child around someone like that."

I growl, pushing my hand into her hair and tipping her head back. Standing over her, I stare hard into her defiant eyes. She's turned on, and I smirk. "*Our* child," I correct her. "We worked hard making him, we should work hard to raise him together."

"So he can become like you and my papa and Benedetto?"

I nod, my lips dangerously close to hers. "Respected, powerful, rich."

"Arrogant, cruel, violent." My lips crash against hers and she allows the kiss for a few seconds before hitting on my chest. I step back and glance at my erection. She does the same, her face reddening. "Take a cold shower," she hisses, spinning around and walking away.

"You're inviting me to dinner?" I ask Blu, and he shrugs like it's not weird. "Why?"

"Because we don't ever do it and this feels like a holiday, so let's do holiday things."

PLAYING VINN

"In case you haven't noticed, I'm trying to get Sofia to come home with me. I don't have time for dinner dates with my second in command."

"Humour me."

I groan, standing and grabbing my jacket. We found a hotel just around the corner from where Sofia and her mama are staying. It's quaint and very country, not at all what I'm used to, and the sooner I get out of here, the better. "Fine. But if this is some plan to talk me out of dragging Sofia back to London, it isn't going to work. My sister is not in charge."

"You don't think Sofia will come back willingly?" he asks.

I shake my head, following him outside. "No. I've booked ferry tickets home for tomorrow afternoon, and she's coming with or without consent. I've been far too lenient as it is."

This town is small and the only place we found to eat was a seafood restaurant with a romantic vibe going on. I glare at Blu as we're seated. He grins back and leans over to blow the centre candle out. "Relax, people might think we're having a lovers' tiff," he jokes.

"They'll witness a murder if you don't shut the fuck up."

"Why have you always got to threaten me with death? It's becoming a very bad habit of yours," he complains.

We're about to order drinks when Gia struts over, dragging Sofia behind her. "Fancy seeing you here," she says, winking at Blu.

"You promised me a Vinn-free night!" hisses Sofia.

"I lied," says Gia, shrugging. Blu stands, and Gia pushes Sofia to sit in his seat.

NICOLA JANE

"I'll be at the bar in case shit gets out of hand," says Blu, slapping me on the back.

Gia pulls up another chair and sits herself on it. "Okay. It's clear you two need an intervention," she begins. For once, I keep my mouth shut because seeing Sofia in a fitted dress, with her hair pinned up and makeup enhancing her beauty, makes me want to hear out Gia's plan. "So, I'll be the judicator. You guys need to talk this out, and we're not leaving here until it's sorted."

"For once, little sister, I agree."

Sofia leans back in the chair, scowling. Gia places her hand over Sofia's. "I know you're angry, and you have every right to be, but you're having a child together and you know how this life works. You can't walk away with Vinn's child."

"He's treated me like crap, and he was planning on killing me."

I shake my head. "Not killing, relocating, *tesoro*."

"Bullshit," she hisses, and nearby diners glance our way. She takes a breath. "You wanted to take my child the second it was born and hand it over to Zarina."

"I felt like she was the only one I could trust at that moment," I say, trying to defend my decision.

"I messed up, I know I did, but as I've already explained, I tried to back out of the agreement and Jessica Cole began blackmailing me. I was scared she'd tell you, and by then, I was falling—" she stops, shaking her head.

"It's okay," Gia encourages. "Be honest, it's why we're here."

"I'd fallen in love with you, Vinn. I was scared she'd mess it all up, and I thought, maybe if I did her one last story, it would be enough for her to leave me alone."

"Things were good between us," I agree, nodding. "That's why I was so angry when the truth came out. I've spent my life unable to trust anyone, but I trusted you, Sofia."

"You can't lock me up and threaten my life whenever I fuck up. People fuck up."

"It was a personal attack, and I was angry and bitter. When I found out you were pregnant, I panicked. It wasn't part of the plan, I wasn't prepared, and locking you up seemed the best solution to keep you safe."

"There are so many things wrong with that sentence. If you hadn't found out, I'd be dead right now. You had a gun at my head. But you did find out and you still locked me away."

"I didn't know how else to deal with the woman I love being pregnant with my child yet betraying me so badly. I needed time to calm down."

"And Zarina?"

"Was a way to hurt you," I admit. "It was childish and stupid. I didn't do anything with her."

"Not because you didn't want to, I'm sure," she mutters in disgust. "If hurting me is what you wanted, you achieved it, because you have hurt me, and now, I can't stand to look at you. It pains me to look at you."

We fall silent, and I notice Gia has tears in her eyes. I nudge her and nod towards where Blu is sitting. She takes the hint and leaves us alone. I grab Sofia's hands and hold them tightly. "And you hurt me," I confess. "I've never been in love. I thought I had, once, but it was nothing compared to how I feel about you. To find out you'd betrayed me from the start . . . I was so fucking angry and I wanted to kill you, but when it came down to it, I couldn't pull the trigger. When Gia burst in and announced you were pregnant, I wanted to shout with relief. I was so happy because a baby meant more time to come up with a plan. What I did was wrong. I see that now."

"If I refuse to come home with you, what will happen?" she asks, looking pleased with herself. She's backing me into a corner. "Because if you really believed that what you did was wrong, you wouldn't have our tickets booked to go back to London."

"Sofia—"

"Have you booked our tickets for London?" she pushes.

"Baby, I—"

"Cut the bullshit. Yes or no, Vinn?"

"Yes," I snap. "Yes, I have tickets booked."

"When?"

"Does it matter?"

"It matters to me," she cries, and we gain more curious glances. "You don't get it. If you want me to come back, it has to be on my terms."

"Then tell me the fucking terms so I can agree and you can come back to where you belong," I growl impatiently.

Sofia stands, giving me a pitying stare. "There's no point. I already know you won't agree."

I watch her march from the restaurant, then Gia rushes over. "What the hell happened?"

"She's trying to be in control!" I snap.

"Then let her."

I shake my head. "I can't."

"It's what she needs to trust you again, Vinn. Why are you so pig-headed?"

"I let my guard down once and look what happened!"

Gia takes my hand. "Vinn, you have to let it go if you want to be in your child's life."

"Why go to all this trouble?" I ask, standing. "She's coming home anyway, and if that means I carry her onto the ferry, I will."

"And she knows that, so why not humour her a little and try some give-and-take tactics. Relationships are about compromise, but so far, you're not compromising at all."

PLAYING VINN

SOFIA

It's raining. I stepped out and the heavens opened. I walk over the road to a stone bridge that sits over a small lake. It's picturesque, and whenever I sit on the stones, dangling my feet over the bridge, I imagine it's like something from a movie scene. "Hope you're not thinking of jumping." I glance back at Vinn peering over the edge. "Not much chance of drowning in there though." I tip my head back and close my eyes. The feel of the rain hitting my skin relaxes me instantly. I know he'll force me to go home with him, and the scariest thing is, a small part of me wants him to. I hate making the big decisions for Mama and myself. I've never had this kind of responsibility, and soon, I'll have a baby to look after too. How can I raise a child when I'm constantly on the run? And then there's other things to consider, like him finding me once the child is born and him running off with it. What if this is my chance to make it right? We've both messed this up, but somewhere along the way, I fell in love with Vinn. Seeing him again made me realise just how much I've missed him.

"I still want to go to college," I announce. "And I want a career at the end of it."

"What about the baby?"

"Women work and have kids all the time, Vinn."

"Okay."

"I want to eat dinner when I feel like it, not at set times."

"What's wrong with everyone knowing when to sit down together?" he argues.

"And I want to redecorate. No more white walls or silk sheets."

"I like silk."

"I want to arrange plans and not have you ruin them or turn up uninvited. I want to make friends who are not scared of you."

"I can't help people feel intimidated by me."

"I want my own bank account and to earn my own money. If things ever go wrong again, I want to be able to provide for my child."

"Things won't go wrong."

"I want to have a say."

He's standing behind me, and for a fleeting second, I wonder if he plans to push me off this bridge, but his hands rest on my shoulders and I feel his forehead against the back of my head. "You do have a say."

"I don't. Not ever. I didn't when I was growing up, I didn't when Dante took me, and I didn't when I married you. I didn't with the pregnancy. I've never had my say and I've never been heard. I will not be like Mama."

"Sofia, you are nothing like your mother."

"I want to skip breakfast when I don't feel hungry. I want to turn down dinner invites if I don't feel like going. I don't want to feel scared of you." I pause, my mouth running away with me. I take a breath and turn sideways so I can see him properly. His eyes are dark and the rain water is dripping from the ends of his hair, down his chiselled face, and gathering on his perfect jawline before falling away. This man is so dangerously dark yet all I want is for him to kiss me. "If you ever pull a gun on me again, I'll wait until you're asleep and I'll stick a knife right through your heart because I refuse to be afraid of you."

He nods, running a finger along my own jaw line. "The thought of you straddling me with a knife over my heart does something to me," he whispers, a wicked look in his eye.

"I want a marriage, not a boss. You are not my boss."

He turns me so I'm facing him and stands between my legs. "You make a lot of demands."

"I'm not sure I've finished."

He licks his lips and my eyes follow the movement. God, I need him to kiss me. "We'll make a list. I'll get Raven to draw up a contract, and you can divorce me and leave if I break it."

I bite my lower lip to hide my smile. "Would you do that for me?"

"First thing in the morning, before we've stepped on the ferry."

"I'm serious though, Vinn. No more games. No more lies. We'll be honest and open."

"I'm deadly serious, Sofia. I just want you beside me. Not behind, not in front, just beside. And I'll get it wrong, I know I will, but I'll try my best to get it right and make you happy. You deserve to be treated like my queen and I've spent too long getting it all wrong. You leaving like that made me see how wrong I got it. Please, come home with me tomorrow."

"And if I say no?"

He glances around. "Then I guess I'll be moving to this little town of shitsville."

I grin. "You'd hate it here."

"I already do."

"But you'd move here for me?"

"I want to be where you are." I know it would never happen, that he's telling me what I need to hear, but it makes my heart happier this way. I'd never outrun him, though I'm not sure I want to, so why am I bothering to try?

I place my arms around his neck. "I kind of miss London anyway."

"There's more places to run and hide there," he points out.

I nod. "More places to hide," I repeat, gently pressing my lips against his. But I'm done hiding.

Playing Vinn was the worst thing I ever did, but falling in love with him was the best. It might not be perfect, and damn, we have a long way to go, but I love him, and after everything,

NICOLA JANE

I'm ready to move on. When we first met, we were forced into marriage, but this time, I'm choosing it. I'm choosing this man ... this fucked-up, crazy man. And he chooses me. Everything else will work itself out.

Epilogue

"Let me have a go," I whisper, taking Mario from Sofia's arms and gently kissing my exhausted wife on the head. "Get back into bed." She doesn't need telling twice. I take a seat in the rocking chair placed in the corner of the room and stare down at my baby boy's moonlit face. Named after his uncle, with his second name being my father's, I feel pride swell in my chest. I wasn't prepared for the rush of instant love I felt for this tiny, precious human. I glance over at Sofia, already sleeping. She's an amazing mother, taking to it like a natural. But being a new parent and attending college three days a week is tiring her out. Luckily, she's got the help of her mama and my mother. In six months' time, she'll have finished her course, and she has a job lined up with Dave Cline. Since taking down Jessica Cole, we've become business associates, and he now handles a lot of my press for the club.

Our marriage has been better. It took a while after we returned from Ireland for us to relax around each other. But slowly, we've built trust again and we're getting along just fine. Better than fine. We never did draw up that contract. Sofia is very clear when she wants something her way, and I've learnt from Blu that giving in to the small things makes refusing the big things easier. It works for us.

NICOLA JANE

One thing's for sure, I spent a long time thinking I loved Leia, then Raven, but it's clear I'd never felt love. Because what I have with Sofia, what we're building together, is real love. She's on my mind every second of the day. I'd do anything to protect her and Mario because they are my world. When I think back to how I treated her in the beginning, it hurts me. I've learnt to be a good husband and father. Some days, I realise, I'm still learning. I'll still mess up, just like she will, but I don't fear losing her like before. I know she loves me just as much as I love her.

I place a gentle kiss on my boy's head. One day, we'll have a whole football team's worth of kids running around, and I can't fucking wait!

THE END

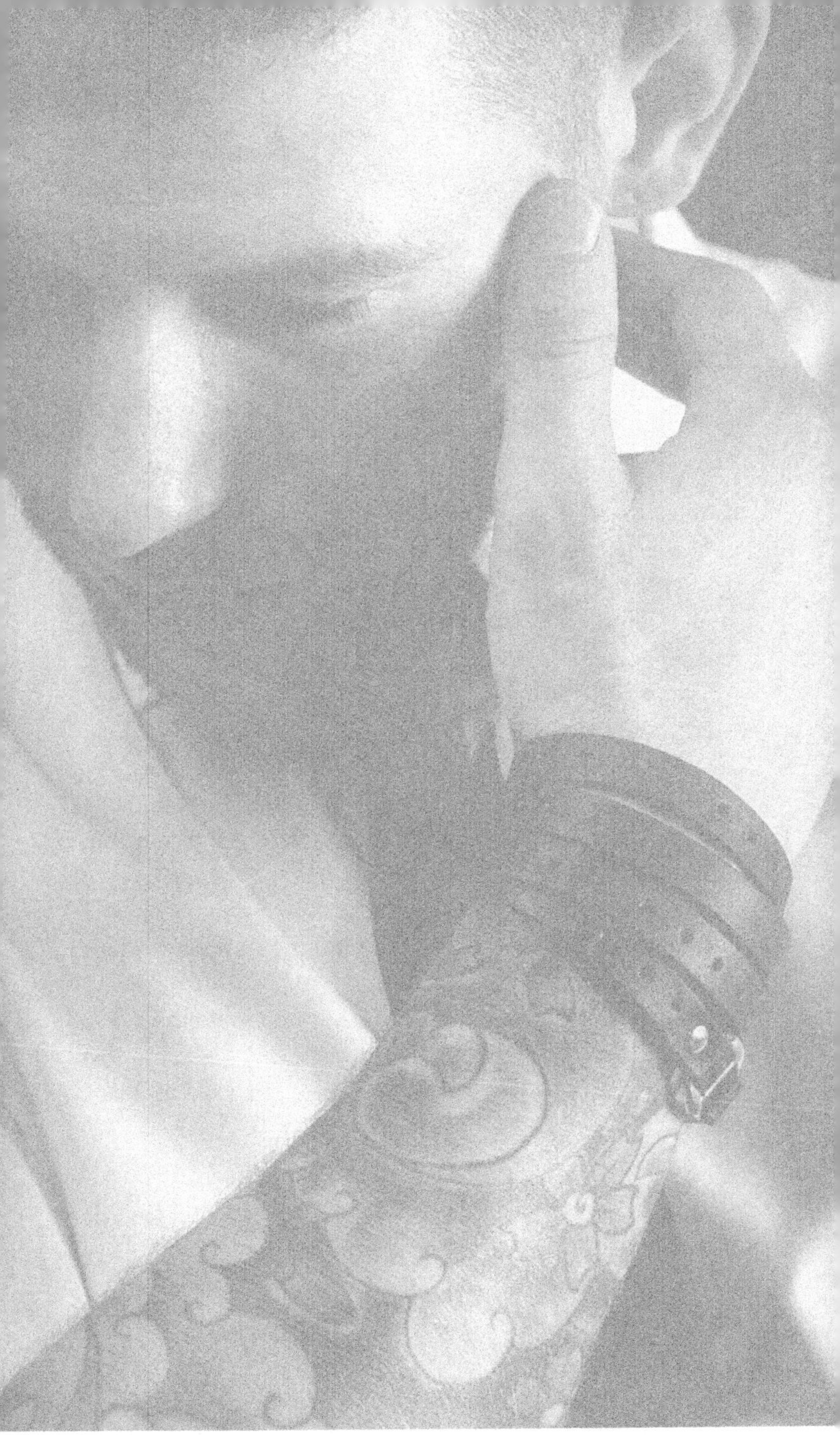

A note from me to you

If you enjoyed Playing Vinn, please share the love. Tell everyone by leaving a review or rating on Amazon, Goodreads, or wherever else you find it. You can also follow me on social media. I'm literally everywhere, but here's my linktr.ee to make it easier.

https://linktr.ee/NicolaJaneUK

I'm a UK author, based in Nottinghamshire. I live with my husband of many years, our two teenage boys and our four little dogs. I write MC and Mafia romance with plenty of drama and chaos. I also love to read similar books. Before I became a full-time author, I was a teaching assistant working in a primary school.

If you'd like to follow my writing journey, join my readers group on Facebook, the link is above. You can also use that link if you're a book blogger, I'd love you to sign up to my team.